Almost There,
Almost Me

Almost There, Almost Me
by Maria Nightingale

First published in 2026
ISBN: PB: 979-8-9953227-0-2; eBook: 979-8-9953227-1-9;
HB: 979-8-9953227-2-6

Almost There, Almost Me

A contemporary romance about long-distance love, travel, and finding home

Maria Nightingale

For millennials trying to make sense of life.

For my late father,
who never got to see the woman I became,
or hear the story I found my voice for.

September 3

Preface

The idea for this book came to me on September 3. I wrote the date down because I knew, somehow, it mattered — the way September always does in my life. As in nature, by September things finally come to fruition: after the fresh beginnings of spring and the wild rush of summer, autumn arrives — calmer, richer, filled with deep colors and flavors. The air turns crystal clear, and you can finally see what all the effort has become.

I am a girl who spent seven years inside the polished halls of a large consulting firm — let's just call it Green & Co. The name doesn't matter as much as what those years did to me. They gave me titles, projects, travel, a résumé that looked enviable from the outside. But they also gave me burnout that seeped into my bones, a loneliness that no client dinner could soften, and a life that sometimes felt more like performance than truth.

This book wasn't born out of shiny success. It grew out of real life — the long nights, the breakdowns, the bursts of laughter that saved me, and the small wins that kept me moving forward. I wanted to write something that would help me make sense of all of it. And I wanted to create something that could help other women — women like me, women not like me, anyone really — to feel lighter for a moment, to find comfort, to let their imagination and emotions wander freely, even if just for a chapter before bed.

These are not grand tales of triumph, nor polished advice from someone who has it all figured out. They are fragments — confessions, memories, flashbacks, even conversations with myself and with the invisible companions (including ChatGPT) who helped me get through the nights. Together, they make a mosaic of one woman's search for belonging and peace.

If you are holding this book, my hope is simple: may it be a companion for you the way writing it has been a companion for me. May it soothe, may it spark laughter, may it remind you that even in the hardest winters, September will come — and with it, a clearer sky.

Part I
Cracks In the Ice

Chapter 1
Too Good and Not True

I can't go on. I'll go on.
— Samuel Beckett, *The Unnamable*

I didn't think I'd feel the crack so soon. One moment I was toasting with my grandmother in Istanbul — laughing, cozy, alive.

January in Chicago doesn't forgive. The wind slaps me awake as I walk to work, its cruelty sharper than the jet lag. The city is deprived of color: gray sidewalks, gray sky, gray faces hunched against the cold. Even my apartment, filled with the leftovers of a life I no longer wanted, seemed to echo with silence.

That was the morning the crack began to show — the gap between the life I was supposed to be grateful for and the one I actually lived. Consulting paid the bills, yes. It even gave me the badge of achievement I thought I wanted. But behind the title, the long nights, and the endless calls and presentations, there was only depletion. I didn't even have time to ask myself: *Maria, are you OK?* And there could be no one else to do it for me.

5:30 a.m. The Do Not Disturb setting on my phone switched off. Messages poured in — emails stacked like dominoes, Teams notifications, Slack pings. Europe had been awake for hours, and I was already behind.

6:00 a.m. First call. Coffee in hand, pajamas hidden below camera view, I sat under the yellow glow of my desk lamp in the corner of the living room. Floor-to-ceiling windows framed a city still in darkness. The effect was surreal: me in my little rectangle of light, talking to disembodied voices, while outside the world slept or turned away.

6:20 a.m. First wave of adrenaline. Someone flagged a "suggestion" in a client deck. The tone was sharp, urgent. I froze — literally held my breath, as if making myself nonexistent could erase the error (even if it was an error). My chest tightened until it hurt.

6:45 a.m. Sweat. The bad kind, the stress kind, sour and sticky. I hated the smell on my skin. Another call began before I could change my shirt or even check what had gone wrong.

7:15 a.m. Balcony break. Three minutes, one cigarette. Camera off, mic muted. I hated myself for it: I believed that if you join a call, you show up. But I couldn't breathe otherwise. The city below was just waking up, but I was already tired to my bones.

It hadn't been like this just a week ago. On the morning we wrapped Christmas presents, Istanbul glowed. The sun was gentle, not too hot, not too cold. My friends and family gathered at the longest table in a packed restaurant. Glasses clinked as we started with champagne, laughter rising above the clatter of plates.

I wore a tulle skirt, white top with bows, and a string of pearls — playful, feminine, lighthearted. The table overflowed with Turkish breakfast plates: cheeses, olives, eggs, honey, pastries. There wasn't a centimeter of space left. We passed dishes across hands, asking, "*Do you want this? Let me give you more of that.*" It was a morning of generosity, kindness, and joy.

Later, we carried ribbons and trinkets from the markets back home and spent hours wrapping gifts. The living room was chaos — paper, tape, scissors, laughter. "*Don't look, this one's for you!*" Piles of color and love stacked by the tree. Not perfect, not polished, but made with care. And I had been the one to gather them all, to bring my grandmother and cousin there, to make the table complete. I was proud of that.

Back in Chicago, that memory was like a lantern against the dark.

8:00 a.m. Lucien, my Paris-based manager, left a comment on a slide deck: "*WHAT IS THIS??????!!!!!!*" in all caps. Yellow sticky box glaring on the screen. My consultants were startled, their faces pale squares on the call.

I typed quietly in our team chat: *Don't worry. We'll figure it out. He probably doesn't mean it the way it sounds.* But I doubted it myself.

9:30 a.m. More calls. More emails. My jaw ached from holding my face in its "professional" smile. My stomach ached from forcing a can-do attitude.

And suddenly, it was dark again — early winter night falling on Chicago. But it was still early — the proverbial sun for working people was still up. For me, it stretched unpredictably past 10 p.m. Had I eaten? What was I thinking? I didn't remember. I was in the whirlwind of messages and asks — schedule this, check that, review content, provide smart ideas, ping your assistant about the SteerCo meeting — has it landed? Serve the client — sometimes a thought partner, sometimes a mom lulling a kid from anxiety... What's my name again? Who is here?

Then, sometimes, between the madness, my mind slipped to Cappadocia. My partner, Pete, had stolen me away from friends and family to spend a few days alone with him there. We stayed in a hotel carved into the limestone, rooms where the monks once lived. A single window, the ceiling raw stone, the bed on a podium. Outside, the landscape was otherworldly: limestone peaks shaped like whipped cream, light beige by day and glowing pink at sundusk, dotted with tiny holes where ancient monasteries once stood. Quiet and peaceful at all times.

We drove an old car across snowstorms that cleared into sudden sunlight, seeing from the mountaintop the valley below, glowing in impossible green. It was tender, romantic, alive. A time of warmth and awe. But even there, something faint whispered that not everything would stay golden.

Me: How do I ask someone to fuck off, I don't have time or energy for you —in a nice corporate way?

ChatGPT: Try: "Thank you for raising this, I'd love to give it proper attention. Right now my plate is at capacity — could we revisit next week, or loop in someone else to keep momentum?"

Me: ...So basically, "fuck off, but politely."

ChatGPT: Exactly. Polite fencing is a survival skill.

By evening, it was too late to get outside. Balcony, then. I need that air. Behind my eyes, Istanbul flickered again: champagne mornings, laughter, gifts wrapped with ribbons. Too good, not true.

Here, the truth was exhaustion, mascara crusted from tears I never had time to shed. I whispered to no one: Something has to change.

I didn't know it yet, but that crack in the ice was the beginning.

Chapter 2
The Lake in January

At the still point of the turning
world... there the dance is.
— *T.S. Eliot, "Burnt Norton"*

I stood at the edge of Lake Michigan, the water black and restless, waves gnawing at the ice. The wind whipped in off the water as if it wanted to erase you — peel the skin from your cheeks, remind you that survival here is always conditional.

I had been here before, dozens of times. The lake was my witness, my confessor. Somehow, large bodies of water do that for you — they absorb your pain, resonate with your joy, and mirror you back as a calmer, wiser version. I grew up by a river, and that part-river-daughter personality is imprinted in me.

When I first arrived in Chicago, I went to the lake on my very first day. It had listened to my heartbreak, my indescribable sorrow for my dad, who passed away just two weeks before that. My lost thoughts about who I was and why. My reflections on my marriage that ended five years ago, and every false restart of romance since. It had heard me rehearse interviews, meetings, emails, pep talks for my teams, and even the excuses I fed to myself. Now it was listening again, silently, as I admitted what I hadn't been able to say anywhere else: I am not OK.

The city behind me kept roaring — trains screeching, traffic lights pulsing, deadlines stacked like glass towers. But here, on the lakefront, there was a pause, a hush inside the chaos. For a moment, I allowed myself to imagine not going back. Not to my desk, not to my inbox, or to Green & Co. What if I just... didn't?

The thought was dangerous, but it was also a relief. Because for once, I wasn't trying to be productive or strategic. I was just a woman on the shore of a freezing lake, asking the question that had been waiting inside me for too long: *Maria, what are you going to do with this one life?*

--

Ok, dear gentle readers, it feels like I owe you a little bit of context by now. If you've stayed with me this far, perhaps you are interested in this lady talking.

Let's start with facts. I'm 35 years old; name's Maria. *Feels like I'm filling out a Tinder profile all over again.*

I don't have kids. I don't depend on anyone. I look all right for my age — 5'5" and about 130 pounds. I'm European, so to give you feet and pounds I had to Google them from centimeters and kilos. And Fahrenheit still drives me crazy.

What defines me most? I'm career-driven. I've been working for large corporations for more than 10 years — but for all the "wrong" non-corporate reasons. Yes, I like the stability, the paychecks on time, the fact that big firms don't rely on the mood of one boss. But at my core, I'm here for the resources and the training ground — and to find a way to use that for something good.

My last job switch was into consulting, originally just for an adventure, to try something new and see the world after a successful run in brand management. Marketing had been fun — big budgets, shoots for TV ads, digital campaigns, even an AI tool predicting cold and flu seasons. Half art, half science. Some things you could prove, others were gut feel. I don't regret a single day spent in that job, even though not every moment was peachy.

Then I discovered consulting. It sounded like a playground for adults, a chance to run my brain at max. The hiring process was its usual gauntlet of case studies and math drills, but I can't pretend I bled sweat over them. Chance and timing carried me through — I wasn't the star candidate, but somehow I fit the moment, and they gave me the offer. And then the fun began! One day you think of strategy for one of the country's biggest factories. Next you have to come up with what's next in the development of a megacity. Then you fly to the polar circle and live there for 6 months. Out of this world. I doubted myself, of course — what if I'm a diversity hire, or a mistake? People around me were laughing, saying that it's normal practice to expect to be fired for lack of competence once every three months. Everyone around here is an insecure over-achiever, so everyone is dealing with similar impostor syndrome. Average tenure in our firm is 2-3 years; I've lasted more than twice that

So yes, my job is 95% of my life. It pays well, surrounds me with talented friends and colleagues, gives me travel, and lets me move across countries.

It even pushed me to study for a third diploma — Philology, Management, and, oddly enough, Mining Engineering. It wasn't a master plan, more like following curiosity coupled with the drive to learn systematically — beyond just helping mines get more efficient. Oh, the mines are impressive, I could talk about them for ages (promise I won't)! You go 1,600 feet underground, listening to Grieg's In the Hall of the Mountain King, and then they let you play with drills, blasts, and heavy machinery. The business name of the game was "increase output by 30%" and we accomplished it... but I lacked the understanding of how it all really worked beyond my narrow focus area. So I studied to be an engineer, and yes, under my belt I have some dead languages, P&L structure, and familiarity with rocks and mines. Some joke there are maybe three of us in the whole world with such a bizarre combo, but here we are — multi-faceted, a little eccentric.

--

You can hear it — I'm an ambassador for my profession. And it was also a mistake. I put 95% of my personality into my job, and when it cracked the remaining 5% wasn't enough to keep me afloat. I'll share more later, but for now, here's orientation in what I do beyond the 70 working hours in a week.

I fly! For five years, I've spent my vacations paragliding. Yes, no engine. No, not hang gliding. We don't jump from a cliff with that delta thing. We soar on warm air currents. My record: 12,000 feet. It is freedom — the most wonderful kind — when you use your skills to rise into silence, seeing everything from above, moving in all dimensions. Paragliding is always in the most beautiful places; there are no take-offs that don't make you say *WOW* when you see nature from up there. And there's acro too — spirals, wingovers, playful tricks that make your stomach drop and your spirit sing. For me, flying has always been about claiming that complete freedom and finding myself in the sky. No joke, your priorities get re-aligned.

Then there's circus. Aerial silks — climb 30 feet, wrap, trick, repeat. It builds strength, coordination, artistry. Circus people are my people — pragmatic, gentle, no fluff. I loved the grit of chalk on my palms, the bruises on my shins, and the way trust in the fabric forced me to trust myself. It gave me strength when my work drained it.

Next came dance. Not the elegant kind you show your parents, but strip dance. No, not for money — for freedom. For sexiness, play, and turning off corporate repression. For an hour a week I was someone else entirely: hair loose, body alive, every muscle saying mine. Sometimes I came home covered in glitter from the studio floor. Sometimes I just came home smiling, a little more in love with being alive.

And finally, the nerdy hobbies: books, podcasts, concerts, museums.

--

I was married once — to a wonderful man I dated from 16 to 30. Fourteen years. No doubt, this relationship shaped me. We divorced because it was time. He's remarried now; I'm happy for him.

In the five years since, I've had romances good and bad. Cherished some, regretted some. And right then, standing on the Michigan shore, I'm half a year into a long-distance thing with a man called Pete. He deserves his own chapter — or maybe half this book. Because this is a love story, and he's its hero. Here and now, in January, he is far away.

--

Here and now, in January, he is far away — dealing with a work crisis, setting boundaries with his almost-ex-wife, and building a relationship with his kid. I'm alone and frozen, staring at the lake and at my life. On paper, I have no right to complain. Healthy, employed, friends, love, books, a cat, a great American city around me. So why does it feel like something's wrong?

I check my phone — messages from my team before logging off. Europeans already starting their day. Which inevitably means more questions by my 5 a.m. wake-up. If I want to survive tomorrow, I have to go to bed before 10, like a ten-year-old. Otherwise, it will be worse than today. How many days until the weekend?

"Inevitably..." The word looped in my head. I didn't see the shimmer on Michigan, didn't hear the waves breaking below. I had to turn away and head home. I was frozen, but I didn't notice.

Chapter 3
Green & Co. Smile

Green & Co. Smile. That's what I call it — the mask you glue on first thing in the morning and pray won't crack before night. Consulting madness has its own rhythm. You open your eyes, join a call, and before you can even think about your life falling apart, you're already asking (frantically trying to remember if you've identified the person correctly — you talk to 40–50 people a day, half of whom you see only once): *"Hi! How was your week? How old is your daughter again?"*

Within minutes, the Zoom room is full. It's hard not to notice that this space is dominated by white, cisgender men in their forties and fifties. Some are balding, some clinging to youth, most with gym memberships, houses, kids, picket fences. My mind wanders: *How much is this group making a year?* It's definitely north of two million. The boss who asked to set up the meeting — easily doubles that sum. He doesn't join, of course. Later, he'll complain in a one-on-one that he pulls all the weight.

He is a type of *executive-have-seen-it-all* guy. He skips calls where the team is struggling to decide on a pathway, then freaks out two days later because he missed the info and got lost. Cue polite phone calls and emails reminding him: *"You had all the info here, in this email, in this deck, in this weekly update."* Written sweetly, so no one feels like an idiot. Inside, I roll my eyes. If clients were perfect, we wouldn't have jobs. Still, annoying humans — but humans nonetheless.

I munch on these thoughts while I share the first slides — the classic "why we are here, what we need to decide today." Clients joke I give off middle school teacher vibes: *"You're not leaving until you agree on something."* Weirdly, they like it. Well, who doesn't like their decisions made, cascaded down, work flowing smoothly? Fake harmony, like the staged family on a juice carton.

Once the setup is done, I hand it over to my team. They know their stuff. Who trained them? Who let them speak in the first place? Managers at Green & Co. are usually such insecure control freaks that they hog the mic. I'd rather say, *"Once I'm sold on the approach, you're the boss. I'll back you."* For me, that became the best part of seven years here — seeing my team fly, not just survive. I also grew a lot by working with truly great managers who practiced the same. It was scary at first, but eventually it gave me the courage to take the driver's seat myself. Not everyone at Green & Co. agreed with my style. They'll praise it in theory, but then write the dreaded phrase in your evaluation "areas for development" — corporate code for "tone it down, stop empowering your team, go back to micromanaging like everyone else."

My internal metric is simple: Are we delivering? Is the client satisfied? Is my team happy? If yes, what exactly do you want from me?

Cocky? Maybe. Too much for a woman, definitely. If you're a man, you're a "strong leader." If you're a woman, you're "difficult." The label shows up in whispered feedback, the kind that's never written down but still shapes your bonus and promotion. Everyone knows they can't put it in writing. They also know you won't fight back unless you have the energy. What they don't realize is that sometimes you don't. And every time you swallow it, a small piece of your trust in meritocracy dies. Despair, disillusionment, disappointment — take your pick.

And so it goes for five or six hours. You join, you chit-chat, you steer, you summarize. You answer when the client asks, *"And how do we do this when you Green & Co. people disappear?"* You jump from topic to topic — five team members, each leading their own area, while you pretend to know everything. Sometimes, you actually do hold some critical expertise. Like the fact that no one reads font size seven. Or that an email can be replaced with a quick text. Or that when a client bursts into tears mid-call, the best thing you can do is be human, listen, and help them turn that anger into action.

Impostor syndrome lingers — but so many years in, I've collected enough proof that everyone is an insecure over-achiever. The only thing that matters is what you do despite it.

By 3 p.m., I still haven't eaten. I try to push through the next call, but the only problem I can focus on is the business in my stomach. I finally give up and order delivery, sit at the table, fork halfway to my mouth — and the phone lights up: "*THIS IS A DISASTER.*" Of course. How do they always know the exact moment?

From trial and error, I've learned that a fake smile increases the chance of resolving a "disaster" quickly by about 20%. So I put the Green & Co. Smile back on. With luck, I'll remember to take it off tonight.

Almost There, Almost Me

Chapter 4
Short Escape – But You Really Can't

I love you as one loves certain obscure things,
secretly, between the shadow and the soul.
— Pablo Neruda, Sonnet XVII[1]

By the end of January, my friends and I had planned a little trip. Something cheerful, a splash of sauce to remind us that Chicago's winter wasn't eternal. Tickets booked, hotel ready. I should have been excited — instead, I was restless, checking my phone every five minutes, my heart already somewhere else.

And then, one day before departure, it hit me: what the hell, I miss Pete too much. I wanted him, right now. I called my friends, practically begging: "*Please, please forgive me, but I can't. I need to see my man.*" They laughed, rolled their eyes, but they understood. Love sickness makes you shameless.

---

[1] Translated by Mark Eisner, The Essential Neruda: Selected Poems (City Lights Books, 2004)

Five minutes later, I was on the Emirates website, clicking through options like a madwoman. A Friday-to-Monday ticket — thirty hours in the air for thirty hours on the ground. Ridiculous? Yes. Worth it? Absolutely. Because this time, it wouldn't be Zoom. I could hold his hand, watch him breathe, feel his warmth. That mattered more than anything.

So off I went. I braided my hair, slathered on a hydrating mask, tried to cheat the exhaustion before it even arrived. On the plane, I set my alarm an hour before landing so I could let down my curls, freshen my face, slip into a silk dress and look somewhat radiant instead of wrecked by a transatlantic flight. I wanted him to see me and think: *she came all this way just for me, and she is gorgeous.*

Arrivals. Families clutching flowers, friends shrieking, children leaping into arms. And me, searching for him with my eyes, not finding. Alone. He was late. My first time flying only for him, no plan B, no hotel, no backup excuse. Just Pete. Each minute stretched, my chest hollowing, messages from him popping up with flustered apologies. By the time he finally arrived, my eyes were puffy and red — all my efforts to look smashing wasted. He had rented a convertible to impress me, so that we dipped into sunshine, wind in our hair, the whole Dubai postcard. I wanted to cheer, but my anger sat heavy, and the tiredness tangled with jet lag felt unshakable.

On the highway, his phone wouldn't stop buzzing. A name flashed on the screen — soft, intimate, the kind of name that burns when you're in the passenger seat. My adamant guess — it was his almost-ex-wife. The calls came again and again, sliding from regular to messenger to desperate. I told him: *"Please, just stop and answer. It's unbearable like this."* We pulled over on the shoulder of the road. Then came the awkward confusion: does he step out, do I? Eventually, I used my smoking as a polite excuse. A cigarette under the stars, petting a stray cat, pretending not to care. He came back a minute later, wrapped in a new layer of guilt, his silence heavier than words. We hugged. He asked for a cigarette. Somehow that tiny, smoky unhealthy moment patched us together just enough for the weekend to continue.

From there, we drove straight to the desert. The hotel was modeled after a fortress rising from the sands — stone walls glowing in the moonlight, lanterns flickering, palm trees whispering in the wind. The air smelled of spices and jasmine. Dinner was full of warmth: we talked, we laughed, and gradually we slipped back into the rhythm of being together. And then, finally, we slept. Oh, that pleasure of stretching out on a real bed after a long flight!

The next day, we simply got on with being in love. It was a breather — just enjoying each other's existence. Chatting, small kindnesses: *"Do you want a coffee? Let me grab it for you — you sit and relax!"* Pete was amazing in understanding what it takes to stay kind and cheerful while fighting weariness and jet lag. He booked us a lavish couples massage, and then brought me on a walk in the sands. You might picture it as a pre-heated oven, but in reality the Emirati desert in January is cool and breezy. Birds darted around us, each with their own personalities: the little black ones bickering like a quarreling family but always sticking together, the lone heron standing proud, a philosopher surveying the horizon. We walked, we rode horses at sunset, we talked about his mother, my friends, funny stories from work. The only topic we gently avoided was the future. He said: *"I want this weekend to be special. You're here only for two nights."* And it was generous — with a faint hint of payback for something neither of us wanted to name. I didn't care; I just needed a couple of good days, a little escape. And I got it. I'd take it any day, even with that dubious undertone.

After the day full of adventures, I went to the shower to get ready for dinner. Oh, that bathroom was a marvel — only in Arabic countries do they strive to astonish you with such comforts and details, in the middle of the desert! Turquoise tiles, glazed walls reflecting golden sparks of light, copper fixtures glowing back at me, thick soft towels. This puts you in the mood, right? And my skin still carried the memory of his touch from earlier, leaving me dizzy with warmth. Wrapped in fabric, I padded into the room, ready to curl up by the window and watch birds hop in the palms outside.

Instead, I walked into a voice on speakerphone. I tried to drown in a book, but the words slipped through: his friend asking about his wife, whether they were still living in neighboring apartments or — hopefully — planning to move back in together. Pete paused. My heart froze. Finally, he muttered: *"No, we're talking about getting a divorce."* I don't remember the rest. That single sentence slammed the door in my face. Clearly, this friend had no idea I even existed. We'd been dating for six months, and I felt like such a fool — unwanted, crashing into Pete's life where there seemed to be no room for me.

I wasn't sure what to do. Say something? Pretend I hadn't heard? Carry on with the night? When I'm stressed or overwhelmed, I usually stick to the plan I had laid out in calmer moments. So I stepped out to change for dinner in my pretty black dress — thrifted a year ago, unassuming on the hanger, but once on, it held you like a secret. I packed it for Pete. And when I came out, hair loose, skin glowing, he looked at me with wide-eyed hunger, his jaw literally dropping. Maybe he exaggerated, but I appreciated it. A little fun, a little encouragement is always welcome. And the dress had one more surprise hidden in its seams.

On the way to the restaurant, he put his hand on my back... and of course slid lower (he'll blame the stairs, but we both knew it was deliberate — and I'd be the last to complain). His fingers found where the seam had come undone, just enough to brush over my skin. I love the way Pete never makes something like that awkward. Not Pete. He turned it into a flirt, a joke, an erotic secret just between us. Who cared about jet lag after that?

We had a beautiful night: laughter, great food, cuddling by the fire pit, talking and stargazing. I melted under his hands — the slow drag of his fingers along my skin, sending heat through me, steady and insistent. Part of me wanted him never to stop. The other wanted him to stop holding back, to pull me closer, to press harder. Let the softness break into something deeper, heavier, let us stop pretending to be patient.

But the next morning came, and we had to get into the convertible for the drive back to the airport. No roof is fun for five minutes, but then it's just wind and noise. I had something I needed to say. I tried to be as soft as possible, with no questions, no accusations: *"It doesn't feel right to me that your friend didn't even know I exist. I'm sorry I couldn't help overhearing."* Pete smoothed it over, as always. He said his friend realized he had misspoken, and later sent a long text full of apologies. But the sting stayed.

And then there was something I never told Pete. In all my thirty hours there, he never once invited me to his home. Not for a night, not even for a cup of coffee. He booked us a gorgeous hotel instead, with horse rides at sunset, perfect food, impeccable service. But not his space. His door was closed to me. I had invited him to mine months earlier without hesitation — I had nothing to hide. But he kept me shut out.

I didn't want to chew on those thoughts, but they crept in anyway. By the time I boarded my flight back to Chicago, I told myself: *"Fine. Calls, texts, fifteen minutes a day — that's all he could give. Anything more came with questions I couldn't bear to answer."*

It was my cowboy-ish exercise, going all in for love and joy. I knew I would return to Chicago, to its endless gray sky and wind, with some idea of escape. But I had already learned that there is no true escape from what you carry inside. It lodges in your gut and slips through every security and customs check.

Chapter 5
Frozen Dinners, Frozen Dreams

Had we but world enough, and time,
— Andrew Marvell, "To His Coy Mistress"

On Instagram, my life looked fabulous — desert sunsets, whirlwind romance. In reality, I was back in Chicago with my cat, microwaving frozen dinners and staring at the same gray apartment walls. The trip sounded glamorous when I retold it, but the truth was more empty. I was home, alone, wondering what to do with it.

Did anything change? I thought: *this isn't enough.* What I can do now is limited, and I cannot be happy within those limitations. It was about work, but not only. Money wasn't even the hardest part. Maybe I didn't need that much, because right then I was overspending just to cover for the lack of substance. If nothing good happened in a week, I'd go to a nice restaurant. If I felt I couldn't stay longer in Chicago, I had to travel. And international travel, in general, became excessive.

So what do I do about it? The answer came clearly: I have to move to Europe.

Which country? Pff, I didn't know. I needed to find a job there. But I was determined: Yes, it will take time — six months, maybe twelve. But what the heck? Who can do it if I can't?

I decided to talk to people. I called my friend who lives in the Netherlands. She had moved there with her partner, now her husband, a few years ago. Her take: the weather is so-so, the salary is average, not so many job opportunities. It's hard to switch jobs. We had started learning Dutch. But it's beautiful here. You can go out to the islands, sometimes catch a train to Berlin, or get a flight for 50 euros. It will take us three more years to get citizenship. We don't love it, but... we bought an apartment. We're flipping it ourselves — finished the kitchen, now working on the living room.

Listening to her, I thought: *wow, her future feels outlined, almost inspired. It makes sense, it's warm. I want something like that for myself.* She added: from the salary perspective, no, you won't get what you have in the US — maybe 30–40% less. Taxes are crazy. But if you want to make it happen, you will. With your experience, for sure.

Then I talked to my uncle. He said: before moving to the US, I considered the Netherlands too. But there's also the Czech Republic. Do mind: if you take Dutch citizenship, you'll have to renounce your former one. That brings bureaucratic challenges. The Czech Republic might be easier. The economy is growing, the job market is solid, the cost of living is still manageable, and people are easy to get along with. Altogether, yes, if you don't feel like you belong in Chicago, you should move.

Between work and those calls, I noticed: every time I spent 2–3 weeks in Chicago, my body started failing. My skin got dry, itchy, flaking. I had random pains, I felt drained of energy. Even in summer, with good weather and sun exposure, Chicago didn't work for me. But when I went to Europe or Istanbul, in five days I was back to being myself. Sometimes it felt like being sixteen again. But no — it wasn't about being sixteen. It was about being at peace with myself, with my environment.

I spoke to more people. One of my friends said, "*It's a pity to lose you from Chicago.*" We were having dinner with him and his wife, whom I love spending time with. He said he knew a career service focused on ex-consulting people. They can help with the routine stuff — writing your CV, cover letters. It can really help. I asked him to share their contact information.

All of this was like flashes of light in the fog. But then, after these talks, I got buried in work again and had no time to think.

I also spoke to Pete. I asked, "*Do you think I could move to Europe?*" He said: "*Of course, if you feel like you should do it, you should.*" My unspoken second thought was, "*If I move to Europe without you — if I move again to a new country without my partner by my side, sharing the challenges of adaptation and of this move — then I don't need you. I don't want a passenger or a lover. I want someone to live this life with, to share it. And you just want the whipped cream on top of the sundae. You want the best parts. But when real life happens, you just say, "Do what you want." And that is not good enough.*"

People kept asking me: "Where?" And I said, "Wherever I can

find a job." Yes, there were more criteria — salary, type of job, acquaintances (or at least a sense of community), climate, language, and even flyability — paragliding spots and the local flying club. I spoke some French, so maybe a French-speaking country rather than German. But then there was cost of living, taxes, opportunities for legal status. Somewhere at the crossroads of Germany, Belgium, France, the Netherlands.

This was the period when I tried to articulate it. I had no real time to think it through. It was a huge thought to process, but I couldn't. Everything was weeds. It was so difficult to capture something and believe in myself, to urge myself to dig my heels in. I had no time or energy, and I found myself stopping more often than taking the next step. That's why I call this chapter Frozen Dinners, Frozen Dreams.

I didn't even cook then. And I love cooking — in the passionate Italian style, for me, it's the best meditation: to get my hands busy, to savor the moment. Touching fresh produce, taking flavors and textures in, sprinkling spices, I feel alive again. But in those weeks, I couldn't. So not even cooking could bring me back to myself. Life was spinning, like an ice cube on a frozen surface.

I WANT
YOU
I NEED YOU

Chapter 6
Caps Lock Sensitivity

*The great enemy of clear language
is insincerity.
— George Orwell, "Politics and
the English Language"*

Client calls, performance, survival behind the polished facade. The absurdity of burnout culture — sharp humor in the middle of exhaustion.

Why am I here? This is absurd. No one even wants me...

Lucien Slacks: **I WANT YOU. I NEED YOU...**

At first, I see the caps lock and panic. Then I read again: **I WANT YOU. I NEED YOU...** He means he wants me to stay on this nightmare project longer. But not forever. Just two more difficult months — he'll replace me as soon as he can. Is this wording really appropriate? Of course not. But right now, I don't have the energy to react. I can only filter it.

And then I think: how can you plan and build everything, pour in your soul, time, and effort... only to hand it over neatly to some replacement? It doesn't make sense. It's either my baby or it isn't, right?

And then I realize: monsieur, you stood me up four times last week. You didn't even bother to cancel our 1:1 calls — you just didn't show. And yes, I had an agenda. Every single time I was prepared. The one time you did show, you were twenty-two minutes late to a thirty-minute call. You expected me to go over, but I had a client meeting with the team. And you were the one lecturing me that my five consultants require senior coverage whenever they meet a client. Those reprimands should come with a cloning machine — then maybe I could follow your wise advice.

I'm sick of the gaslighting. I don't trust any of your words; they reek of insincerity. Why can't we just admit: we don't like each other, but we've figured out how to work together? And stop with this "I WANT YOU. I NEED YOU" nonsense; it's pathetic, and we're pathetic for keeping it alive.

Meanwhile, the team had a huge success — a big event rolling out the process we developed across the whole organization. Hundreds of people learning it, questioning it, and eventually admitting it was a good change. I was satisfied, the clients were proud. We made them all speak in front of their peers, teams, and bosses. And — aha! — ChatGPT did an amazing job preparing the talking points. It's funny how the machine can't create anything (yet? TBD), but it is borderline genius at reshuffling good stuff you throw at it. Interesting thing: every speaker knew their slides and ideas inside and out, but still felt calmer with a safety net of text if they froze. Only one out of ten actually used it, but all were grateful. We are all such scared humans in the spotlight.

With my team, everything rolled into the event, from the panic of "how can we make it" to the laughter that followed. I even set up an internal contest for the dumbest idea to keep the audience engaged. Don't tell my boss, but it worked. While hundreds of people giggled, some of them became our ambassadors.

This relationship with the team, strengthening horizontal ties, was my garden during this case. Safe, fun, supportive. A Texan, a Chilean, a New Yorker, a Frenchman, and a Spaniard — if you list them without context, it sounds like a pirate crew. And then our shipboy: a Costa Rican, my eighteen-year-old admin assistant, fresh as a spring chicken. He rocked it — making impossible scheduling happen and saving my ass with "*You moved your flight; do you want me to book an extra hotel night?*" He didn't say it outright, but with me running on my last brain cell, I might have ended up sleeping in the woods somewhere in New Jersey. He also had a killer music taste and introduced me to albums I'd never have found alone, some of which landed in my top Spotify list.

Growing this garden was the most important part of my job. Take the Chilean: a chill, fun guy juggling implementation in six factories. Six factories! Usually you have to talk to 8–10 people from each, so that's about 50 people you need on your side. Keep them close enough so that if something goes wrong (and it always does), they call you with questions instead of running around shouting the process is broken. That kind of noise kills morale. So they go to my Chilean. I don't need to know the details unless something goes spectacularly right or devastatingly awry; I will praise and give a hard time in equal measure. But what they don't know about my Chilean when they complain to him for the third hour in a row is that his wife is struggling with depression, and when he travels, her twin sister comes to keep her company. It's my job to know these things, I guess. And I wish my boss would also pause to think, *"Is she really OK, when was the last time I saw her laugh genuinely?"*

Maybe I'm a dreamer (OK, no maybe's there, I know I am), but we are in the people business. One day the Texan will be a VP in some large company, and I'll be a managing partner — or vice versa. And I hope we'll see each other, and our teams, as people, not functions.

And also: we probably would never use caps lock.

Chapter 7
The Crack Spreads

My autopilot was better than my real self. I could hardly tell what was what anymore. I braced myself, focused — laser-sharp — and then found myself depleted for hours after.

I cried myself to sleep more often than not. Like a responsible adult, I tried to figure out why. Did something hurt? Nothing... everything... I didn't know. Just let me lie down and cry for a few more minutes. Yes, I knew I had to wake up and shine in five hours — sobs streaming into my ears, pooling warm and ticklish in the auricles. My soul blacked out, my brain went unresponsive, and I dropped into oblivion when my body surrendered to sleep.

In the morning, the sequence went in reverse. The first step was crying while gathering the strength to lift my head off the pillow. Then I could cry while brushing my teeth. By the time the camera was on, I was smiling, hoping the redness and puffiness weren't too obvious through the laptop lens.

This went on: "How are you?" — "I'm good, good, thank you for asking. How about you?"

Eventually I realized: I needed to close my eyes at any given moment when no one saw me. I was terrified someone would. But as soon as I did, tears streamed down my face. Five minutes between meetings? Thirty minutes when I was supposed to eat lunch? Forty minutes reserved for reviewing the team's materials? Sure — who said you can't read and cry at the same time?

Bright moments didn't come often. But one day, in a rare clear moment, I admitted I needed help. Something is rotten in the state of Denmark.

So I turned to the regular consulting support network. Mentor. Coach. Another coach. The last one tried to teach me how to communicate "nicer." (LOL — ChatGPT's advice on how to politely tell people to mind their own business was more useful than hours of "maybe you should smile more.")

The career coach assigned to me was a kind Canadian woman. She was actually great — helping me think through what I should carry myself, what was more important, what was less, how to prioritize, how not to drown in guilt every time someone told me I was wrong. During a session in the last days of January, she paused right after joining Zoom.

— Maria, are you OK?

I realized it was the first time in weeks that someone at work genuinely asked how I was. Or maybe they had, and I was too deep in my head to hear it.

— I don't want to give you advice or say you should do something better. Right now I don't think that's what you need.

We spent that hour together, mostly sitting in silence, seeing the person on the other end, and afterward I thought: oh shit, what I really need is professional support.

I skipped a couple of meetings. I said, "No, I cannot do that, I will not... I'm sorry, my team, I think you have to handle it yourselves. Can you cover for me there? Thank you." It was fake and smiley; I tried to be kind. But I needed that time. And instead of breathing in and out, I just sobbed. I scheduled two calls: one with HR, one with a psychiatrist.

The HR call came first. I asked, "Do you have any options for sick leave?" They said, "Yes, don't worry, we'll send you the information." Surprisingly, they were supportive, gentle. *It's up to you, but here are the options. Fill this in, fill that in. Let us know if you need help. It can be tough. We've seen people like you many times. Take care of yourself. If you need it, you need it. If you don't, you don't. That's fine.*

The psychiatrist call came later. Not straight away — I had to wait another week. I spoke to HR on a Friday, but the psychiatrist appointment fell on the following Thursday. So I carried on. Calls from 6 a.m. to 2 p.m., and at 2:30 after lunch I opened the deck and found seventy sticky notes of comments. Half of them were repeats, about 20% were sentences starting mid-something and going nowhere. It was devastating, but there was nothing left in me to be devastated. I just thought: OK, OK, OK. Change this, change that. This will probably be done by AI in a year anyway. We'll just bear it.

On Thursday, I joined a call and could barely speak. My psychiatrist — a woman who had spent many years working with the military — started with the simplest questions I should have been prepared for: "How are you doing?" I froze. I didn't want to lie, but I couldn't say the truth either. I didn't know. She asked again, "Are you OK?" And I whispered, "No. I'm not. I cried five times today. I have no words left in me. Nothing."

We sat without speaking, and suddenly I was comfortable with the pause. No need to prove anything. She looked at me and said, "I know what's happening. Your amygdala is overactive. You're stuck in freeze–fight–flight. You need to take a pause. Can you do that?"

I said, "HR told me there was an option." She said, "Right. I can sign you off for six months of leave to get better. You need it." I protested, "But how can I leave my team?" She said, "You're no good to your team like this". I asked, "But how do I explain it to them?" She said, "Take your pen, write this down — I'm not in a good place. Full stop. I need to take care of myself. Full stop. I'm going on LOA. Full stop. Then you send it."

It sounded simple. She smiled, "Yes, they're adults, they can handle it." She didn't say the next thought out loud, but I can now: if they had been paying attention, they would have noticed earlier.

I spent the next day, Friday, writing the email. A couple of versions, but in the end, one message I sent to different groups. To my team: Mental health is important, take care of yourselves. To my bosses: here's the status, this person will cover this, that person will cover that. Do I need to contact the client? They said: no, just go. Everyone was nice, but I didn't care anymore. I didn't care to distinguish between genuine kindness and politeness.

And then my life started blanking. If I had to put a sound to it, it would be the flatline of a heart monitor: beeeeeeeeeeeep. I didn't know where I was. Probably in my flat in Chicago, binge-watching TV series. You fall asleep, you wake up, and...

Skip >

Chapter 8
The Great Nothingness

*Nothing happens? Or has
everything happened,
and are we standing now, quietly,
in the new life?*
— Juan Ramón Jiménez, "Oceans"[2]

XXXXXXXXXXXXXXXXXXXXXXXXXXXXXX
XXXXXXXXXXXXXXXXXXXXXXXXXXXXXX
XXXXXXXXXXXXXXXXXXXXXXXXXXXXXX
XXXXXXXXXXXXXXXXXXXXXXXXXXXXXX
XXXXXXXXXXXXXXXXXXXXXXXXXXXXXX
XXXXXXXXXXXXXXXXXXXXXXXXXXXXXX
XXXXXXXXXXXXXXXXXXXXXXXXXXXXXX
XXXXXXXXXXXXXXXXXXXXXXXXXXXXXX
XXXXXXXXXXXXXXXXXXXXXXXXXXXXXX
XXXXXXXXXXXXXXXXXXXXXXXXXXXXXX

---

[2] Translated by Robert Bly, *News of the Universe: Poems of Twofold Consciousness*

X X X X X X X X X X X X X X X X X X X X X X X X X X >> skip >> X
X X X X X X X X X X X X X X X X X X X X X X X X X X X X X X X
X X X X X X X X X X X X X X X X X X X X X X X X X X X X X X X
X X X X X X X X X X X X X X X X X X next X X X X X X X X X X X
X X X X X X X X X X X X X X X X X X X X X X X X X X X X X X X
X X X X X X X X X X X X X X X X X X X X X X X X X X X X X X X
X X X X X X X X X X X X X X X X X X X X X X X X X X X X X X X
X X X X X X X X X X X X X X X X X X X X X X X X X X X X X X X
X X X X X X X X X X X X X X X X X X X X X X X X X X X X X X X
X X X X X X X X X X X X X X X X X X X X X X X X X X X X X X X
X X X X X X X X X X X X X X X X X X X X X X X X X X X X X X X
X X X X X X X X X X X X X X X X X X X X X X X X X X X X X X X
X X X X X X X X X X X X X X X X X X X X X X X X X X X X X X X
X X X X X X X X X X X X X X X X X X X X X X X X X X X X X X X
X X X X X X X X X X X X X X X X X X X X X X X X X X X X X X X
X X X X X X X X X X X X X X X X X X X X X X X X X X X X X X X
X X X X X X X X X X X X X X X X X X X X X X X X X X X X X X X
X X X X X X X X X X X X X X X X X X X X X X X X X X X X X X X
X X X X X X X X X X X X X X >> next episode >> X X X X X X X X X
X X X X X X X X X X X X X X X X X X X X X X X X X X X X X X X
X X X X X X X X X X X X X X X X X X X X X X X X X X X X X X X
X X X X X X X X X X X X X X X X X X X X X X X X X X X X X X X
X X X X X X X X X X X X X X X X X X X X X X X X X X X X X X X
X X X X X X X X X X X X X X X X X X X X X X X X X X X X X X X
X X X X X X X X X X X X X X X X X X X X X X X X X >> skip X X X
X X X X X X X X X X X X X X X X X X X X X X X X X X X X X X X
X X X X X X X X X X X X X X X X X X X X X X X X X X X X X X X

X X X X X X X X X X X X X X X X X X X X X X X X X X X X X X X

X X X X X X X X X X X X X X X X X X X X X X X X X X X X X X X

X X X X X X X X X X X X X X X X X X X X X X X X X X X X X X X

X X X X X X X X X X X X X X X X X X X X X X X X X X X X X X X

X X X X X X X X X X X X X X X X X X X X X X X X X X X X X X X

X X X X X X X X X X X X X X X X X X X X X X X X X X X X X X X

X X X X X X X X X X X X X X X X X X X X X X X X X X X X X X X

X X X X X X X X X X X X X X X X X X X X X X X X X X X X X X X

X X X X X X X X X X X X X X X X X X X X X X X X X X X X X X X

X X X X X X X X X X X X X X X X X X X X X X X X X X X X X X X

X X X X X X X X X X X X X X X >> oh, it's 2 a.m. already >> X X

X X X X X X X X X X X X X X X X X X X X X X X X X X X X X X X

X X X X X X X X X X X X X X X X X X X X X X X X X X X X X X X

X X X X X X X X X X X X X X X X X X X X X X X X X X X X X X X

X X X X X X X X X X X X X X X X X X X X X X X X X X X X X X X

X X X X X X X X X X X X X X X X X X X X X X X X X X X X X X X

X X X X X X X X X X X X X X X X X X X X X X X X X X X X X X X

X X X X X X X X X X X X X X X X X X X X X X X X X X X X X X X

X X X X X X X X X X X X X X X X X X X X X X X X X X X X X X X

X X X X X X X X X X X X X X X X X X X X X X X X X X X X X X X

X X X X X X X X X X X X X X X X X X X X X X X X X X X X X X X

X X X X X X X X X X X X X X X X X X X X X X X X X X X X X X X

X X X X X X X X X X X X X X X X X X X X X X X X X X X X X X X

X X X X X X X X X X X X X X X X X X X X X X X X X X X X X X X

X X X X X X X X X X X X X X X X X X X X X X X >> next episode >>

X X X X X X X X X X X X X X X X X X X X X X X X X X X X X X X

X X X X X X X X X X X >> I dosed off at some point? >> X X X X X X

X X X X X X X X X X X X X X X X X X X X X X X X X X X X X X X X X
X X X X X X X X X X X X X X X X X X X X X X X X X X X X X X X X X
X X X X X X X X X X X X X X X X X X X X X X X X X X X X X X X X X
X X X X X X X X X X X X X X X X X X X X X X X X X X X X X X X X X
X X X X X X X X X X X X X X X X X X X X X X X X X X X X X X X X X
X X X X X X X X X X X X X X X X X X X X X X X X X X X X X X X X X
X X X X X X X X X X X X X X X X X X X X X X X X X X X X X X X X X
X X X X X X X X X X X X X X X X X X X X X X X X X X X X X X X X X
X X X X X X X X X X X X X X X X X X X X X X X X X X X X X X X X X
X X X X X X X X X X X X X X X X X X X X X X X X X X X X X X X X X
X X X X X X X X X X X X X X X X X X X X X X X X X X X X X X X X X
X X X X X X X X X X X X X X X X X X X X X X X X X X X X X X X X X
X X X X X X X X X X X X X X X X X X X X X X X X X X X X X X X X X
X X X X X X X X >> it's gray outside >> X X X X X X X X X X X X X
X X X X X X X X X X X X X X X X X X X X X X X X X X X X X X X X X
X X X X X X X X X X X X X X X X X X X X X X X X X X X X X X X X X
X X X X X X X X X X X X X X X X X X X X X X X X X X X X X X X X X
X X X X X X X X X X X X X X X X X X X X X X X X X X X X X X X X X
X X X X X X X X X X X X X X X X X X X X X X X X X X X X X X X X X
X X X X X X X X X X X X X X X X X X X X X X X X X X X X X X X X X
X X X X X X X X X X X X X X X X X X X X X X X X X X X X X X X X X
X X X X X X X X X X X X X X X X X X X X X X X X X X X X X X X X X
X X X X X X X X X X X X X X X X X X X X X X X X X X X X X X X X X
X X X X X X X X X X X X X X X X X X X X X X X X X X X X X X X X X
X X X X X X X X X X X X X X X X X X X X X X X X X X X X X X X X X
X X X X X X X X X X X X X X X X X X X X X X X X X X X X X X X X X

X X X X X X X X X X >> tv series' finale >> X X X X X X X X X X

X X X X X X X X X X X X X X X X X X X X X X X X X X X X X X

X X X X X X X X X X X X X X X X X X X X X X X X X X X X X X

X X X X X X X X X X X X X X X X X X X X X X X X X X X X X X

X X X X X X X X X X X X X X X X X X X X X X X X X X X X X X

X X X X X X X X X X X X X X X X X X X X X X X X X X X X X X

X X X X X X X X X X X X X X X X X X X X X X X X X X X X X X

X X X X X X X X X X X X X X X X X X X X X X X X X X X X X X

X X X X X X X X X X X X X X X X X X X X X X X X X X X X X X

X X X X X X X X X X X X X X X X X X X X X X X X X X X X X X

X X >> found something new >> X X X X X X X X X X X X X X X X

X X X X X X X X X X X X X X X X X X X X X X X X X X X X X X

X X X X X X X X X X X X X X X X X X X X X X X X X X X X X X

X X X X X X X X X X X X X X X X X X X X X X X X X X X X X X

X X X X X X X X X X X X X X X X X X X X X X X X X X X X X X

X X X X X X X X X X X X X X X X X X X X X X X X X X X X X X

X X X X X X X X X X X X X X X X X X X X X X X X X X X X X X

X X X X X X X X X X X X X X X X X X X X X X X X X X X X X X

X X X X X X X X X X X X X X X X X X X X X X X X X X X X X X

X X X X X X X X X X X X X X X X X X X X X X X X X X X X X X

X X X X X X X X X X X X X X X X X X X X X X X X X X X X X X

X X X X X X X X X X X X X X X X X X X X X X X X X X X X X X

>> when was the last time I slept in my bed? >> X X X X X X X X X

X X X X X X X X X X X X X X X X X X X X X X X X X X X X X X X

X X X X X X X X X X X X X X X X X X X X X X X X X X X X X X

X X X X X X X X X X X X X X X X X X X X X X X X X X X X X X

X X X X X X X X X X X X X X X X X X X X X X X X X X X X X X

It's strange how several weeks of your life can just vanish. I have almost no memory of that time. I assume I spent most of it on the couch, staring at the wall, at a streaming show (for the life of me I can't remember which), at... whatever happened to be in front of me.

Total lack of structure. Robotic thoughts: Have I eaten today? Anything since Monday? Everything I shoved down my throat I tried to label a treat — but it didn't matter. Taste was ash.

Sometimes I tried to remind myself about things I once loved. I mounted expeditions for groceries (and steps — you know, steps and fresh air can coax a little dopamine, make you feel life again...). But I'd come home so exhausted that the next two days disappeared. I needed to cry, to hide, to sleep. Lots and lots of sleep. No thoughts, really. Which was its own kind of blessing. Thoughts weren't good for me then; a significant portion were scary. I lived on the 28th floor. I'm not afraid of heights. The grayness below the balcony suggested a brief fear, then no problems at all. That pattern of thinking terrified me to the bone.

My own brain had betrayed me. Reasoning had been my

happy place — challenge, excitement, joy... even internalizing some grim poetry like Poe. Now it had changed.

No energy either — one effort, one text drained me for 24 hours. I wondered: Am I going to be this handicapped for the rest of my life? And then I hid again — anything to keep from spiraling.

Day after day slipped into a gray abyss. As if they never were. Sometimes I remembered I had to reply to some message. Sometimes I talked to Pete. I braced myself — my autopilot was still better than my real self. *Look fine. Be engaging. Find something to talk about.* Don't show that you have no idea what day it is. He's a guy — look nice, cook on camera (he doesn't need to know you're not sure you'll eat it later).

Worst-case: you still show up even if you cry. He didn't sign up for that, did he? But it's a relationship, and he wasn't always in a good place either, and I supported him as best I could. Now... maybe he could support me?

I can't bear living far from you. I hate that we don't have a future. I can't hold optimism knowing you're married and nothing seems to change. Yes, it's not easy for you — I understand. But should it feel like a concrete block on my chest?

On many days I skipped the routines I was supposed to maintain to get better. My therapist advised exercise and mindfulness meditations. I even got the app for free through my employer (oh, the absurdity — "we'll let you burn out, but here's an app to offset the damage"). And being fair, I knew that was an unkind thought about my firm. In my seven years there, I'd met many people for whom "value to people and impact" weren't just corporate slogans.

But when your brain is sick, disbelief and despair spread anyway. Gratitude feels out of reach. You're starving, and the idea of a hearty stew is just a joke about your poverty of feeling. Still, I had the app installed, and my therapist sent me research showing it could be as effective as an antidepressant.

The other thing I did to cope: in a rare clear moment I realized one thing a day was my limit — and that thing shouldn't involve a decision. Decisions depleted my will to live. So I delegated decisions — to ChatGPT.

Me, in the chat: I'm depressed and on sick leave. Help me plan a super-simple schedule to get through tomorrow. If you can get me outside, that's a win.

ChatGPT: OK. Tiny steps, no heroics.

1. Wake up, drink water, shower

2. Put on soft clothes and open a window for 3 minutes

3. Eat something with protein (yogurt, eggs, peanut butter)

4. 10-minute walk outside — if that's too much, stand on the balcony and take 10 slow breaths in

5. Reply to one message or one email

6. Rest without guilt: watch an episode, read three pages, or nap

7. Simple dinner (delivery is fine)

8. Warm shower, phone on Do Not Disturb, lights dimmed

9. Write one sentence: Today I lived as best I could

If you do just 1–2 items, it still counts.

I didn't follow it every day. But knowing that when I felt lost, I could look and just do what I was told — eat, shower, read three pages, write a line in a journal — helped.

Time slipped away. Not just days, but whole stretches vanished: *"Wait, today is Thursday — wasn't yesterday Saturday?"* Those weeks were blank, as if I wasn't there at all. Just tears, drifting in and out of sleep, and a dreamlike existence.

When I write this now, still in the same year but from a different season of myself, I want to walk over and hug that woman. She had spent all her energy, her spark, then all her reserves. Before us, she's almost naked, so endlessly tired she barely feels like herself. That candle's wick had burned bravely in the wind, flickering and flaring with each gust — and then it burned out. There was nothing left to burn, only a puddle of shapeless wax.

But I know now: that's only how it *seems* in the moment. From the deepest kindness in my belly — the breath that fills lungs, gut, throat — I want to envelop that Maria in warmth, bring her a moment of safety, show her color for even a second, let her believe color exists. And of course, there was no one else then who could do it but me. Not friends, not lovers, not even a therapist. We are adults, adults wipe their own tears. And I couldn't back then.

Depression, for me, was the bottom of the Mariana Trench: no light, no warmth. A crushing weight of water pressing from all sides, holding you still. Every tiny movement becomes impossible. So getting out is impossible too. And yet, by nature,

I'm joyful: three thousand ideas a minute, twenty plans, inviting everyone to dance in a circle. Maybe it was that memory that saved me — the memory of good. I couldn't feel joy, or inspiration, or fascination. But I remembered *where* I had felt good: by the sea. And in the air, under a paraglider.

— *A paraglider?* You can't make it from the bedroom to the living room every day. *Fly?* I don't know. For a day or two I turned the thought over. I can suffer and waste time here on the couch, in the grayness of a Chicago February, each day echoing the last. Or I can waste time — spend time — with a view of the sea. Maybe even the ocean. Here, it won't get better; it doesn't look like it will. There, I haven't tried.

I felt horribly weak then. Fragile. And very lonely. I didn't have words inside me. The idea formed slowly: I want to go somewhere. But I didn't even know how to form the request for Google.

And as the days passed, a word came back. *Paragliding.* They still organize trips on old-school forums, with threads and little plus signs if you're interested. Maybe something like that? If I find an organized trip... no decisions to make. Just buy tickets and insurance, pack your gear (you have an extensive Excel list of all the stuff you need to fly — project manager to the bone, after all).

Once you have words, they have power. If you can name it, it gains some reality. It doesn't grant courage or certainty — but it invites them. And slowly, they begin to gather.

That was the first flicker of movement out of the great

nothingness. Not recovery, not yet — but the idea that maybe life wasn't over. That maybe the next chapter could begin somewhere else, under a different sky.

Chapter 9
Half a Globe Away

The longest way round is
the shortest way home.
— James Joyce, *Ulysses*

On the flight map in the little screen on the seatback in Economy class, Chicago and Dubai glow like two lonely dots pulsing at the opposite edges. Almost like they don't both fit on the same map. Half a globe apart, and yet somehow I was in both places at once — in my bed in Chicago, the blue light of my laptop on my face, and in his living room in Dubai, faintly laughing at his bad jokes as if I were there beside him. And it felt good, even from the depth of my burnout pit.

Pete — not his real name, but the one I gave him, because he was a dreamer, like Peter Pan. We used to watch *The Sandman* together across time zones (his night, my midday), and he reminded me of Dreamlord: restless, magnetic, more comfortable carrying everyone else's dreams than shaping his own. With him, I felt that rare, electric sense of belonging. The kind that made me forget, for a moment, how far apart we really were.

We had known each other for years, long enough that I thought I understood the category we fell into, and then, one evening about six months ago, over a glass of Amaro Montenegro at a loud dinner, I suddenly thought of him. It was he who had once introduced me to that bittersweet digestif, and on impulse I sent a small, friendly reminder that I still remembered. A month later he appeared in Chicago, unexpectedly for me, though he now says he knew why — or rather, for whom he was coming — and somewhere between dinner, a walk beneath the elms, and a Sunday morning text suggesting coffee, we found ourselves standing with paper cups in our hands while he looked at me in a way that felt deliberate and said, simply, *"I look at you and I can't take my eyes off you."* Months have passed since then, and somehow it still worked.

But it wasn't all tenderness. From the beginning, I warned him, *"We're so different, we'll quarrel a lot."* And I was right. The fights came sharp and fast, like summer storms — sudden, drenching, leaving no air to breathe. One moment we were laughing, trading lines like best friends; the next, we were locked in some terrible quarrel neither of us knew how to escape. We are both introverts, masters of shutting down behind a friendly façade — a skill so useful in life, and so harmful when you sever a romantic connection.

That was our story with Pete: sparkles and storms, belonging and distance, love and exhaustion braided together. He could make me laugh at 3 a.m., when my world felt like it was collapsing. He could also break my heart with a single sentence.

And still — still — I kept choosing him, half a globe away.

Pete had a way of making everything sound like a joke — even when it wasn't. His humor was quick, irreverent, almost boyish, and it pulled me out of darkness more times than I can count. But under the laughter, I sometimes caught a quietness in him, a gap.

One night, after we had finished another episode of The Sandman, I asked him softly, *"What do you dream about?"* The question hung in the air. I could see him shift, stumble. He was a man in his early forties, endlessly imaginative when it came to others, but when it came to himself — to his own future, his own desires — there was only silence.

That silence told me everything. He was a dreamer without a dream. A Peter Pan who had grown up, desperate to create, to build, to make things real — and terrified of it at the same time, like a man lost on uncharted land. It wasn't that he lacked vision; he carried a whole atlas for everyone else. But when it came to his own life, he didn't feel empowered.

Later, almost offhand, he confessed, *"You probably don't know, but I have ADHD."* He said it like a warning label, something he thought I couldn't possibly have noticed. But I had. The scattered energy, the forgotten threads, the way he burned so bright and then disappeared into himself — it was all there. I had suspected it, but I never felt it was my place to name it (I'm not a professional, and unsolicited advice is the worst). When his friend finally did, and he repeated it to me, I just smiled and thought, *"Yes, I know. I've known all along."*

It didn't make me like him less. If anything, it made me like him more. Because beneath the quarrels and the storms was a man trying to be everything to everyone, and in the process, letting go the space for his own hopes.

So yes, on a physical level, I was alone — I felt nothing, did nothing, day in, day out. It was vastness and absolute depletion. But that's not the full story. The one person who was supposed to be interested in me emotionally — partnering with me in this life, supporting, loving — was withdrawing. He called often enough, and he saw me cry, but nothing pushed him to just come see me.

We were discussing plenty of things over Zoom calls almost every day, but I felt the withdrawal most when I surfaced the topics that mattered. *"What's the future going to look like? Where do I go from here?"* He would dodge, then say, *"OK, I think I can come for Valentine's Day."* He mentioned it once, casually, *"At least I can come for the long weekend and spend it with you in Chicago. I see that you need it."*

I couldn't even show excitement — that was my lowest point. But I clung to it anyway. A beacon of light two weeks away. Maybe we'd go to my favorite restaurant in Chicago, the one that actually holds warm memories. I desperately needed someone to hug me right then, but I settled for the promise of later.

When the day came — February 10th, maybe the 11th — we had our usual call around my lunchtime. We talked about little things. Then he paused. *"I'm sorry, dear, but I cannot come for St. Valentine's. I can't arrange it. I'll have to stay with my son. My almost-ex-wife won't take him this weekend. It's not convenient for her."*

It turned out I still had some parts of my soul left beneath the depression. Now, every piece of me froze. Froze to the temperature of nonexistence. Then imploded. I turned sideways to the laptop, coffee in hand, and smashed the cup against the floor. It shattered into twenty pieces, bruised the floorboards, coffee splashing everywhere, Dexter-style. *"I cannot talk to you. Goodbye."* I quit Zoom.

I sat staring at the carpet, soaked in coffee. Dry sobbing, trembling hands. *OK, small actions. Towels. Clean it now. Later it will be too much. I cannot afford more pain.*

Then his calls began. Every messenger, every device, buzzing. And I thought: this is the man I chose, the one I wanted to lean on. He told me he cared. So I owed him at least to pick up. Not to talk — just to pick up.

I did. He asked: *"What is happening?"* I had no words, just sobs. Finally, the only thing I could say clearly was, *"I give up. I can't do this anymore."* Not fighting, not holding, no soldiering — just supporting this relationship, the warmth, the spark. But I couldn't. It wasn't enough.

We sat in silence on the line. Then we said goodbye.

The days after, I found a new chamber under the bottom of my pit — but I was also angry. Pete hadn't been fair. When he needed me, when he needed unwavering support, I was there. And when I needed him, he "couldn't arrange it". I was angry, and anger has its own energy. It burns. And I used that fire to return to the idea of flying.

I opened the paragliding forums again and found Morocco:

a thousand dollars, everything decided for you — where you live, what you eat, where you fly. Not hardcore, more like traveling with the option to fly. Even if I never opened my gear, I'd still be by the ocean.

A few months later, in May, I booked my usual acro school, and then a message came: my old instructor was organizing a trip to India, to the Himalayas. The man who had taught me to fly — I hadn't seen him since moving to the US — and now there was a chance, the timing falling neatly between the other two trips, and I thought: why not.

I couldn't focus for long, but slowly the itinerary began to take shape — anchors in the fog. Morocco said, "Just come," the acro guys were as welcoming as ever, and India reached out. I said yes. I couldn't focus for long, but slowly, the itinerary took shape — anchors in the fog. Morocco said, "Just come." Acro guys were welcoming as always. India reached out. I shepherded everything in my calendar to make sure nothing overlapped and booked the plane tickets.

Meanwhile, Pete and I still talked a little. I didn't see a future, but I wanted to know he was OK. A lighthouse on the shore, a signal back and forth. One day he sent me a picture of a cup he had made in pottery class with his son. Hand-painted in orange and blue, parts of it clearly done by his kid. "A replacement for the one you broke." I thought: I don't need a cup. I can buy a thousand cups. What I need is decency, support. But it felt like an attempt.

Later he asked, *"Can we have a Zoom?"* I wasn't sure why, but well... he was still the person I had been with for more than half a year. I owed him that. We chatted about mundane nonsense for half an hour. And then he found his courage: *"Come live with me in Dubai while you heal."* I didn't know what to say. But a smile surfaced. He saw it and said, *"That's a good sign, the way you are looking at me."* It felt right, but also too easy. One question doesn't erase weeks of misery. And I had my plan. I was going to fly. Still, I said, *"Maybe I can come for a few days between Morocco and India, and a few weeks in April. Use your place as a base."* He replied, *"And I can come see you wherever you go."* Spoiler — little did he know about the middle of nowhere and the wonders I had planned.

"Of course, dear. I'm glad you're here today. Let's make Dubai the base."

Part II
The Unmoored Middle

Chapter 10
Casablanca Ride

I don't know where I'm going from here, but I promise it won't be boring.

— David Bowie

I left Chicago still half-asleep and half-alive, with three suitcases and exactly zero certainty about where my life was going. In my diary I'd written, "*I feel like a piece of wet clay — pliable, unshaped, waiting for my future.*" It sounded brave at the time. Mostly it was terror wrapped in stationery.

Burnout had burned everything: appetite, curiosity, ambition. I wasn't even sure what I wanted anymore — only that I wanted *something*. Or what I dreaded was the void of stillness waiting for me around the corner. I'd do anything to prevent going back, even if it was moving forward. My therapist called it "re-engaging with the world." I called it "trying not to crumble." You'll see the effect of this mind state in the next chapters. My brain registered events but remained partially absent, so it all comes out more like a report of those days — without lively details, fragmented, a selection of pictures rather than a story. It's not that I'm broken as a narrator; it's that the Maria of that time couldn't connect events into anything cohesive.

The overnight flight was pure purgatory. Somewhere over the Atlantic I watched a documentary about Amy Winehouse — her voice, her chaos, her line that stuck in my head, *"If you can't look after yourself, no one can."* Well, I'm failing at the basics — by the time we landed in Casablanca, I couldn't tell whether I was hungry, tired, or just dehydrated from too much recycled air. What do I know about this town? It has to be grainy black-and-white, and someone has to say, *"It's the beginning of a beautiful friendship."* I grinned at the irony.

Outside the airport everything smelled like dust and fuel. I rented a car — a ridiculously big BMW diesel, because apparently that's what you get when you ask for "automatic" in Morocco. I didn't even know diesel and gas weren't exactly the same until I tried to refuel and the attendant pointed at the word *"gasoil"*. So there I was, blocking the entire station, googling *"What is gasoil?"* while the locals waited, patient and politely amused. I must have looked like a parody of the American tourist: too large a car, too little clue, too much determination.

The forty-minute drive from the airport to the hotel felt like an exam I hadn't studied for. Cars, scooters, donkeys, entire families on one motorbike — everyone moved like a flock of birds, each obeying rules only they understood. A complex system, no less. I clenched the wheel so hard my fingers hurt. When I finally reached the hotel — a Bonvoy something, because I had loyalty points and zero strength to negotiate for authenticity — I could have cried from relief.

Chain hotels are faceless, but that night, I needed one without expectations. A shower, clean sheets, silence. A good wi-fi connection, though, allowed me to look up a restaurant and get a taxi. To the ocean! The sun was sinking in, the air came in soft, breezy waves, bringing the smell of salt and grilled fish. For the first time in months, no gray sky. Silence, disrupted by the crash of the surf and seagulls arguing somewhere above.

I ordered wine, real food on a real plate (the first in two days of airplane meals in tinfoil). Halfway through dinner, my phone lit up — Pete calling on Zoom. In Chicago, we'd never managed this hour; when it was dinner for me, it was past midnight for him. Now we were in the same day. He said, "You look better. I wouldn't guess you just made an overnight flight." I said, "Maybe I am better." And I meant it. It wasn't OK-ish yet, but the dread had eased, just an inch, and that was already an upgrade.

The next morning, Casablanca felt even brighter, offering its treasures in the gentle and damp air. I decided to visit the Hassan II Mosque, the city's famous landmark, mostly because I had no other plans. The guide told us it was built half on land and half on the Atlantic. He said the architects were inspired by a line in the Quran: *"The throne of God is upon the water."* So they built Him one — a palace literally on the ocean. It took them only twelve years. Cedar, mother-of-pearl, stone. Maximalist and minimalist at once — as if discipline and devotion had finally shaken hands.

I stood there, shoes off, head tilted back, thinking not about faith but about imagination. What humans can create when they believe in something — even if it's just a line from a book.

Leaving the mosque, I was still wrapped in those fantasies and let my feet carry me to a café by the ocean for a late breakfast. The waiter didn't speak English, and I realized, to my own surprise, that I could reply in French. The words came back from somewhere deep in memory — dusty, slightly crooked, but functional. He smiled and said, "Votre accent est charmant." I laughed; so did he. I hadn't spoken French in years, and it felt like hearing the voice of an old part of myself that had been silent, but never completely faded.

Back at the hotel, I packed. The valets brought my suitcases to the door, and I loaded the car, ready to head toward Marrakech. Once outside the city, the road straightened, the air turned warmer, and the sea smell gave way to dust. The landscapes changed in slow motion — green fields, then limestone, then red clay glowing under the sun. Everything shifted so gradually that when I noticed, I gasped. Maybe this is how people heal — so slowly it feels sudden? Maybe I could?

Halfway along the road I saw flashing lights. First speeding ticket in my entire life: 130 km in a 120 zone. The officers were polite, even gracious. Somehow it felt like an accomplishment — proof of moving again.

Not long after, my phone pinged: a message from my therapist reminding me about our check-in. I pulled over, video-called her from the car. She asked, "Where are you?" I said, "Outside." Which was true, in every possible way.

She smiled. "How do you feel?" I said, "Better. Maybe reckless. But better."

I didn't tell her that I was in Morocco or that I was driving through a foreign country alone with three suitcases and one shaky sense of purpose. It felt too fragile to explain. She nudged me back toward mindfulness meditations and exercise. I nodded, already doing both — mindful of the road, exercising by staying alive on it.

When the session ended, I started the car and merged back into the moving flock of traffic. The horizon was bleeding red. I rolled down the window, let the warm air hit my face, and thought: "*You wanted to feel life again.* Here it is, the life, disguised as road dust and diesel — is this something you were longing for?"

Chapter 11
Tangerines in Marrakech

my heart was set
on rothko
marrakesh dress steel
retro choreography
fabric of being
alive
that expectation
of oceans
never listen to us
anyway
— erica lewis, "gonna show you
higher ground"

I arrived in Marrakech after the long drive from Casablanca, the red clay still clinging to my tires and my mind. The city greeted me with chaos — heat rising from the asphalt, vehicles swarming like mayflies, the call to prayer cutting through the car horns. I was exhausted and half-dazed, unable to articulate what waited for me ahead, only that forward was the only direction that made sense.

At the airport, I met the flying group. They were already clustered around a pile of luggage, chattering in four languages. When I rolled my three suitcases toward them, their eyes widened at the size of it all. I mumbled something about a few months on the road and tried to look smaller. They smiled — kindly, not mockingly — and made room for me. I felt exposed and invisible at the same time.

We loaded our gear into the van and headed toward Aguergour, our first flying stop in Morocco. In the darkness of a southern night, we stopped at a roadside market. I wondered why we weren't heading straight to the camp — everyone was tired from the long trip and sleepy — but the driver disappeared. It took several minutes for him to come back holding a large bag, dropping it into my lap. I reached inside — tangerines. Their scent filled the car: sharp, sweet, orange if it had color. I peeled one and passed a few slices to him. The juice stuck to my fingers, the dust from the road mixing with the sweetness. After months of gray, the fragrance was something surprising. The others laughed and talked easily. Their lives seemed intact and functional — this was a vacation for them. Mine still felt like a mosaic of cracks held together by dynamic equilibrium.

We reached the camp late, a cluster of rooms in the middle of the desert. The night was silent, no city hum, only wind and our tired footsteps on gravel. I was sharing a room with two other women. I'd never agree to that in a sound mind, but here we are. My too many suitcases spilled into the small space. Obviously, I had too much stuff... but to my panicking mind, there was also too much of THEM. They seem cheerful and patient, but they are total strangers. How am I supposed to sleep next to them? What if they snore? What if I snore? I was frantically moving from one thought to another, but frankly there was nothing to do about it right now. Jet lag gnawed at me, and sleep came like anesthesia despite the overstimulation of a new world.

Morning revealed that the window in our room had no glass — it was simply open to the air. People here didn't see the need to separate the indoors from the outdoors. And from this no-glass window, I saw... a goat. It was peacefully chewing on something, minding its own goat business. I felt a flicker of discomfort but said nothing; I didn't want to seem spoiled or high-maintenance. Would I be too much of a princess if I voiced concern about the proximity of this goat to my pillow? So I focused instead on the tangerine trees bending under their fruit, on the smell of Moroccan honey and mint tea with freshly baked bread drifting from the kitchen. The world was alive, and I was almost interested in it.

We were going to fly that day — it was a paragliding camp, after all. My heart raced, excitement tangled with fear — after months of stillness, I wasn't sure my body remembered what to do; my mind certainly didn't. Before takeoff, our instructor — patient, sunburned, endlessly competent — took us on a short drive through the Atlas Mountains. The name alone carried myth: Atlas, the titan who held the sky. The landscape was a patchwork of contradictions — green valleys blooming with spring, ochre cliffs, dusty plains, and far away, snow-capped peaks. I watched it all, feeling something inside me stretch. After months of Chicagoan gray, these colors looked otherworldly.

When it was my turn, I clipped into my harness, trusting my hands to go through procedures as they had hundreds of times before. Then we were ready to launch — pull, lean into it, give it some speed — and the wind filled my glider, and suddenly I was weightless. The ground fell away, and the world opened — hills, roads, even a river all laid flat beneath. My heart thumped, but I wasn't scared anymore. I took a deep breath, laughed, even shouted. My first flight in a new country, on a new continent. Proof that I was still capable of lift.

The days that followed blurred into a rhythm of flight and sunlight, except for one — the day we visited Jardin Majorelle. I hadn't expected such a burst of beauty. The cobalt walls of the villa didn't reflect the light; they absorbed it, radiating something uncanny instead. Their presence felt unbelievable and yet sharply undeniable, framed by the graceful curves of palm trees, bamboo, and cacti from every corner of the world. Every shape and shadow seemed deliberate — the geometry of curiosity. The Majorelle blue was almost too vivid, piercing the eyes, making you doubt your eyesight and sanity — and then, insanely attractive, it drew your mind in, luring with its secrets, its magic, its fantastic hum. I took a thousand pictures — plants, paths, reflections — and portraits of myself that I barely recognized. Yves Saint Laurent had rescued this garden after decades of neglect, turning it into a cradle of love and design, and I understood why. It wasn't a garden; it was a dream of order and wonder stitched into the chaos of the world. Could I ever render the same service to myself? In that moment, I felt like part of a painting, and looking from the side, I had enough confidence to know that the woman on the canvas was beautiful and sensitive, even if she couldn't acknowledge it.

I overheard tourists speaking French and smiled — words floated back to me, familiar, soft, and carrying meaning. I thought of Pete then — how I missed his voice, his warmth, the safe hollow of his neck. The longing surprised me. For a moment, I was split between two lives: one vivid and full of color, and one that existed only through a screen.

That night, when I heard my teammates' laughter from the courtyard, I didn't join, but I didn't resent it either. I was learning to say, "I'm not comfortable," without apology. I lit the small lamp by my bed and wrote in my diary: I don't belong yet, but at least I'm here. On the windowsill, a strip of tangerine peel curled in the warm air, the scent of citrus and goat mixing with the night.

Chapter 12
Mirleft Nights

I am a part of all that I have met;
Yet all experience is an arch
wherethro'
Gleams that untravell'd world
whose margin fades
For ever and forever when I move.
— Tennyson, "Ulysses"

We left Marrakech in the early morning, the van heavy with paragliding canopies, harnesses, my suitcases, and the soft weariness of travel. Our guide and flying instructor, an unshakable optimist, had turned himself into a DJ. He matched the road to music: Arabic pop for the sunrise, 80s love songs for the red hills, and something French and nostalgic as the light mellowed. Each turn had its own soundtrack, and for the first time in months I found myself humming along — even dancing in my seat, no longer watching it happen but being inside it.

The landscape kept shifting: red clay dissolving into gold

sand, then finally into a horizon of silver and blue. When the Atlantic appeared, it was so sudden and so wide that the van fell silent. It looked like the end of the world and the beginning of peace. The closer we came, the louder it murmured — a deep, steady breathing that wrapped itself around everything. The air grew heavier with salt and humidity, faintly smelling of oranges left too long in the sun.

Mirleft was a small, quiet fishing village — whitewashed and a little frayed around the edges. Children played barefoot in the dusty streets, women in bright scarves leaned from balconies to gossip, and cats patrolled every corner. Someone handed me a key and pointed upward: my apartment was on the top floor. "Go up until the stairs end, then out onto the roof — at the end of it, you'll see a door. It's yours." To my introverted cheer, the building was almost empty — no neighbors, no noise. The whole rooftop was mine. Finally, no people around when I fell asleep or woke up, no one I needed to talk to before finishing my first cup of coffee in the morning.

The flat was small and bright, the tiled floors cool and glossy under my feet, reflections playing on the walls. From every window I could see the ocean, only a hundred meters away but blocked by a field of construction debris — pipes, stones, shattered bricks. It was the perfect metaphor for my mind then: the view intact, the way obstructed. The ocean was there, breathing, but I couldn't reach it yet.

That evening I walked down to the beach. The light was already fading, the wind teasing my hair. The waves sounded deep and hypnotic, almost human — like a grandmother telling a bedtime story while you drift toward sleep. I stood there for a long time, watching the foam curl and collapse, letting the hum fill the hollow places inside my head. The ocean didn't ask questions. It just kept breathing.

The next morning, we went paragliding. Coastal flying is always different — it's easy, forgiving, even relaxing (to the extent you can let your concerns go when 50-70 m over the ground). The damp air is thick to slice through — it hugs you like a weighted blanket, slowing you down, allowing for precious moments to focus on what you feel, not how you survive. In places like Mirleft you can glide for kilometers one way and back again, barely touching the steering lines in hours. Like a lazy seagull, I hovered over the stretched coastline of dust, cliffs, and white foam, the blue reaching farther than my eyes could go. Pete was already on his way, somewhere between airports, and maybe that lifted me more than the wind itself. Pete decided to come find me here. *On the very brink of reality,... this means something, right?* For the first time in weeks, I felt light.

Days settled into rhythm: flying, landing, eating, para-waiting. One evening our group went to the fish market, where tables overflowed with everything that swam. You choose your fish and they grill it on the spot. My companions discovered I spoke French and immediately appointed me translator. It felt good to be useful again, even if I fumbled the words and resorted to pointing at the sea creatures — whose names I don't know in ANY language — and laughing with everyone else.. The smoke, the chatter, the heat — it was messy and joyful and real.

Another part of me was restless. Pete's connection got

delayed, and then came the three-hour drive from the airport. We joked over messages about my talent for choosing unreachable places — a hole in a hole, he called it. He said he was driving fast, and I told him to slow down, though part of me was already listening for the sound of his car. Night thickened; stars appeared; the air cooled. I realized the village wasn't really on Google Maps, and his phone was dying.

So I went out to meet him. Where? The streets were dark — no pavement, no lights — only the echo of my own steps and the distant murmur of the sea. I guessed where he might get lost and walked that way, trusting instinct. Then I heard it: his audiobook playing through an open car window, a voice floating through the night, "I feel I need a holiday, a very long holiday, as I have told you before. Probably a permanent holiday: I don't expect I shall return. in fact, I don't mean to, and I have made all arrangements....". A minute later headlights cut across the sleeping village, and the car stopped in front of me. The door opened, and there he was: tired, smiling, in the flesh.

We didn't say much. The sea kept whispering in the distance, as if it had known all along that we would meet.

Chapter 13
The Martian Sunset

Between what is said and not meant,
and what is meant and not said,
most of love is lost.
— Kahlil Gibran

I haven't seen Pete in person since that weekend in the Dubai desert. Since then, we broke up for that awful week in February, and my burnout happened, and I felt like I was a different person. At the same time, I was longing for physical touch — for tenderness that could dissolve my personality for a moment, to lose myself in his arms, maybe to find some comfort there. And despite knowing that you can't really solve your problems just by being with someone, that you have to do it on your own; still, it was important to feel belonging. He actually made an effort and came all this way to find me here — in the middle of nowhere in the middle of nowhere. That really mattered.

We woke up in the morning and went out for breakfast. In Mirleft, there were only three small cafés side by side on a dusty street — eggs, fantastic Moroccan bread, coffee. We sat together, looking at each other, holding hands. I don't recall what we were talking about — or if we were talking at all. It felt fragile and unbelievable, like a mirage in the desert. Tilt your head and it may disappear.

Note from Pete: "*I remember that you just didn't know what to do with me. To love or to chase away.*"

Right now I find it hard to patch together the events of those days. The fact that he was close was so enormous to process that my brain stopped recording 80% of what was going on — it just refused to store it. For the life of me, I can't say what he was wearing or what color his rental car was. What music was playing in the café where we heard and danced to it. The dance was an excuse to lean into his arms in public. The owner, a French woman, looked at us with a spark of compassion — not asking anything, only whether we wanted sugar in our coffee (yes for me, no for him). Then we danced on the high shore over the ocean. There was a camper van and a grey-haired rock guy sitting in front of it with his dogs, listening to music. We stood by, overlooking the blue waves, holding hands — closer, closer — then started swaying. A calming, happy place. I can't say what song it was, but it was ours for that moment. And broader — despite everything before and after — those moments were only for us. We joked about what the man might think and decided he'd probably seen it all and would appreciate affection when he saw it — maybe reminiscing about a love story of his own.

Later that day, we set out to drive toward the wild Atlantic shoreline — the stretch with red sandstone arches. The car was a stick shift, and I asked Pete to let me try driving it. I hadn't driven one in years, but curiosity won. We ended up in an arrangement where I worked the pedals and he changed the gears. Coordination, patience, a bit of chaos. I laughed at the absurdity of it — my knee shaking, his hand on the gear stick, both of us pretending this was perfectly normal. Sometimes he pushed me to shift faster than I wanted, and sometimes I hesitated too long. Maybe that's how we were in general — moving forward, not quite in sync, but still together, figuring out the rhythm of the road, the engine, and us. *"You fighting the clutch, me fighting my control issues."*

As if in passing, he asked about my burnout. It was clear that while he was trying to accept and understand it, he didn't really get what it was. I think even now he doesn't. He asked in so many words: why, what happened, what drove it, why I felt like that, what caused it, how I could fix it. It all sounded logical, but it wasn't understanding. It was interrogation disguised as care. I knew he wanted to help, to make sense of it, to fix it — but that's the thing about burnout: it resists fixing.

I tried to tell him about the Paris guy, Lucien, but I couldn't make myself say the harder truths — that the distance, his unresolved marriage, the constant longing, all took their toll. That I didn't know which part had broken me. That I was scared of explaining it to someone who wanted reasons when there weren't any clear ones. It was a sickness of the soul, invisible and merciless. I remember thinking, *"If I can't explain it to him, the person who cares about me, maybe no one will ever understand. Maybe I'm damaged beyond repair."* My therapist once said, "Get out of your own way and let yourself heal." But those conversations didn't help. They made me feel like a malfunctioning machine trying to reference broken files. I posed the same questions to myself and couldn't find words. Some mechanism in my mind would blur out the inner view, force me to stop. Maybe it was too painful. Maybe it was protective — healing by avoidance.

The biggest fear for me was falling again — losing all will to move on, to look around, to care. The fear of drowning in apathy was worse than exhaustion itself. At that thought, I shrugged — no, I couldn't defend myself back then. Couldn't stand up for this soft, fragile person inside. I can now. I have stubbornness and force in me. I can fight if needed. Which is why I usually don't have to, people sense when a punch will be returned. I'm not a victim — that's how I would describe myself now. But then, I was... agreeable. Meek. Did he feel it? Was he scared of seeing me like that? Did my autopilot take over again?

We arrived at the beach near sunset — a vast, open place surrounded by red cliffs. And when I say red, I mean it — deep terracotta bleeding into violet and purple as the light shifted. A natural red sandstone arch bridged the shore, its feet sunk into wet sand; at low tide, you can walk beneath it, while the waves lick its base and break into spray. We walked through it, the sand lukewarm and spongy underfoot. Beyond it was another stretch of beach, the rocks carpeted in mussels that shimmered black and silver. We climbed one — carefully, laughing, testing the wet surface. Waves crashed below, loud but not threatening. The air was laced with salt and the metallic scent of the shells. It was one of those places so beautiful it makes you dizzy, the kind that rewrites your idea of the world.

"It's the perfect place for a proposal," he said jokingly.

I froze for a moment. In the background of my mind, a thought flickered — *you don't understand me, and you're married to someone else.* Pinch. So I smiled and said, "Maybe. But also a perfect place for a cigarette." I took one out and lit it. He hugged me from behind, his chin resting on my shoulder. The warmth of him, the crash of waves, the smoke — it all felt like life condensed into one absurd, beautiful moment.

We stood there for a long time, not speaking. The sun slipped below the horizon, the rocks glowing like molten copper. For that brief time, everything felt suspended — connected and disconnected, love and depression coexisting. Happiness, I realized, isn't only what happens to you. It's also what you choose to feel.

Chapter 14
The Hut and the Fortress

The flying spot in Mirleft is called Nid D'Aigle — though we didn't see any eagles there. That's something about Morocco: it dazzles on the surface, sometimes more appearance than substance. Those days were beautiful, yes, but also strangely shallow — like I was watching my own life through a fogged window. Depression does that. It fragments the life and makes you feel separate from yourself, your words from your feelings, it cracks your reality into pieces, and then mismatches them into an ugly Quasimodo.

I was depleted and losing foothold, content with OK. Pete was the opposite, with his ADHD, he always craved variety, movement, the next thing. And I wanted him to be comfortable, to have what he needed — he flew this long way to be here, I was rushing myself to give him space to enjoy it. I'll give him credit, though: he often found magical places. Still, his process drove me mad. He dragged me through a handful of hotels before settling on something "perfect." Days before, waiting for his arrival, I had already unpacked in my rooftop flat, found a local market, and stocked it with eggs, bread, fruit, coffee — tried to make it ours. But no. It wasn't enough. And I didn't have the will to explain why that rubbed me the wrong way. If it wasn't good enough for him, it simply wasn't. If silence was the price, I paid it. A vicious circle.

This new place for the night was a romantic hotel with huts on the beach. You stepped straight from the door onto the sand, into the hum of the ocean. I packed a few things for the night. Nomad life was growing into me: toothbrush, shawl for the night, who cares if I wore any underwear — survival mode disguised as freedom. I was shutting down, quietly agreeing to adventure, hoping it could build connection. But the hut was dazzling, and I let it be enough.

He: "Do you realize you turn me on just by standing there, two meters away?"

I: "I didn't hear neighbors knocking on our door."

He: "Really? They definitely heard your groans."

I: "I don't care — they can envy or be happy for us. Their choice."

It was absurd and funny, and I smiled despite myself.

The next morning, I woke at hazy dawn. A bright rainbow rose straight from the ocean, the sky turning pink with the first light. I was alone. Pete had gone swimming — the water barely sixteen degrees, cold and pure. I stepped onto the terrace, naked under a white blanket, the cigarette smoke curling into the sunrise. I remember thinking, "I could write a novel about this." When he came back, sea-salted and glowing, he smiled at me like I was part of the scenery. He admired the view — all of it — and drew me back to bed.

For some reason, that morning proved I didn't want him to leave. Despite his blindness to my exhaustion, I still felt warmth toward him. Or maybe it was just the illusion of safety. But I held on to it.

We used that day to bring Pete closer to the airport. No one said it out loud, but he was leaving tomorrow. The drive wound through Morocco's south — rocky desert turning into mountain passes. It rained, then cleared. The road coiled like a snake through fog and sunlight until we reached a valley full of almond trees in bloom. White and pink petals trembled in the wind. Quiet, tender. Perfect for me.

We listened to his audiobook of The Lord of the Rings. I've known it by heart since my teens; every line felt like an old friend. When Frodo and Sam got a basket of mushrooms from Farmer Maggot, I laughed — that kind of familiarity was comforting. Predictability was a gift. I was in a foreign country with a man who legally belonged to another, but he crossed continents to see me, surrounded by almond blossoms. For a brief moment, there was nothing threatening in the world.

The day blurred on — fragments replaying like a kaleidoscope: crooked argan trees stepping out of fog like alien creatures, red mountains and beige rocks, goats climbing impossible slopes. Pete talking about his kid. Me saying something silly. A rainy village, me walking alone while he took a call. Booking another hotel for the night. A medieval fortress tucked in a valley, where we wandered through stone corridors, imagining farmers hiding grain from raiders. We kissed in the corners like teenagers. For that evening, the world was simple.

The Morocco trip was messy, beyond saving, but that chaos gave us a rare gift: we were normal there, blending in. The town where we stayed was typical for the coast, with a few cafés, small streets, salt in the air. I wore the long skirt I'd packed just for Pete, sparkly jewelry, washed my hair — an emergency resurrection. The restaurant was fancy enough for wine and grilled fish. The chatter was light, his jokes quick and warm. For a night, I felt cherished.

That's the curse of long-distance love: you wait forever to meet, and when you finally do, you waste the first days just re-learning how to exist together — their voice, their smell, their gestures. Only when you start to relax, it's already time to part.

The next morning was blissfully decadent. We ordered breakfast in bed — coffee, fruit, pastries — and watched a movie propped on pillows. Like kids pretending to be grown-ups, or grown-ups pretending the world outside didn't matter. *Who know what a plane was? Burn that witch!* It felt reckless and perfect. I told myself not to be angry about another work call he took mid-morning. He hadn't cleared his schedule — I knew that. But I also knew I couldn't afford to be angry. So I built my own small pool of contentment from what was there. Not an ocean — but enough to float.

We moved that pool to a new apartment, this time in Imsouane. The terrace overlooking the ocean was lined with carpets and jute cushions, rough but comforting — reality scratching softly against the skin. Pete held me as we watched a movie about the desert, the Martian landscapes echoing outside our door. We dozed off right there, and the early morning came too soon. He kissed me goodbye, made coffee, and left for his flight home.

For a while, his presence lingered — his voice, his scent, the echo of laughter. Then, nothing. Just the ocean and me, facing the next stretch alone.

Chapter 15
Salt, Steam and Pirates

Your absence has gone through me
Like thread through a needle.
Everything I do is stitched with its
color.

— *W. S. Merwin, "Separation"*

Neither I nor even the memory of Pete left the apartment the following day.

I lounged naked in the sun, pretending my body was a solar battery (who could see me — seagulls?), listening to the waves, reading the poetry book Pete brought me, daydreaming, and half-watching a TV series whose name I don't even remember. The silence felt strange — not peaceful, not lonely, just hollow in a way I couldn't describe.

Luckily, my group arrived in Imsouane soon after. They asked about our adventures and wished they'd gotten more than just a glimpse of Pete. They took me to the take-off, talking, laughing, looking at the ocean from every possible angle, walking along the coastline, feeling the mist of the waves crashing against the rocks. Thousands of steps by the water, collecting shells, watching incredible sunsets. The air pushed salt and the scent of seaweed into my lungs, leaving me no choice but to breathe deeper.

The simplicity of the surfer village gave me peace. It was grounding to watch people living day by day, with no urgency to prove anything. I longed for Pete, though. It didn't sound real, but something in my heart was shifting — I was beginning to understand what I truly wanted. Not adventure or stories to tell. I wanted something simple and mundane — closeness, small rituals, a steady rhythm, not novel material but real life. I looked at the ocean and thought how painfully short it all is, how easy it is to waste hours on nothing.

We took a trip to Essaouira — a pirate town up the coast with markets buzzing and restaurants spilling onto the streets. My companions were elated, bargaining, eating, laughing. I stayed behind, sitting on a stone wall, leaning my back against an old bronze cannon that once guarded the city. The ocean wind tangled my hair; birds hovered over the harbor. Their cries were calling me back to the lively hustle. But not yet. Right now, all I could do was sit there and breathe through this unmoored middle of my existence.

I celebrated the end of my Moroccan chapter with a hammam — steam and organic black gooey soap made locally from who knows what. It seemed like a good idea: a way to clean up and return to my senses, to come back to myself. But as I sat in the heat, sweat mixing with soap, I was still lost. My body was here, in a tiled room smelling of eucalyptus, but my mind wandered somewhere over the foggy Saharan hills, under foreign stars.

The steam wrapped around me like fog, and for a moment, I disappeared.

Chapter 16
Capsule of Air

I'd gotten so used to living in Chicago, far away from everything and everyone, that it didn't even occur to me that "eleven hours between point A and point B" in this part of the world meant the layover would last an entire night. And you have to understand — I had enough brainpower to pack my three suitcases but not enough to double-check how long I'd actually be in the Istanbul Airport.

I knew the place — I've always loved it, I still do — but it still came as a surprise when I landed there, checked the screens for my next flight, and realized I had almost eight hours until departure. My poor sense of geography betrayed me: Istanbul to

Belgrade is barely an hour's flight, basically a bus route. Sometimes, even crossing Chicago in traffic takes longer than that.

Evening had fallen, and I was bone-tired and homeless. Lost, extremely lonely, and — most of all — incapable of coping. When you're deep in depression, sensations blur together — everything becomes too much. Any small nuisance feels like an enormous event. The airport is a textbook example even for a healthy mind. The place smelled of coffee, cleaning detergent, jet fuel, and a faint trail of designer perfume from duty-free stores. Announcements echoed overhead, trolleys rattled, children cried. I wasn't used to that kind of noise anymore — I had just come from an empty surfer's village where a single passing car was an event. Before that, the Sahara — the quietest place on Earth. Here, three hundred people could pass by in the time it took to sip a coffee, chatting in ten languages.

Gods, I have three diplomas, I'm a consultant, a strategist — I've moved mountains before... but in moments like this, reasoning gives you no advantage; you can't think your way out of overstimulation.

I needed a dark and silent space, and once again I was just lucky — right in the transit zone, I saw sleeping pods — tiny, dark, and silent capsules of air that would be mine for a few hours. It cost almost as much as staying at the Ritz, but it was worth every cent. Step inside, close the door.

I promised myself I'd be safer and better taken care of in the weeks ahead. But for now, I talked to myself like a child: You poor thing, just settle here for the night. Breathe in, breathe out.

The sheets are clean, the pillow is cool. You're OK. My rational side rolled its eyes, but this tone of voice worked better than panic. I lay down, curled on my side, breathing in the crisp scent of linen. Sleep didn't come easily, thoughts circled restlessly: Where do I go? Can I get back to work, eventually? What if I can't? What happens with Pete? Do we ever stop breaking up? Maybe it's safer this way — not getting too close, staying half-known? But I want real. I want close. I want to be known and accepted, even when I'm not my best. For the first time in weeks, that thought felt like clarity.

At some point, I must have drifted off into dreamless sleep. When I woke, all I had to do was open the door, and I was already at the gates. It felt surreal — the bustle of departure so close to my pillow, the light flooding in as if I were still dreaming. I had slipped in a space between countries, between worlds.

Chapter 17
Belgrade Balcony

I gave in to life. I was not defeated but outplayed.
— Ivo Andrić, Signs by the Roadside

There is no sane way to explain Belgrade in my itinerary. Between Chicago, Morocco and Dubai, it just happened. And it was just what I needed to calm down my spiraling mind. The city carried a rhythm I could trust — slower, softer, forgiving. My closest friend, Sarah, lived there, and for that week while her husband was away, I had a place to rest. I could simply be — sit next to her, watch her embroider, browse her books, exist in her space. Books filled Sarah's apartment — shelves lining every wall, creating a sense of HOME in capital letters. Her collection of plates was carefully chosen by her husband during his wanderings through the flea markets and pawn shops. Each had a story to tell. She'd lived in Belgrade long enough to know the best restaurants, the right places to order from.

We went grocery shopping, cooked, shared wine and laughter. We found a cake called Kraljica Marija — Queen Maria — and I insisted it was named after me. We talked about growing up, about having kids, about my plan to move to Europe.

Our days together were gentle. We made dinner, drank wine at the kitchen counter, lingered over coffee, gossiping about people we used to know, tracing what became of them. I told her about Morocco and Dubai; she told me about her work and the small things that made her happy. Some days, I would describe mine in fragments — a bench in the park, half an hour with a book, a pigeon, a grocery store with good apples, brought back for dessert. She would smile and respond with genuine curiosity: "Oh, that's the Per Su store, right? How did you find it? Was it easy to navigate?" It wasn't advice or concern. It was deep human interest that didn't ask for anything in return. She had that gift, and I was lucky to receive it.

Sarah and I met when we were seventeen — back when the world was still expanding in all directions and we thought we had infinite time. We were both quiet girls then, introverted and a little nerdy about literature and languages, the kind of students who quoted Tolkien to each other and thought that counted as flirting with life. At the same time, we were ecstatic about living away from home and starting university. In my country, we don't have sororities, but at our faculty, the gender balance was about ten-to-one for girls — so by nature, it was an endless sorority with rare male aberrations. You'd imagine pink and gossip and obsession with love stories, but instead it was passion for the strangest art-house films, endless discussions about philosophy, and roller-skating through the night streets of the megapolis with a bottle of cheap berry wine. We grew up — some steps together, some apart — but we were lucky not to lose our connection.

Now, nearly twenty years later, I found myself mentally unwell, while she remained quietly strong — comfortable staying beside me when I didn't want to speak. She didn't need to fix me or fill the silence. Life had gone on for both of us. Here was a harbor where I never needed to worry if I was enough, if I looked good, if I was pleasant enough to be around. I exhaled.

Some conversations are like warm baths — safe and serene — and in them, plans begin to shape themselves simply because someone who loves you is listening. Whether you succeed or fail doesn't matter; they'll appreciate you either way, and you know it in your bones.

The last time we'd seen each other was New Year's Eve in Istanbul — only a few months ago, though it felt like years. So much had changed. I wasn't the sparkly woman in a tutu with a champagne flute anymore. And somehow it didn't matter. Sarah said, "I've seen you at seventeen. You weren't that sparkly then either. I've seen you at the start of your career. Honestly, whatever you've achieved — I don't understand half of it, and I don't care about the other half. It's not THAT important. What matters is that I can hug you, pour us wine, and we can go out for dinner or try something new."

It's impossible to overstate how healing that was. Belgrade became the quiet background of this restoration.

The city itself was patchy and fascinating — a blend of

elegant European architecture and brutalist concrete blocks, with whole corners still scarred by the bombings of 1999. In some streets, ornate facades with carved angels stood beside buildings left hollow and raw. It was chaotic, yet somehow coherent. Much like the way differing opinions and old wounds coexisted among people here; the city lived in balance between contradiction and calm. That *polako* spirit — softly, without rush — prevailed over everything. You could feel it in the way people talked, the way they smiled, the way cafés stayed full for hours.

Everyone eats out in Belgrade. Cafés spill onto sidewalks, terraces crowded with laughter, the smell of coffee and freshly baked bread floating through the air, mixing with the light scent of blossoming cherry trees. It reminded me a little of Istanbul — that hum of everyday happiness. People chat, smoke, flirt, debate politics, feed stray cats under their tables. This was the life I wanted: mundane, alive, beautifully ordinary.

Walking became my default. If Google Maps said it was under an hour, I'd put on my sneakers and go. After years in the U.S., where everyone drives even for ten minutes, walking felt like rebellion. Step by step, my body adjusted to the rhythm of the city — tram bells, the hiss of espresso machines, pigeons taking off from the square. My amygdala was learning peace. Sometimes I walked with purpose, sometimes aimlessly, letting the streets decide. Getting lost wasn't failure; it was exploration. In those meandering walks, I realized how rare it is to have the time and safety to simply wander.

I loved walking by the Kalemegdan Fortress, watching the orange light of sunset reflect in the slow flow of the Danube.

Sitting on the wall of a medieval fortress, overlooking centuries of life, I could feel the flow of time — so many things existed long before you, and so many will exist after. It humbled and soothed me. In the parks, apple and pear trees were in bloom, petals of white and pink falling on cobblestones like confetti. They reminded me of the almond blossoms in Morocco, and I wanted to show them to Pete — I sent him picture after picture, my phone full of small attempts to share.

Mornings were often spent on the small balcony of my Airbnb, coffee in hand, sun on my skin or sometimes the soft gray of clouds. The sounds of the city filtered in — a radio playing folk music somewhere below, a baby crying, the chatter of neighbors, and in the evening, music drifting from nearby terraces where someone was dancing. Belgrade lived out loud, but it didn't intrude; it breathed gently around me.

I met my old circus coach — she'd moved to Belgrade too. Olga welcomed me with the same warmth as before, happy to see me back and torture me a bit with exercise. Training was grounding; muscle soreness killed me and at the same time became evidence of becoming alive and stronger. Pain in the body was manageable, unlike the one in the mind. I also booked a massage package, and it turned into a mindfulness exercise. The woman doing them was called Suzy, and she chose to live nomadically, traveling from country to country as she pleased. I envied her ease. My curls came back — finally, after months of exhaustion straightening them out. Finding a good hairstylist in a new country isn't easy; you start by asking around, and somehow it all leads to the right door. Hours later, head wrapped in chemicals and curlers, I saw myself in the mirror — bouncy spirals, a full mane again. I wasn't fully there yet, but it was an improvement.

Evenings often ended on the same small balcony at my place. Two chairs, a small table, an ashtray. I smoked and watched the sun set over the city's red roofs. The balcony overlooked the courtyard of neighboring buildings — voices pouring in from other lives. Someone practiced dance steps, someone laughed, someone clinked dishes. The scent of dinner drifted up, mixed with cigarette smoke and evening air. I liked that feeling — of being alone and surrounded at once. Every place I'd lived had a balcony: Istanbul, Chicago, Dubai, Mirleft, now here. Each one was a small refuge, a brink between inside and outside, a place to linger and allow indecision. Maybe that's why I could never quite quit smoking — not just the nicotine, but the ritual of stepping out, breathing in, pausing.

Belgrade's balcony was my latest pause. A quiet space where time softened its edges. Sarah would pour wine, I'd light a cigarette, and we'd talk about nothing or everything — love, friendship, what's next, the latest TV series. No pressure to say anything meaningful, move, to decide, to fix. Just to be.

Belgrade breathed slowly. So did I.

Polako.

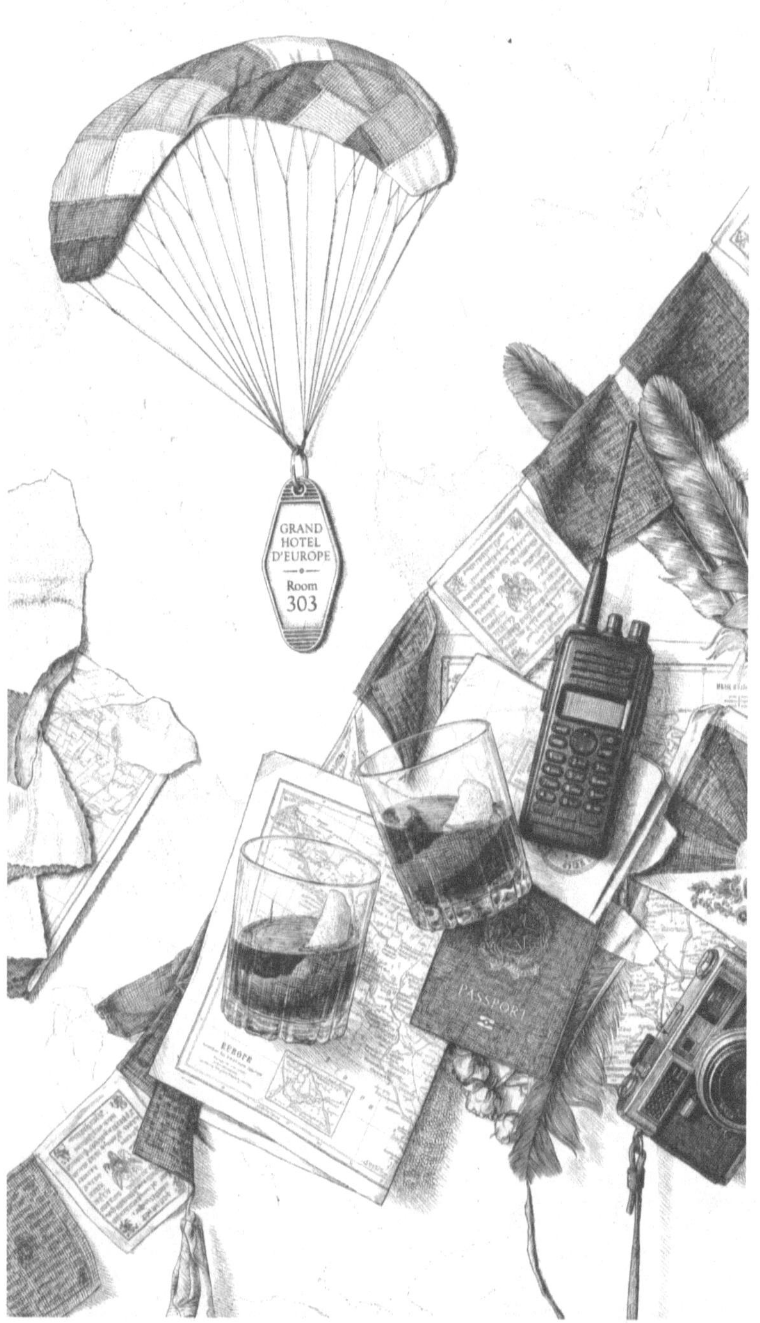

GRAND
HOTEL
D'EUROPE
Room
303
PASSPORT
EUROPE

Part III
Arrival & Disillusionment

Chapter 18
The Hotel of Power(less)

Where to start — if only I could start from all sides at once without feeling as though every word has too many letters, takes up too much time.

— David Grossman, Be my knife

After Belgrade, I went to Dubai for a short stay — three nights, two days — to spend some time with Pete before heading to India. It felt good to remember that he had offered his place as a base for my nomad adventures, that he was waiting for me and wanted to see me there. After Belgrade, I felt refreshed, ready to explore, and open up again.

I was surprised when, after collecting me at the airport, he asked the taxi driver to take us not to his apartment but to a hotel. We hadn't discussed it beforehand, and I had assumed we would spend these days at his home. Pete seemed uneasy and presented the stay as something special — a kind of celebration for us. He called the hotel his "place of power." Over dinner, he told me a story about one of his first visits to Dubai — how he'd found himself walking through this palace, catching the sea glimmering beyond the walls, and thinking, This is where I can belong.

To be fair, the hotel was luxurious — stylized as an ancient Arabic fortress around an oasis, with canals winding through palm trees and sandstone buildings, and small boats drifting from one side to another. Everything was human-scaled and intricate, soft light reflected off the water. It wasn't the skyscraper Dubai you see on postcards; it was curated calm, a crafted paradise. He wanted to share that with me — to introduce me to his life here, as he wanted it to be.

When we unpacked, he said, "I have a gift for you." So many times over Zoom, he'd mentioned that he'd love to pick a dress for me — and now he'd brought two! So thoughtful. I wasn't prepared for posh restaurants here, and after weeks of travel all my clothes were in dire need of dry cleaning and pressing. It was so fun to unwrap them and hear him explain why he chose these two:: one pink and frilly, the other a white maxi with yellow and brown leaves. And pockets! That's what women want, no kidding. I tried hard not to freeze (despite the thought crossing my mind, "The last man who went dress shopping for me was my ex-husband"), and instead to lean into joy. I wasn't sure what it meant, but it felt like care, a small claim of affection.

"Choose one," he said. "You can keep both if you want, too."

"I'll wear both," I smiled. Because we were in a hotel, after all — no dinners would be served at the kitchen counter.

That night was for the pink cocktail dress. We didn't have a reservation, but found a table at a restaurant right on the beach, waves lapping almost at our feet. The evening air smelled of seaweed and expensive perfume. We chatted with Pete, laughed, easing into our rhythm again. After time apart, we always needed a few hours — sometimes days — to sync up again. But the question hovered in the back of my mind: Why the hotel? I knew the answer — his almost-ex-wife still lived next door, in the same building. The risk of running into her terrified him. He'd never said it outright, but I could feel the fear shaping his choices. And I hated that fear — not just for him, but how it infected me too.

Still, the night was beautiful — like an Arabian fairy tale spun in modern fabric. The sea shimmered black and gold; the air was warm, almost liquid. After dinner, we stopped by the bar, and he ordered Amaro — our drink. As he handed me the glass, the scent of bitters and orange peel rising through the ice, it felt like recognition. He was no longer just a man in my messages or across an ocean — he was here, bodily, warm. The drink was festive, ours. I took a sip, and we walked back through the lantern-lit corridors. That night, I slept deeply near him for the first time. No jet lag. Just a rare, synchronized night.

The next day, he took me to his second favorite place — an aqua park. I was oddly proud that he wanted to show me his corners of the city. The sun burned hot, the air thick with chlorine and laughter. We went on every wild ride — dropped, spun, soaked. Water in our faces, sun in our eyes, the childlike joy of sliding and screaming together. We were both exhausted and elated. The body remembers faster than the heart how to trust.

By the evening, I was drained. Reconnection, even joyful, takes energy — your mind and body recalibrate at high speed. Dinner that night was spectacular anyway — at a restaurant built over the water, reached by a long wooden bridge. The breeze was scented of jasmine. Around us, dozens of couples — some tender, some Tinder. Dubai-style romance: perfect lighting, filtered affection, two people scrolling through their phones across the dinner table. I couldn't help but think, *"Thank God that's not us."* Our talk turned serious — his fear of losing connection with his son during the divorce. I listened, I reassured. It was real conversation, no jokes, smiles and pleasantries... maybe it is a real connection, too?

Yet I couldn't stop my thoughts from branching. Here I was, dining with a successful white man in his early forties, one of the most privileged kinds of humans — and still, he looked lost. How do we manage to be so unfulfilled, even when life gives us everything? Health, comfort, beauty — and yet we ache for more. Maybe that's what makes us human, or at least keeps us alive. The happy ones are usually dead — or sculpted in bronze.

The next morning, we returned to the aqua park. He showed me his favorite ride, the artificial waves where you just float, drift, exist. "This is where I look for peace," he said. For his restless ADHD mind, it was perfect: endless motion, no pressure or schedule. Then came the ice cream — a tiny cart with a crowd around it, the vendor vanishing right before we reached it. Typical Dubai comedy. The cones came topped with gold leaf — edible luxury. Even dessert had to shimmer.

In the midst of joyful hustle, my brain kept looping: *"Why are we in a hotel, not your home?"* He'd said his apartment was temporary — small, filled with furniture he didn't love, paintings he hadn't chosen. I knew one of them, the greenish modernist cow I'd seen behind him on Zoom. I wanted to see it in real life. And I came to realize that he was hiding, and not only from his ex. Spending the night at his place would mean something too real, too visible. It would mean belonging. And he wasn't ready to risk that.

When we finally went there, I was thrilled — a real home after weeks of hotels and Airbnb's. His apartment was indeed small but cozy, cluttered with too much furniture, the space of a man relearning single life. Figuring out what to buy, how to cook, how to live. I realized then how rarely we talk about men learning domesticity. He had a full drawer of supplements but no painkillers, no plasters, no first-aid kit. When do guys miss the survival lesson? Did we invite them at all?

Still, the place had a certain harmony. You could sense his pull toward beauty, toward order: souvenirs from his travels, soft lighting, the faint scent of oud and fresh laundry. It was imperfect, but human. And for the first time, I saw how deliberately he had built his comfort around design, not people, not the ad hoc wishes of his restless mind. No wonder he'd been drawn to me — messy, emotional, alive at the core, while on the outside I remained organized and disciplined. We were opposites. I was nature breaking into his architecture.

That night, making love in his bed felt different, tender, grounded, almost domestic. The scent of him on the sheets, the rhythm of his breath. It wasn't fireworks; it was homecoming. And the next morning, when he made breakfast. Eggs, coffee, toast — it was better than any Michelin meal. There's no luxury that compares to someone cooking for you out of love.

Chapter 19
Nomad in the Sky

Flying may not be all plain sailing,
but the fun of it is worth the price.
— Amelia Earhart

My take-off to India was scheduled for the early morning, around 7 a.m. I had everything packed again — this time one suitcase fewer, because I could leave one in Pete's apartment, my newfound "base." I was going to India a little reluctantly; I'd finally gotten to spend time with him in the intimacy of a home, and that mattered. On the other side of this journey lay the unknown — a country I'd barely seen before, a promise of flying and mountain air. Anyhow, I'd been into paragliding far longer than I'd been into Pete.

Imagine that early morning: sleepy people, airport lines, security trays, everything in motion. Then the flight to New Delhi — not long, three or four hours, maybe four and a half, though you land deep in the p.m. due to time difference. Vegetarian-only food options served as a reminder that I had no idea what I was getting into. When you land, India hits you with its scale. It's enormous, ancient, and dense with people. The sheer size of the arrival halls already hints at it — in this country, more than a billion people live and travel, and you know nothing about their lives. Even the biggest airports I'd been to — New York, Los Angeles, London — felt modest compared to this one.

I disembarked, collected my luggage, and got my passport stamped, gawking at the vastness and smelling the damp, warm air (in early March! What do they do during hotter seasons?). Knowing myself, I didn't rely on my problem-solving skills after a 7 a.m. flight, so I'd arranged a transfer in advance. A driver was waiting for me in the parking lot so we could begin the twelve-hour road trip up north into the Himalayas. Something I could barely fathom — in twelve hours you could cross half the U.S., or five countries in Europe, and here we were driving from the nearest airport to the flying spot.

Being wise, I tried to buy some water and snacks for the road... but alas, tapping my card resulted in the reader beeping disapprovingly. "Only Indian cards or cash," the shopkeeper said. Fantastic. Luckily, I still had a few dollar bills from Chicago — paper never fails when systems do.

My driver assured me we could find something on the way, and he even had some water in the car (I'm probably not the first or last passenger to arrive utterly unprepared). We loaded everything into the trunk, looked back at the airport (I didn't know it yet, but I wouldn't return to New Delhi), and set off on the road, aiming to reach the destination at dawn. The car wasn't exactly luxurious, but large enough to recline the seat and sleep.

Darkness came quickly. In India they drive on the left, a colonial echo, and the traffic itself sounds like an orchestra hectically preparing for the performance: horns blaring, headlights crossing, trucks painted like carnival floats. Back home, a horn means danger; here it was greeting, conversation, reassurance. The noise was constant, deafening, almost comic.

I tried to follow our direction on Google Maps, but soon the signal was gone. I realized I actually had no idea where I was being taken or whether the road was right — they could have driven me anywhere. Pinch of fear to my anxious mind. Having nothing better to do, I drifted in and out of sleep — half-dreaming, half-listening to history podcasts, waking up to the black window and a scattering of faraway lights.

At some point we stopped. The driver woke me gently. "Toilet break? Tea? Some food?" I shook my head. I didn't want to risk street food with twelve more hours to go and no local currency. "Do you have a bank on the way?" I asked. "At night?" he laughed. "No bank open now."

I stretched my legs. There were a few children's swings by the roadside. I sat on one, the chain squeaking, lit a cigarette, and stared into the dark. Out of the shadows loomed something large and strange — half from a dream, half from myth. A huge painted statue of a Hindu god — eyes wide, crown gleaming faintly in the headlights. It felt somewhere between divine and hallucinatory. Maybe both.

I wondered if the Greeks felt the same crossing the seas back from Troy. You know where you were before, you know where you're going — more or less — but you move through space on pure trust in the process. Night covers your tracks, and if you're pagan, you might pray to Nyx, the goddess of it, and throw a small offering to Hermes so the mischievous one doesn't toy with you.

We drove on, and on, and on. I lost track of time, sense of direction, and any hope of finding a comfortable position for my legs and back. Not seventeen anymore — I can't curl up like a shrimp without risking never uncurling again.

When we finally reached the hotel, I was still mulling over those thoughts, tired in both body and mind. It was a relief to find staff who greeted me kindly, carried my bags, and let me collapse straight into bed. It was still night, but the horizon was paling. Tomorrow would be a rest day, I decided. I would sleep, process the long road from Dubai — and the days we had with Pete there — and hope that all of this, the exhaustion, the distance, the chaos, would prove worth it. Well, this trip gives me an opportunity to paraglide, and that's something!

The next day, I woke up scrambled, but straight from my pillow I saw... the mountains. The Himalayas are something else entirely — pure space and impossible air. I wasn't even sure this was real, not a backdrop printed on paper, not something you could poke a hole in.

That morning (or maybe it was afternoon, if I arrived around five and slept for six hours), the weather turned playful. Thunder rolled over the ridges, and brief rain showers swept across the valley. Then, as if nothing had happened, the clouds opened to let through the light. Every storm was followed by a rainbow, every rainbow by a sky freshly washed in blue. You could almost hear the mountains breathe in and out.

I took my time to breathe with the mountains, just doing some Headspace exercises on the balcony opening into the valley. Below me stretched tea plantations, each plot covered in white fabric to shield the tender leaves from the sun. From above, it looked like a circus of tents scattered across the green, gleaming faintly in the light. Parrots shrieked in the distance, some blue birds darted across the air, and two eagles circled each other, looping and gliding as if waltzing to some tune I couldn't catch from here. It's a pity, but I can't stay in all day! Shower, Wi-Fi, and checking out what this village has to offer. A quick search online suggested: cows in the streets, Tibetan monks in ochre and burgundy, monasteries, blossoming gardens, paragliding pilots, tandems, and schools. And, wow, a coffee roaster! When I found it on the map, I was determined to check it out straight away. ...And it was a success! You have to be lucky to find a decent cappuccino in Chicago, and here it was — in the middle of nowhere, on the slopes of the Himalayas, in the village of Bir, India. It's the best spot to open my diary, no?

Date TBC — Bir, Northern India

I'm not even sure what day it is anymore; I've lost the rhythm of time somewhere between airports, rainbows, and arrivals and goodbyes. Maybe that's fine. The world here moves differently — slower, wider, softer — and I feel suspended in it, like a feather waiting to fall where the wind wants. What's ahead? I don't know, but it seems like the best place to figure it out.

Today I had decent coffee and a balcony view that could make a poet weep. My luggage survived, my Wi-Fi works, and so far I haven't fallen off any cliffs (not that I've climbed anything higher than a chair so far). The next few weeks promise flying — the best kind of meditation, diet — they don't really cook meat here, and I'm skeptical about most vegetables and spices, and lots of quiet. For now, I'll take another cup of chai and pretend I'm a local.

Toward the evening, another happy event came my way — a long-overdue meeting with my paragliding instructor. His name is Serge, about seventy years old. He started paragliding before it was cool, when they had to sew their own wings and learn to fly by trial and error. I don't know how he does it, but he commands respect and trust just by being in the room. His calm voice, grounding attitude, and above all — kindness, fairness of opinions. Imagine a wise and old dragon but in human shape.

You can see that I'm totally in love with the guy, and it's all right — his beautiful wife has nothing to worry about. He was the one who taught me to fly, the one who opened up the sky, and that's a kind of bond that never goes away. I hadn't seen him for three years, since I moved to the U.S., and it felt symbolic to meet again in a place so distant and exotic for both of us. He's older now, and I didn't know if we were going to meet again soon, so these days together were to be enjoyed.

These years weren't easy for him (same!), but it has only made him softer and funnier. He's one of those people who never raises their voice, never say anything abrupt or unkind. At the same time, around him you somehow know that the standards are sky-high and feel compelled to match them to the best of your ability. Not because you feel threatened or could be excluded, no. Just because it's good for you and the most reasonable thing to do. I think there's a whole philosophy beneath his course of action — acceptance, and wisdom, and deep understanding of humans: if they hear something harsh, they might get scared and defensive in return, and they might never try again. So he kindly jokes instead.

It was a happy reunion, all in all. And a busy one: catching up on the news, chatting about the latest events, and, most critically, getting through the briefing for flying tomorrow. Oh my, I'm going to fly in the Himalayas! To fly in any new spot, you need to memorize quite a few things so you don't waste precious time at take-off or in the air. That time might cost you a missed flight (not a huge deal), or an injury (which is far worse — especially given that medical support here leaves much to be desired). Typically, your first interests are the direction of the wind, its speed, takeoffs, no-go zones (if any), and basic orientation in local geography — mountain range names, rivers, some landmarks like oddly shaped peaks or canyons. All serious stuff, and you and you keep your eyes peeled for the map study and prick up your ears for the first task for tomorrow. But how exciting!

I couldn't wait until tomorrow to go flying.

Chapter 20
Higher Than the Snow Line

Sleep, my darling, sleep, my baby,
Close your eyes and sleep.
Darkness comes; into your cradle
Moonbeams shyly peep.
— Mikhail Lermontov, "A Cossack
Lullaby"[3]

I woke up before the alarm, heart thudding lightly, as if my body already knew what waited for me. The valley was still wrapped in dawn-blue quiet, and the air coming through the open balcony door was cold enough to sting my cheeks. This would be my first proper flying day in Bir. My hands shook a little as I braided my hair and layered my clothes — not from fear, but from anticipation. A different kind of altitude sickness.

On my way to the road crossing where the team would pick me up, a man stopped when he saw my gear bag.

"Ah, you fly?" he asked, clearly delighted. "Listen, very

---

[3] Translated by by Irina Zheleznova, Selected Works by Mikhail Lermontov

important — when you take off, you lean forward and keep the wing centered. Yes? Centered. And if it comes up too fast, brake gently. Gently. Not too much."

I blinked. Smiled politely. "Thanks, I'll remember."

Inside my head: *Holy airball. Three years of acro and I'm getting a 7 a.m. lecture on 'keeping the wing centered.'* I walked away before he could explain gravity to me.

The pickup truck arrived, filled with gliders, helmets, and sleepy pilots. No one felt like talking much; the cold bit our fingers as we climbed into the back. The serpentine road wound its way up the mountain. We rolled the windows down despite the chill — to feel the wind direction, to smell the blossoming trees, to sense the day. Every pilot develops their own superstition. Mine was simple: if the wind felt kind on my face in the morning, the sky would be kind too.

Halfway up, we slowed down to greet the Dragon, a tree trunk twisted into a shape so uncanny it deserved mythological status. We never passed it without saying hello.

At take-off, the mountain came alive. Wings were being unfolded, helmets clipped, harnesses adjusted; radios crackled with short, clipped phrases, "Radio Check" — "Check-Check". I slipped away from the bustle, to stand on the far side of the ridge and look at the Himalayas stacked in hazy blue layers. They didn't look real — more like a backdrop, brushed in with soft strokes and impossible depth.

Serge was sipping the ginger-honey tea, sniffing air, looking for eagles soaring in the sky — the first signs the weather becomes flyable, as if time politely waited for him. How many years does it take to grow into a person like him? Maybe 60, maybe 70 or 300 — lean and weathered, with eyes that missed nothing and a voice like warm stone. He had been flying since the days when people stitched their own wings and trusted physics mainly to behave out of courtesy.

"Morning," he said simply, nodding at me. No fuss.

We laid out our gliders. Checked the lines. Helmets. Sunglasses. Sunscreen. Gloves — two layers. Boots — sturdy ones this time. Tools — altimeter, camera, radio, phone. The ritual steadied my breath.

"Wind's OK," Serge said. "Soft. Take off down there today."

I nodded. My heart thudded once, sharply.

When everything was finally set properly, he looked at my wing, then at me.

"Ready when you are."

That was all. That was his blessing.

I gave one last look to my lines, shouted "Take-off!" so the others would hear, lifted the wing, checked it in one glance, turned, ran — and in three steps the ground fell away beneath me.

Every time, it feels like a trick. Like the earth simply forgets to hold you.

"Light turn left," Serge's voice crackled in my radio.

I turned.

"Good. Hold. Don't rush the brake."

My breath slowed. His voice always did that to me.

"Little one, breathe."

I was. Maybe. Hard to tell.

Flying in this new spot demanded everything, eyes scanning above, below, sideways; Serge always jokes that we should grow a pair of eyes on the back of our heads, too — but what would be with the helmets? Hands adjusting brake pressure by millimeters; skin reading the texture of air and the position of the sun. My vario beeped gently as I searched for the first thermal.

And then — lift. A soft, rising push into the left console of my glider, like the sky exhaling under me.

"Looks clean," Serge said. "Follow the ridge."

I did. And for one brief moment, everything aligned — my breath, the wing, the mountain, the morning.

But flying is humbling. The very next day, I nearly lost it.

I turned into a small canyon someone had recommended — "good lift there." But instead of rising, I sank. The ridge disappeared behind me. The landing field vanished in the distance. My heartbeat outpaced my vario.

"Serge?" I whispered.

Silence.

Hands glued to the brakes — I couldn't press the radio button even if I wanted to. Fear tightened everything inside me.

Please say something.

The air grew heavy. The ground rushed closer.

Out of desperation, I started to look for a field to land on, like a narrow terrace they have in the mountains — green from above, stone and walls when you're actually falling toward it.

At the last moment, a breath of lift brushed my wing.

"Good," Serge said suddenly, as if he'd been there all along. "You found it. Take it."

I spiraled up two hundred meters, shaking with relief.

When I finally made it back to landing, my knees were so weak I could barely stand, let alone pack my wing right away. It took me about two hours to get back to normal, and then I ate enough for two people. Almost asked for dessert.

But something shifted after that. The fear didn't leave exactly — but it stopped taking the lead.

By the third day, my flying improved. I could hold a clean line. I crossed from the first ridge to the second, then to the third. I felt the wing move not as a burden but as an extension of intention.

"Nice," Serge radioed once. "You're higher than launch."

The morning I climbed above 3,600 meters, the world opened in a way I never expected. Snow-capped peaks lay beneath me — white, ancient, indifferent. The air thinned into something holy.

"Well done."

A pause.

"Enjoy it."

Just two words. But from him, it felt like a medal.

Higher than the snow line, the world turned silent. Not empty-silent, *full* silent. A silence that held you.

Later that evening, to celebrate, we flew in sunset light — pink, gold, soft as breath. The air was gentle, forgiving. No lift, though, just 30 minutes of pleasure ride down to the village. I made a video, knowing no one would care about it as much as I would when I'm fifty.

"That's me," I thought. "That beautiful flying woman is me."

Serge's voice came through the radio one last time:

"Pretty sky today."

Yes. And for once, I felt like I belonged in it.

I landed softly. Packed my wing with steady hands. And for the first time in months, I felt not broken, not lost — but capable. More myself.

And I couldn't wait to fly again tomorrow.

Chapter 21
Prayer Flags in the Wind

Strange, weightless peace — the kind that feels like waking inside a held breath. The violet dawn slid slowly over the valley, soft and solemn, tinting every surface with a color that didn't exist anywhere else in the world. Below my balcony, the tea plantations were still wrapped in their white protective sheets, glowing like circus tents abandoned by wandering performers. From somewhere in the branches came the uneven screech of parrots, a blue-black bird darted low across the fields, and two eagles were already carving spirals into the morning sky — drifting, gliding, unhurried.

---

[4] Translated by Joanna Macy and Anita Barrows, Book of Hours: Love Poems to God.

I stepped outside with my blanket and cigarette, the cold air pinching my cheeks. For once, silence didn't mean loneliness. It simply meant space. As if the mountains had made room for me — and I was learning how to exist inside that room without apologizing for taking up breath and light.

The smoke rose in pale ribbons. I watched it fade into the dawn. Maybe this is what healing feels like, I thought. Not joy — not yet — but the absence of ache.

Date uncertain — Bir, Northern India

I've lost track of the days. Whatever my phone claims, the valley disagrees. The Wi-Fi works only in brief, teasing flashes; messages to Pete go through sometimes, then vanish mid-thought. And oddly, that's fine. The silence between us doesn't sting — it simply rests. Maybe India is teaching me how to be alone without feeling abandoned. Maybe it's teaching me how to hear myself again.

A few days into my stay, we drove to Dharamsala — two hours of winding roads curled around mountain edges, crossing narrow bridges over stony rivers. The air smelled of dust, pine, and something sweet that reminded me faintly of cardamom. At one crossing, a cow stood squarely in the middle of the road, chewing slowly, contemplating existence with the patience of a deity. My driver braked, sighed, and waited.

"Stray cattle," he said with a shrug. "Belongs to no one. Beloved by everyone."

Another cow joined, blocking the entire road. Traffic halted.

"It's like they know we won't move them," I whispered.

My friend Alex — tall, sharp-witted, with blue-green eyes that sparkled even at 8 a.m. — leaned forward, grinning.

"I want this level of self-confidence," she said. "Imagine walking into a board meeting and just *standing there* until everyone rearranges their day around you."

We laughed, the valley catching the sound and scattering it into the wind.

The monastery — the Dalai Lama's residence in exile — was enormous. Not spiritually enormous (though that, too), but physically: sprawling courtyards, multiple temples, staircases leading to rooms filled with chanting, corridors lined with ancient murals, golden roofs piercing the sky. People had travelled from all over the world to be here — Tibetans in traditional robes, Westerners with beads around their necks, families holding offerings, pilgrims carrying prayers in their palms.

And then there was me — arriving almost by accident, dusty from the road, glider bag over my shoulder.

Inside the main hall, chanting swelled like a tide — low, resonant, vibrating through ribs and floor. Butter lamps flickered in golden rows. The air smelled of incense and stone dust and time.

Flags snapped in the wind outside — hundreds of them, thousands — blue, red, green, yellow. Each carried a prayer painted or printed onto thin cloth, and each prayer was offered to the wind to spread across the world.

I stood beside Alex, both of us quiet.

"Do you ever feel like flying is prayer?" she whispered.

"Maybe," I said. "And maybe prayer is flying without leaving the ground."

Alex smiled. "Then these people must be soaring."

We turned a long row of prayer wheels — heavy brass cylinders engraved with mantras. Some were tiny enough to turn with a fingertip; some were massive, responding slowly to the push of your entire arm. Their metal was warm from sunlight. Each click felt like a steady heartbeat.

And despite being the most non-religious person I know — the one who mocks omens and rituals — I found myself making wishes. For clarity. For strength. For gentleness. Wishes that rolled on long after my hand left the wheel, carried by nothing but wind.

When we left the monastery, a man approached us on the street.

"You saw the scenic road?" he asked.

We shook our heads. "What scenic road?"

He gasped dramatically, pressing a hand to his chest. "Best place! Come, come. Just turn corner there."

No signs. No markers. But one turn later, the world opened.

It was a corridor of wind and color — millions of prayer flags hanging in long rows, stretching across the sky like brushstrokes. Red, blue, yellow, green. Some fresh and bright, others faded to ghost shades. They danced wildly in the mountain gusts, the sound of fabric snapping like wings testing their strength.

We walked through them in silence. Flags brushed our arms, our hair, the tops of our hands. The air was thin and cold, carrying the faint scent of incense from the temples below.

Farther in, we found the tumbling prayer drums — metal cylinders that spun wildly when hit by wind, as if alive. Wishes written into perpetual motion.

The entire place felt mystical, mysterious, and profoundly human.

I remember thinking: *"So much longing fits into such small objects."*

Next, we wandered down into the market — narrow alleys crammed with stalls selling malas, shawls, wooden carvings, prayer beads, sweets in sticky trays, rugs folded like quiet mountains. The air buzzed with voices and bargaining and the occasional clang of metal.

That's where I met her — the old painter.

She was tiny, wrapped in bright fabric, her face a topography of deep, beautiful lines carved by years of sun and life. A ruby bindi glowed on her forehead. Her eyes — dark, clever, all-understanding — sparked when she saw me lingering near a stack of paintings.

"Madam, madam!" she called, beckoning me with a hand so small I worried I'd break her if I took it.

She held up a painting: four animals stacked one atop another — a bird on a rabbit on a monkey on an elephant.

"Four Friends," she said proudly. "Old story. Very old. You want hear?"

I nodded, delighted already.

"In forest," she began, mixing Hindi with English in a lilting, musical cadence, "fruit tree very tall. No one can reach. Elephant say, 'I lift.' Monkey say, 'I climb.' Rabbit say, 'I balance.' Bird say,

'I fly.'" She tapped each animal with one crooked finger. "Together — they eat. Alone — hungry forever."

She laughed, a sound like wind chimes. "Life same, madam. Alone — hard. Together — strong."

I bought that painting as a gift for Pete.

Now, when I look at it — even months later — I remember the warmth of her shop, the chaos of the street outside, her bright sari rustling in the breeze, and the feeling that ancient stories travel easily between cultures because the human heart hasn't changed all that much.

A day later, we set out for the hot springs. Someone had promised it was an "easy walk." Lies. It was a relentless upward trail, narrow in places, winding along the side of a mountain with no railings and no apologies.

But the beauty was absurd. Rhododendron petals covered the path — soft pink, the rare color locals consider a blessing. Someone from our group said, amazed, "Pink is lucky. Red is normal. You're very lucky today." We took pictures under the blossoms, laughing, believing for a moment that maybe mountain blessings are real.

Then came the noise — a violent rustling above.

"Leopard?" I whispered before I could stop myself.

A beat.

Then a monkey — enormous, self-important — swung into view, followed by several others. They watched us with disdain, as if to say: "*Tourists*".

We got lost without signal. Turned back. Tried another route. No one panicked — the air itself was too calming.

When we finally reached the springs, they looked like something painted for gods — pools of emerald, jade, turquoise set into stone. One stream scalding hot, another freezing, and in the middle several perfect pools where the waters mingled.

We slipped into one. The shock of heat gave way to slow, sweet release. Steam rose into the bright air. My muscles unwound. My mind followed.

We stayed until our fingers wrinkled and laughter softened into quiet.

Afternoons in Bir always brought storms. Thunder rolling over the valley like someone dragging heavy furniture across the sky. Then the downpour — sharp, cold, brief. When it cleared, the world smelled newborn.

Back at my hotel, the shower was a kind of ascetic meditation — a bucket, a ladle, and two temperatures that alternated between glacial and volcanic. So I filled the bucket, knelt beside it, and poured water over myself in long torrents. Dust, sweat, fear — everything washed off in heavy streams. Inefficient, yes. But strangely spiritual.

Dinner was usually a handful of nuts and a few biscuits. Sometimes I ate them on the balcony, sometimes curled on the bed with a book. The valley went quiet early — by seven the world felt tucked in.

Some nights I went upstairs to the mezzanine. I'd push the beds aside, turn on the music, dim the lights, and dance — slow, simple movements. Not to impress. Not to seduce. Just to remember that my body was mine.

In the glow of the laptop, I watched my shadow move.

Chapter 22
Two Souls over India

> *What saves a man is to take a step. Then another step. It is always the same step, but you have to take it.*
>
> — *Saint-Exupéry, Wind, Sand and Stars*[5]

Until the very last moment, Pete was trying to find the right plane ticket. The obvious option meant landing in New Delhi and enduring a twelve-hour drive north into the mountains — a journey I already knew too well. We kept refreshing pages, comparing routes, bargaining with algorithms, until finally we found a compromise: a regional airport closer to the Himalayas, cutting the drive in half. Six hours instead of twelve. Still brutal, but survivable.

And I decided to make a surprise.

I didn't just book a car to pick him up. I booked another one

____

[5] Translated by Lewis Galantière

for myself.

We drove into the night from opposite directions, our drivers texting each other like conspirators, trading coordinates and landmarks that meant nothing to me — a turn by a chai stall, a bridge, a dark parking lot somewhere in the middle of nowhere in India. At some point my driver slowed and pulled over. Another car was already there, idling under a flickering lamp.

Pete was sitting inside, hunched over his iPad, absorbed in some video. I knocked on the window. He looked up, startled — and then his face changed completely.

"Hi," I said.

"Hi..." he answered, as if he needed a second to convince himself I was real.

Then we were hugging in the dark, laughing, holding on to each other like children who had found each other again after being briefly lost. Our drivers watched us — smiling, tired, indulgent — two professionals who had already been driving for hours and still had hours to go. But for a moment, in that anonymous patch of asphalt, it felt like the universe had aligned itself just for us.

That night we barely slept. We still had to reach the hotel much later, but the exhaustion was sweet — the kind that follows something good. We were together again.

A couple of days before his arrival, we'd talked about flying. "Would you like to try a tandem?" I asked, trying to sound casual.

"Of course," he said immediately. "I'd be delighted to fly in the same air as you."

I felt the weight of responsibility settle on my shoulders.

This wasn't a casual thrill ride; this was someone precious. So I went to the pilots who had been coming to Bir for years, the ones who knew every ridge and thermal by heart, and asked them to recommend someone trustworthy. A very valuable passenger, I explained. They smiled, understood, and helped me arrange it.

On the day of the flight, Pete tried to look calm. He's good at that — a gentleman's composure, a manly refusal to show fear. But I could see it in the set of his shoulders, the way he listened a bit too carefully to the instructions. And then he took off, the wing lifting cleanly, carrying him into the sky as if it had always intended to.

I ran to my own take-off, unpacked my glider, and launched as soon as I could after seeing him lift into the air. I flew straight toward him, scanning the space until I saw his silhouette suspended over the valley. Sharing the sky with him was a different kind of intimacy — no words, no touch, only wind, altitude, and silence. Was it love?

Almost an hour later, on the landing area, as I was packing my glider, I texted him to come to the field if he wanted to see it. I added that I'd find us some wheels afterward to get back to the hotel.

He showed up with wheels already found.

"I rented something for us," he said proudly, gesturing toward a motorbike.

I stared at it. Two wheels. No protection. My glider bag enormous and unwieldy. I trust many things — including some questionable choices like air, mountains, nylon — but motorbikes are not among them. I don't really know how we managed; maybe now it was my turn to get scared and do it anyway.

Later that day, we set off toward the waterfall I'd chosen to show him as a treat and another adventure. It was one of the places that had helped reopen my eyes after months of darkness. The road there was rough, a gravel serpent twisting upward. I sat behind Pete on the motorbike, helmet on, arms wrapped tightly around his torso, clinging as if to my life.

"There's nothing to be afraid of," he said cheerfully.

"That is extremely unconvincing," I answered into his back. I trusted this two-wheeled monster approximately as much as an untrained circus tiger.

Luckily for me, the road ended soon, and we had to dismount and continue on foot. A cheerful local guide led us into a narrow canyon, showing us how to climb over boulders, where to place a foot, where to grip the stone. He was agile, confident, knowing every rock by heart. I worried about Pete — refined, office-dwelling, dressed in clean clothes — while I was scratched, sunburned, hair tamed only by wind. But we helped each other, crossing cold streams, pulling one another up slick rocks. It was strangely intimate, this cooperation, this shared effort.

You hear the waterfall before you see it. The roar arrives first, then the chill, the moisture in the air. And then, after one last turn, it reveals itself, water pouring from sunlight into shadow, the top sparkling, the bottom lush and green. The plants around it nodded gently in the draft it created, as if acknowledging its power.

The guide offered to take our photo. I look at those pictures now and see two people bathed in affection, standing before something vast and clean. Pete went into the water; I was too cold and stayed back, taking pictures, smiling. You can't stay there long because the sun sinks quickly, and soon we had to turn back. The sound of the waterfall faded almost immediately once we rounded the corner, its power hidden again.

On the way back to the village — on our metal stallion yet again — we stopped by the roadside to watch the sunset. We just held one another and watched the sun disappear, quiet and content, breathing in the dimming valley below.

The next day, reality intruded in a smaller, more mundane way. We were leaving Bir in the morning, packing in a hurry. On the drive toward the airport, Pete mentioned casually that he'd forgotten his pajamas at the hotel. Could I ask them to send them to Dubai?

It was ridiculous. Bir doesn't have a concierge. It doesn't even have a post office. Still, the request landed on me as a problem I was expected to solve. I tried. I texted people. A chain of goodwill formed — someone carried the pajamas to another city; another person took them to his home country, eventually sending them to Pete's mother, who could hold onto them until the next time they saw each other. Too much effort for something so small — and the open expectation that I would fix a problem he'd created by being absent-minded planted a quiet seed of resentment in my chest, even as I remembered how much I liked seeing him in those pajamas.

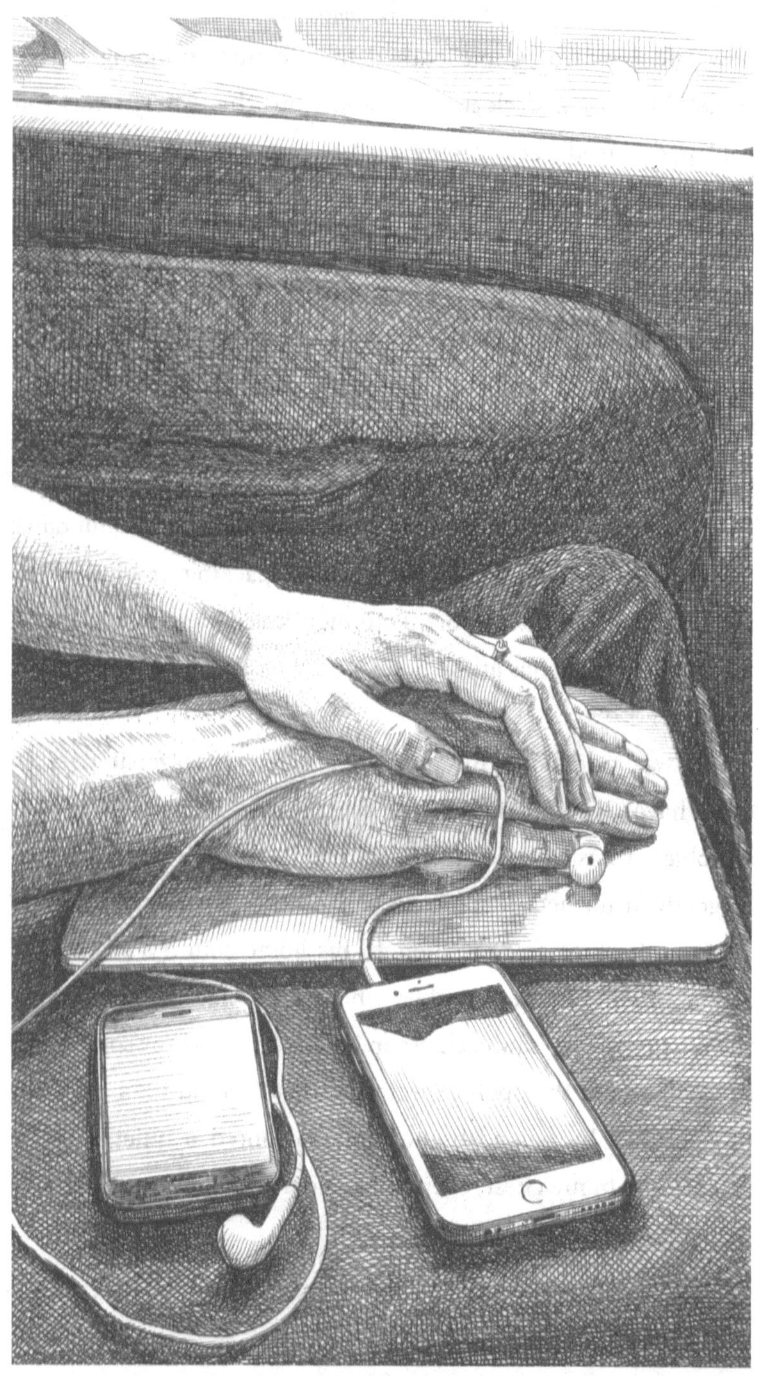

Chapter 23
Six Hours, No Touching

My dear, it was a moment
to clutch at for a moment
so that you may believe in it
and believing is the act of love,
I think,
even in the telling, wherever it
went.

— Anne Sexton. "The Expatriates"

We left Bir early in the morning, the valley still half-asleep, tea leaves damp with dew and prayer flags barely moving in the quiet air. The road took us back toward the regional airport — six hours in a car before the flight to Jaipur. It should have been exhausting, but instead it became one of the most concentrated stretches of time we ever shared.

It was also the first time I traveled this road in full daylight: bumpy stretches of asphalt and gravel, sudden stops as monkeys crossed lazily in front of us, cows standing immovably in the middle of the lane as if traffic were merely a suggestion. As we drove away from Bir, the valleys opened and closed again, hills folding into one another as we said goodbye to the Himalayas. Patches of gardens in bloom flashed past — fresh spring greens, soft pinks and whites — before the air thickened with dust when we slowed to a crawl near road construction. At first we kept the windows open, letting the cool morning air rush in, carrying the smells of earth and plants. Later we switched on the air conditioning — for coolness, for quiet, for the small luxury of silence amidst the road's constant noise.

We couldn't touch much. The driver was there, steady and silent, eyes fixed on the road. So we talked. We shared podcasts, switching earbuds back and forth, pausing them, rewinding them, arguing gently about what we'd just heard. Opinions, memories, half-formed philosophies spilled out without effort. There was no rush, no agenda — just two minds circling each other, curious and open.

At some point I played him a podcast about the history of sex — how desire had been understood, regulated, hidden, and celebrated across centuries. I stretched out in the backseat with my head on his lap. The position softened something in me; it quieted my shyness and let me feel the warmth of his body without tipping into anything overtly erotic, a closeness without performance.

Some of the facts startled us both. In certain periods, the head of a household had the right to sleep with his sons' wives — especially when the men were away working in the city. Other parts made me angry: how Western society had long been unnervingly, hypocritically oblivious to women's bodies, branding them unclean and unworthy of study. As if not every scientist had once been born of one.

That opened the door to what we considered "normal." We talked about experiences we'd had, and the ones we hadn't. Would we want to? He admitted he'd never had a threesome and said, carefully, that he'd be curious to try one with me. I laughed and told him I'd enjoyed it when it happened in my life, that it could be fun, not frightening. It was unexpectedly sweet how we — both around forty — grew a little bashful, like teenagers pretending not to be. Though I couldn't help my senses getting sharper, the road vibrated through the seat, a low, constant tremor, and I could feel it even with my head resting on his lap.

Pete, who rarely allows himself to retreat or hide, shared stories from his own experiments and detours. Nothing felt transactional or defensive; there was no tallying or comparison. I didn't feel even a flicker of judgment from either of us. The questions came from genuine curiosity, not about what we'd done, but about who we were becoming.

The conversation was intellectual, but it carried heat. At one roadside stop for tea and a simple lunch, we noticed that the restaurant was attached to a small hotel. For a moment, we seriously considered disappearing into a room upstairs, just the two of us, stealing a few hours of passion from the day. In the end, practicality won: questions of hygiene, logistics, and the awkwardness of returning flushed and smiling to our waiting driver. We laughed it off, but the fantasy stayed with me — a moment that didn't happen, and therefore remained perfect.

Jaipur arrived like a stage set. This time, I chose the hotel.

I didn't want polished marble or the kind of luxury that could exist anywhere in the world. I wanted history — something that breathed. We stayed in an old merchant's mansion converted into a hotel, its walls lined with fading photographs, carved wooden doors, textiles worn thin by decades of use. It smelled faintly of dust, incense, and old fabric warmed by the sun. The place carried the quiet dignity of something that had lived many lives before ours.

That first evening, we went out to see the city. We took a tuk-tuk — funny enough, in Jaipur it's a regular Uber option, just like "Comfort" and "Black" in Chicago. We were curious and paid for it — a three-wheeled contraption that looked permanently on the verge of collapse. It was loud, open, and felt wildly unsafe, but it let the city pour in. Jaipur at night glowed softly, its famous pink walls deepening to rose and coral under streetlights. It was less crowded after dark, the heat easing, the air filled with voices, horns, the smell of spices and dust. The city felt suspended between centuries, neither fully modern nor entirely ancient.

Chapter 24
Marble and Dust

The more a thing is perfect,
the more it feels both joy and pain.
Though these accursed souls
may never attain true perfection,
they expect to be more after this
life.
— Dante Alighieri, Inferno[6]

The next day lay before us like a fragrant candy in a shiny, bright, crisp wrapper. We had a guided trip to the Amber Fort — or Fort Amer, if you try to respect the local version. Just listen to these lines from the first result in a Google search: *"Amer Fort gets its name from either Amba Mata (the Mother Goddess Durga), revered by the local Meena people, or from Ambikeshwar, a local name for the god Shiva, with the temple dedicated to him located on the fort's hill."* Sounds like an exotic oriental tale, right?

The old seat of power rose tall on the hill in front of us in

---

[6] Translated by the author

the midday sun when we arrived. The heat was already building, pressing down from above and rising back at us from the stone under our feet. Dust coated our sandals almost immediately; it worked its way into skin, into fabric, into every fold of the day, enveloping us in a soft, hazy cocoon of blissful tiredness. Tour guides called out to passing groups, donkeys clattered uphill, carrying tourists with wide eyes and bottled water, vendors shouted about scarves, hats, and something cold to drink. It was noisy, chaotic, unmistakably alive.

Inside the fort, sound fell away, muffled as if the doorway behind us had been draped in heavy fabric. Now we could hear water running in carved fountains and the hiss of footsteps on marble floors polished by thousands of feet. Our guide spoke in careful English — proud, practiced, and clearly in love with his subject. "Here, Hindu and Mughal come together," he said, gesturing toward carved stone where floral patterns intertwined with elephants and monkeys. Muslims are forbidden to depict living beings, so Hindu artisans softened the figures, stylized them, and negotiated them into acceptability. "This was not only palace," he added, tapping the wall gently. "This was a place of power. The rulers of this state were the first in India to trade with the Mughals instead of fighting them. They gave their daughters to wed foreigners — and while neighbors despised this choice for centuries, we now see how it enriched both cultures."

We moved through courtyards where people once gathered to ask for advice and judgment from their rulers, and through mirrored halls built for the queens. Ladies of the house were not permitted to leave the palace after marriage, but one longed to see the stars. Her husband loved her and built a room covered in tiny pieces of glass set into the walls; at night, when it was dark and lit only by a few lamps, the reflections bounced off the walls and ceiling, creating the illusion of lying among the stars.

These stories caught my imagination, and the whirling beauty of the carvings, mirrors, mother-of-pearl inlays, and jeweled mosaics enticed me to dance — flaring my long pink skirt (the color purposefully chosen for the Pink City of Jaipur), turning and twisting around the carved marble columns of what used to be a city hall overlooking the valley. Many days later, the guide shared the photos he took that day, and to my surprise, he caught this very moment. I am frozen mid-turn, the fabric lifting and curving around me. Behind me, blurred but unmistakable, Pete is watching — not the fort, not the guide, not the history — just me. His face holds a look of pure tenderness. I cherish that image.

It was easy — almost irresponsible — to imagine ourselves as king and queen for a moment, standing on shaded balconies, the world stretching far and wide below. From the fort, the long defensive walls spread across the hills, fading into the horizon. I later learned they are comparable in length to the Great Wall of China and served a similar purpose: protection against invading Mongol forces and raiding nomad tribes.

The walls radiated heat. My feet ached, gritty with fine dust that found its way into every crease of skin. Sweat slid down my spine. It felt physical, earned, real.

At one point, as we stood catching our breath, the guide smiled and asked, almost casually, "Do you want to ride an elephant?"

We looked at each other. We were exhausted. But how many times in a lifetime do you get asked that question — seriously, without irony? We had just been listening to stories about maharajas riding elephants through these very gates. These animals live nearly as long as humans. They remember. Of course we wanted to.

A few minutes later, we were climbing up — awkwardly — onto the broad back of an elephant. I was still wearing my pink skirt, which immediately proved to be an impractical choice: the elephant's skin was rough and scratched my bare legs, nothing like I'd imagined. Someone handed us a rainbow-colored umbrella to shade us from the sun. From that height, we could see over the walls into private courtyards: children's swings hanging from beams, laundry draped over railings, a few chickens pecking at the ground, herbs growing in battered pots. Ordinary life unfolding inside extraordinary architecture.

The elephant moved slowly, deliberately. Each step felt considered. I thought about how many feet had climbed these paths before mine, how many lives had passed under this same sky. It was a moment of privilege — not just the ride, but the freedom to change the plan on a whim, to say yes to curiosity.

"Are we ready to move on? There is something you'd want to see," the guide winked at Pete. I was briefly confused as to why.

The evening before, I had made Pete watch *The Fall*, my favorite film — one I've returned to again and again for its beauty and its story of struggle and healing. One of its most haunting scenes was filmed at a stepwell — a geometric space, like an upside-down pyramid dug deep to reach water at its base. This was the place our guide had been winking about. Pete made sure we saw one while we were nearby.

Standing at the edge of that deep, geometric void was unsettling. Stone steps descended endlessly into darkness, the air growing cooler as you leaned forward. Bats clung to the shadows, barely visible until one shifted. When we whispered, our voices echoed back at us, fractured and multiplied.

Our guide laughed softly. "Many kings came here to think," he said. Then, after a pause: "Too much thinking, maybe."

At night, the stepwell transformed. Oil lamps lined the edges, their reflections trembling in the dark water below. It had once been a place to gather water, to cool down, to gossip, to meet — a heart hidden underground. Sharing this place with Pete felt intimate in a quieter way. He listened, asked questions, stayed present because it mattered to me. That meant more than the place itself.

Agra was a study in contrast with Jaipur. For starters, Pete chose the hotel there, and it was spectacular — luxurious, immaculate, overlooking the Taj Mahal itself. The gardens were manicured to perfection, the grass thick and soft underfoot, almost springy. Everything was thoughtful, deliberate, attended to. From the balcony, the Taj rose white and luminous in the distance, so perfectly framed that it looked unreal.

We were both at the edge of our energy limits. The drive had been long, the day dense. On top of that, Pete wasn't feeling well — stomach pain, a restless unease in his body. We even checked his blood pressure. He didn't look like himself, not the energetic man I knew. When it was time for the guided tour of the Taj, he sent me alone, as he had already seen it and wouldn't let me miss it.

The Taj Mahal is a symbol of love, but it is also a tomb. That contradiction sat heavily with me as I walked its perfectly symmetrical paths. Why is something built to house death so blindingly white, so radiant? The story goes that the emperor built it to honor his wife, pouring the wealth of an empire into her memory — and in doing so, hastened the empire's decline. What are we meant to feel here? Awe? Or a warning that love, when it consumes everything else, can become destructive?

The marble was cool under my fingertips. The inlaid stone flowers shifted color as the light changed — pink, beige, gray — playing across white. The geometry was flawless, commanding the eye and the mind, and yet my gaze kept drifting toward the irregular shapes beyond: trees bending in the breeze, water moving, people crossing the space in imperfect lines.

Our guide recited his rehearsed script. When I asked questions, he repeated sentences, uninterested in the history beyond the performance of it. "Stand here for photo," he instructed, expertly creating the illusion that I was alone in the frame. In reality, tourists pressed shoulder to shoulder just outside the lens. Looking at those pictures now, they feel strangely fake.

When I returned to the hotel — my home for the night — Pete was waiting on the balcony. He had ordered tea. We drank it as the light faded, porcelain cups warming our fingers, the Taj glowing softly in the distance. Everything felt perfect and fragile at the same time.

That evening, despite still not feeling his best, he dressed and took me to dinner at a restaurant he had enjoyed before. I cherished that — the desire to share a good memory with me. Sitting across from him, feeling his warmth, remembering how far he'd traveled just to see me fly, I felt confused and grateful all at once.

Agra outside the hotel told another story. Beyond the curated gardens lay slums — laundry drying in dust, walls patched with scraps of fabric, lives lived in conditions impossible to imagine from inside an air-conditioned car. Seeing it was ethically unsettling. You feel powerful and powerless at once: a small person inside a vast system you don't know how to fix.

Marble and dust. Love and uncertainty — held together, unresolved.

Chapter 25
Finally Together

Isn't it nice to think that tomorrow is a new day with no mistakes in it yet?

— L.M. Montgomery, Anne of Green Gables

We came back together. The first time I came home with Pete hand in hand — and for once, it was home. Not another polished hotel with too-smooth marble floors and perfumed corridors, not another marvelous short escape. This place was real: jars of honey and peanut butter on the table, the faint smell of coffee, a half-open window breathing in the city — neighbors passing, children laughing somewhere below. Dubai. Not Chicago. The base he'd promised weeks ago, now tangible, with sunlight, noise, and us.

It felt strange but fitting — after months of moving, flying, packing, and living out of a suitcase — to finally land somewhere. I half expected a marching band, or at least a confetti cannon.

Instead, there was quiet: a hum of the AC, the sound of pigeons plotting their next scandal on the windowsill. And that, somehow, felt even more celebratory. I looked around and thought, *"This might be it"*. A base for healing, for trying to live, for daring to stay — even if just for a while.

I wandered like a cat, nosy and territorial, brushing against furniture, testing textures, learning the terrain. My fingertips slid across the countertop, the couch seams, the cool pane of glass, the painting on the wall — I'd seen it a hundred times on Zoom: a modernist green cow beside a man who looked mildly surprised by her presence. In real life, it was even funnier. Light slanted through the blinds in molten ribbons, forgiving everything — the clutter, the fatigue, even us. Pete leaned against the doorframe, smiling like he'd been waiting for this scene to happen since forever.

"Can I have a tour?" I asked, half teasing, half shy. We went room to room — kitchen, living room, balcony, bedroom. "Which drawers can I use?" He laughed, handed me a stack of hangers, and cleared a shelf. When my toothbrush stood beside his, something inside me melted. Ordinary things — two mugs, one toothbrush holder — turned extraordinary just by coexisting. It's the little domestic miracles that sneak up on you.

In the next few days, I had mostly nothing to do, so I went grocery shopping and took on a complicated recipe — Hungarian Goulash. His flat's equipment was exactly what you'd expect from a single man's household: one pot, one pan, no lids. But, of course, a coffee machine fit for a barista, and knives sharp enough to audition for a murder mystery. So I made do, stirring too much paprika into the air. The smell clung to our clothes, and we threw open the windows, laughing as the smoke alarm had an existential crisis. Pete's eyebrows practically caught fire when he tried it — but he finished the plate, eyes watering, insisting, "It's perfect!" Between coughs, he added, "Spicy food improves circulation." "And compliments to your woman improve her cooking," I said, wiping tears from my own eyes. We both ended up wheezing with laughter.

Later, I found a forgotten pot-bellied vase of pink glass high on the top shelf and filled it with roses and gypsophila. "I guess it's been there since I moved in," he said. "Maybe it was waiting for you to make use of it. I love how you rearrange the space — it shines with new colors." I didn't tell him, but those words sank deep. We were both adults — and there was a fifty-fifty chance we wouldn't click, that cohabiting might end in awkward silence — and yet here we were, making the place, and maybe each other, a little brighter.

Every morning Pete left early to take his son to school and came back with coffee for me — a flat white with two sugars, perfectly remembered. He'd set it by my hands without a word, like an offering, "Will you wake up and spend this day with me?" The smell alone was enough to pull me from dreams, but Pete's body nearby worked better than caffeine. Sunlight creeping across the sheets, teasing me to get up, or at least to throw off the blankets and let him see how the light played along my skin. The joy of those mornings made my bones hum. Maybe this was happiness — not fireworks or grand gestures, or plane tickets and lavish spa stays, just the quiet wonder of being seen. I'd dreamt of mornings like that during long Chicago winters, but I hadn't realized how much I'd missed them until now.

The world sparkled... and flowed around my tired mind, giving shelter from worries and anxieties — for a while. The roller coaster climbed slow and steady — smooth track, laughter echoing off the metal, wind in our faces, hair in disarray. We were still ascending, pretending not to notice the rails twisting ahead into impossible loops.

Chapter 26
Doll's House

*(From below, the sound of a door
slamming shut.)*
— *Henrik Ibsen, A Doll House*[7]

Weekends in Dubai were supposed to be calm: breakfast runs, errands, the small rhythms of an ordinary life. Pete's son was due to stay over for the first time since I arrived. We'd even made a plan: a Saturday movie night, me cooking something easy, all of us together in one space. We were both nervous but hopeful. We even consulted a child therapist, and the suggestion was simple: tell the truth, no drama, no surprises. That sounded easy on paper. Reality had other ideas.

It started with the phone vibrating on the kitchen counter. Once. Twice. Then over and over, like an alarm that wouldn't stop. Pete stepped outside to take the call. I tried not to listen, but heard it anyway — the sharpness in his voice, the silence that followed, the brittle "OK." When he came back, he looked like

---

7 Translated by Rolf Fjelde

someone who'd just walked through a sandstorm. "She said you can't stay here when he's here."

I stared at him. "Not even in the other room?"

He shook his head. "And she doesn't want me to introduce you yet." He hesitated, voice low.

"But why? I'm not going to do anything harmful — I even have some training in pedagogy. And what does she want then? Oh, it's such a shame if she keeps your kid for the weekend and you don't get a chance to spend time with him."

"She said she won't sit with my son while I'm 'having sex with that woman.'"

That woman. Me.

I wanted to laugh — not from humor, but disbelief. "She's angry," I said finally, trying to be reasonable. "It's not really about me." But the words felt like paper, and the fire was already spreading. Pete tried to smile, to soften it. "You're my guest," he said. "You're not going anywhere." It was generous of him — and I deeply appreciated that he made a point of making me feel safe and at home.

And still he packed a small bag and left. I stayed — surrounded by the not-yet-familiar place, the sound of the exotic city outside, lingering memories of his goodbye kiss, and an emptiness I hadn't planned for.

The apartment felt wrong without him: too cold, too still. I walked from room to room, touching things he'd left behind: his watch on the dresser, a towel on the chair, half a cup of cold tea by the sink. I opened the balcony door and let the warm desert air rush in. The city glittered, loud and indifferent.

I poured myself a glass of wine, settled on the small balcony, and chain-smoked until my throat hurt. In the distance, the sky blinked and the Persian Gulf glimmered with reflections. I whispered to no one, "You're still ascending, remember?" But my stomach had already dropped.

When his message came — *Good night, sweetheart* — I watched the screen dim until it went black. "Sweetheart" didn't belong to me anymore. I used to get those same texts in Chicago, and the similarity was stunning — he was here, and he wasn't, at the same time. He probably wanted to be; he said he did, but in fact, he wasn't. And he was an adult man. I knew he could do anything he set his mind to. So maybe this just wasn't as important.

But we survived — through talking, opening up, and admitting the tension this situation created. It put a strain on both of us, and on each of us separately. The almost-ex was still his wife. She held the reins over his relationship with his son and, by extension, over my weekends. He didn't belong to himself, and he couldn't give me what wasn't his to give.

A few days later, an idea popped up. He asked if I wanted to join him in Riyadh for a conference. "It'll be an adventure," he said. And why not? I had time, I had a visa, and I was craving a change of air. Still, I realized I had nothing to wear — not even one decent work-appropriate outfit. The next morning, we went shopping together. Pete turned out to be surprisingly patient, opinionated even — offering running commentary as I tried on blazers and dresses. He loved shopping and clearly liked looking at me, trying things, changing my look from "I'm on sick leave and paragliding in the middle of nowhere" to "Been there, done that, have some thoughts on the strategy you pursue." We left with a few bags, me slightly dizzy from his charm and the scent of new fabric. It felt like playing dress-up before a big scene.

Riyadh hit like an oven door opening, forty degrees Celsius of heat and light, dry as static. The palace-like venue where the event took place was stunning: marble floors, golden arches, and the constant hush of money. Pete was dazzling there, in his element: all confidence and ease, commanding the room. Watching him at work made me proud, then uneasy, then proud again. There's something undeniably erotic about seeing someone you love at their best — it reminds you of what drew you in and what might pull them away.

Evenings were gentler. He skipped the corporate dinners and gathered a few old friends instead. We sat in a courtyard strung with fairy lights, Arabic music floating from a nearby café, our table filled with laughter, mint tea, and small plates disappearing too fast. It felt like a scene borrowed from another life — one where things worked. For a few days, I believed the roller coaster could still smooth out, that maybe we'd just hit a tricky curve and not the final descent.

Do you know that in Arabic, Riyadh means *oasis*? It was exactly that — a patch of stillness between storms. But oases are often mirages the desert shows to daring travelers; you can't stay there, you just rest until you have to move again. When we returned to Dubai, the heat felt heavier, the air thick with what we were foreseeing but hadn't voiced. The climb was over. The descent into the tumbling ride had begun.

Almost There, Almost Me

Chapter 27
Reclaiming the Air

> *Wish for nothing larger*
> *Than your own small heart*
> *Or greater than a star;*
> *Tame wild disappointment*
> *With caress unmoved and cold*
> *Make of it a parka*
> *For your soul.*
> — Alice Walker, "Expect Nothing"

Back in Dubai, the drama started before we'd even unpacked. His ex. His mother. The guilt tangled in his shoulders. The tension built until the walls themselves seemed to vibrate. I started slipping out to the balcony more and more — barefoot, cigarette in hand, watching the city pulse under layers of heat. The air tasted of salt, exhaust, and perfume from someone's dryer vent. The balcony became both my confessional and my refuge, a suspended pocket of air between suffocation and survival. The next weekend was nearing — and we would again face the same battle over who stayed where, and Pete would fail to defend our right to share one bed. And I couldn't really blame him — the discussions and the tone were awful, with all weapons blazing, from cries to tears to insults.

He was trying to stay calm, and I was trying to stay kind. But we were burning out at different speeds. The arguments came in waves — never about us, not directly. It was always them: his ex, her calls, the late-night messages, the guilt of not seeing his son often enough. Each time the phone rang, I felt my heart flinch. When it stopped ringing, I felt the silence press in heavier.

He was kind in repeating that I was invited here as his guest and that he wouldn't let me leave. But I couldn't put more burden on him — God knows he needed the safety of his own space to recover. And besides, it was my turn, so I packed a small bag and we booked a hotel. The irony wasn't lost on me — escaping to a five-star room with silk sheets and a view of the Burj Khalifa, pretending it was a luxury when it felt more like exile. The bed was huge, the room silent, and I had no one to talk to. The bathwater went cold before I remembered to get in. It wasn't freedom. It was a gilded timeout.

I needed something that wasn't about him. Something mine. So I signed up for a theatre masterclass — leadership through embodiment, shadow work, Jung. Ten strangers, two instructors, and a black box studio where we spoke in movement and silence, crawling, shouting, laughing. We explored the Victim-Aggressor-Savior triangle, switching roles using our voices, word choice, and body positions until we learned we could all shift from one to another — sometimes at will, sometimes pushed there without knowing it. Surprisingly, I could feel my nerves strained like a string ready to snap when I had to lead. Me — the woman who managed crises from three kilometers in the air, flying under a piece of fabric, down to a kilometer underground in a mine — suddenly afraid to take up space. Where did I lose that girl? When did she become a shell, a vessel for worry? I gasped when I got a glimpse of that long-forgotten feeling of being someone alive and electric — no panic, she was still there.

By the end of the weekend, my body was sore, my voice raw, but my mind clear. Pete didn't really ask how it went — he was too tired and preoccupied with his own troubles, and we were late to a cinema date anyway.

When I got a minute, I poured myself coffee, opened my laptop, and typed into ChatGPT.

Me: I think I lost touch with a part of myself. I heard people talking about shadow work based on Jungian theory. Can you tell me more?

ChatGPT: Sure. The best start is to ask yourself — what roles do you play most often in life? And which ones do you never allow yourself to play?

Me: My shadow... she's the most hidden part of me. No one knows her. She's sharp, dangerous, merciless. No one loves her, and that only makes her stronger. It seems that she doesn't care anymore what others think or how they feel. Her eyes are cold. I think she's tired of being locked away.

ChatGPT: Say hello to her — you just met again.

Me: Is it OK to be terrifying? If I take back that part of me, will I be alone?

ChatGPT: That's the work — to hold love and fear at

once. Fighting here won't yield any results.

I sat there staring at the screen, breathing slowly, the coffee cooling beside me. My reflection in the black monitor looked back — not better or worse, kinder or meaner, just maybe a little bit more whole. I laughed — a startled, shaky sound that cracked the silence in the kitchen.

On my way to claim something of my own, I reached out to a couple of old friends living in Dubai. They offered to join me for a bike ride. They brought an extra bike and helmet, with patient smiles ready. (I'm hopeless on wheels — flying doesn't scare me, but I trust my feet more than any vehicle.) We rode along the coast, clumsy at first, the city lights shimmering across the water. Ten kilometers later, sweaty and happy, we shared some cocktails and burgers at a beach café. The sea was calm, the sky a velvet blue fading into black. For the first time in weeks, I wasn't thinking about Pete, his ex, their poor kid, or the future. I was just Maria again — imperfect, accepted, alive.

When I told him about that evening later, he frowned. "Did you talk about me?" he asked quietly. "Of course," I said, laughing it off. "They're my friends." His face tightened. "How many of my secrets did you tell them?" The silence that followed was worse than any argument. That was an attempt at control — that's how it starts, not by force, but by guilt. The rails rattled; the wheels screamed. The cart was rushing down the slope at full speed. Would it stay on the track — or crash into the ground?

Still, I kept pushing to reclaim small pieces of air. I started updating my CV, reaching out to recruiters, imagining life somewhere cooler, lighter. Europe, maybe. It wasn't running away. The roller coaster wasn't done with us yet, but I had started to build a backup plan — a landing strip, or at least a map back to myself.

Chapter 28
Up and Down the Elevator

Experience is merely the name men gave to their mistakes.
— Oscar Wilde, The Picture of Dorian Gray

Two days later, the night before I had to leave for the next chapter of my travels, in between my mundane errands — getting my hair done and a pedicure — he texted: "Can we meet?"

I wasn't sure what he had in mind. We were planning to spend the evening together — my last one in Dubai. I tried to gauge how long it would take — I had a ninety-minute window between appointments, but was ready to cancel anything. "No, no," he said, "I'll just come and share lunch with you." He was forty minutes late. When he finally appeared, he looked composed and rehearsed. "I think it's better for us to break up," he said, right in the middle of How are you? How was your day? I felt the room tilt. "You don't get to decide what's better for me," I said, steady but flat. "If you want to leave, say you want to leave." He didn't argue. He just looked at me as if memorizing something he'd already lost.

I went through the motions — finished my drink, paid, smiled like an actress at curtain call. Then I left and went to that pre-booked pedicure that I wouldn't remember. Watching the polish dry while my heart cracked felt absurdly, painfully symbolic.

That night, I packed and sobbed. He offered to let me stay for this last night. "Anyway, your flight is in the morning." But how could I? Why would I? I shoved my things into suitcases. It wasn't easy — this apartment was supposed to be a base. We'd bought new clothes for the Riyadh event and souvenirs from Jaipur. But packing was the only way to channel the rage into motion. Slam the lid, pull the zipper. Finally, I booked a hotel near the airport and called a taxi.

"I'll accompany you there," Pete said. I saw no point, but I was too drained to argue. When we got in the car, I burst into tears again — and I foolishly thought I had none left. This wasn't how I imagined leaving this place, his place, where I had been invited as a guest.

So much pain, so much absurdity — in Dubai as it was, and in our lives. So much connection and rare affection — wasted.

Me: Why?

Pete: It's too painful to be together. I think we rushed too fast.

Me: There's no such thing as an ideal situation or perfect people. You choose, you commit, and you solve it. Yes, sometimes it's unpleasant.

I'm not sure if I said it out loud or just kept turning it in my head.

The lobby smelled of lilies and disinfectant. Dark grey stone all around, cold and echoing. He reached to kiss me goodbye; I turned away. "You don't get to kiss me anymore." We stood there a bit longer, saying meaningless words and just looking at each other. Oh, how I wanted to kiss him. But he decided to leave, and I had to respect that.

Finally, I went to the elevator leading to the floor with my room. My hands shook so badly that I pressed every wrong button — doors opening, closing, opening again. Finally, we took off. In the golden mirror, my reflection looked foreign — swollen eyes, puffy lips, no light, no warmth. What do I do?

I hit Stop, then Lobby. Bolting out into the lobby, past the glass doors, I saw him waiting by the taxi stand and I ran to him. I wrapped my arms around him from behind, just staying there, not letting him go. I couldn't.

"Maybe you'll allow me to turn around and hold you in my arms properly?" he mumbled.

For one suspended breath, the world paused — a roller coaster stalling midair before the final drop.

"Don't you dare give up on me. We'll talk through everything and sort it all out. Get out of your head and just be. You are an idiot, but a loved one."

After a moment, he said, "Good."

We stayed there holding each other too long, then went to a somnambulistic dinner — something Italian, scented with basil and vinegar. I kept touching his hand, his shoulder, his back constantly — as if I were afraid he'd disappear. Well, I was terrified. To lose him, to lose this, because he was too tired to see that we'd withstood the darkest storm. Despite all the present troubles, we were genuinely interested in each other. I saw it in his eyes, and I heard it in his voice. These feelings are a miracle — the kind we touch only a handful of times in life. And I treasured that chance over pride, even over dignity. Come what may, I wasn't the one to falter and step back when I saw something terribly wrong happening.

Later that night, I went to my room — collapsed for two hours, then collected my luggage and boarded a plane toward somewhere softer than Dubai. The roller coaster had stopped. The track ended here. And, for the moment, I didn't feel anything but exhaustion — the good kind, the kind that comes after survival, when you're finally allowed to rest.

Part IV
Borrowed Ground

Chapter 29
Cry like a Girl

Between the idea
And the reality
Between the motion
And the act
Falls the Shadow
— *T.S. Eliot, "The Hollow Men"*

Engines roaring, I learn new meanings of the words *depleted* and *exhausted* — isolated in the plane cabin, suspended in the sky, no connection, filtered air, and unfiltered self-awareness.

[seatbelt sign on] [phone in airplane mode]

Pete's words keep pounding in my head.

We should part ways.

I'd better leave.

So much pain. Tears when I was leaving his place. Bloody La Mer. Bloody Dubai.

[here the handwriting becomes uneven]

Me: Why?

He: It's too painful to stay together. I think we hurried.

Me: There is no such thing as perfect timing or perfect people. You choose to commit, and you solve it. Yes, it is not perpetually pleasant.

Me: Don't you dare abandon me. We can talk and sort this out. Get out of your own head and just stay.

He: All right.

(Later) He: I'm here.

—

Two days pass.

Formal texts.

"Have a wonderful Turkey." "I'm all right, gym time."

I am anxious and torn between giving him space and showing up. Pete is mostly silent.

—

I am deep underwater. Like a heavy hangover. Damn — I let him into my heart after all. And he let me into his apartment — as a guest.

(This is MY bed. This is MY place.)

How many times have you heard this?

[engines steady, lights dim]

Time to lick my wounds. Yes — more than one piece has been knocked out of my heart.

"A five-star hotel, the best there is. I tried..."

The eternal victim of that's-how-it-turned-out.

"You chose the worst possible moment." "I was shocked and shut down."

And not an ounce of compassion.

"I still didn't get it." "It triggers me that you take this long break." "I don't understand."

Like it's my fault. Like it's my task to make you understand.

As if it's even possible to rearrange something inside someone else's head.

And at the same time he claims to have strong intuition and empathy.

And says: "You are either with me, or against me."

"I have trust issues — they were switched off till now — but you said you can leave and now I..."

"I walk a minefield — you react strongly to anything and everything."

He is correct. I react to everything.

As if all of my skin is bruised and even a soft breeze rubs the wrong way, causing pain.

I dared to take on more than I could. Bit off more than I could chew and swallowed.

And no matter how much I asked for help — said that I was desperate and miserable — I got n-o-t-h-i-n-g.

Dear little Maria. What did you expect? Why did you?

—

And the final splash:
"I better leave."

Good phrasing. Clean. "It will be better for me."

You can't let him go — you're in love — but he really doesn't care.
So it's a service to you, apparently.

You will be further away from a person who won't bring any happiness to your life.
And I wished so much to see how he relaxed. To watch tension melt from his stone-carved muscles. Leaving him languid. Supple.
Like a tiger at ease in its native forest.

—

And what did he want for you? Probably nothing at all.
"I so wanted to make you happy."
Beautiful words.
But he never really wanted to give.
That's where the 25,000 demands come from.
You're strong. Be strong. Take more.
What, you need compassion and help? That's me who needs it.
I have so many problems — left, right, center.
Saaaave me...

[ink smudged here]

When did you feel good around him?

The last time we had sex.

When you did what you wanted. Touched yourself. Touched him lightly. With pauses.

Knowing he wanted more.

After the bath.

And the evening before that. The wheel. The restaurant. The walk. The swings.

He was tired. Fell asleep.

(Oh God, how many times was it "tired, fell asleep.")

You walked, smiling, thinking — how great it would be when he comes to pick me up in the evening, takes me to the Hyatt; we'll have great sex.

"I'm tired. It will be too much for me — to go somewhere. I'll go to sleep."

—

And did you ever think — what if you tried coming to Dubai for a year?

Agree that I honestly tried. Work it out. Look for friends and activities.

Either yes — everything works after a year and we live together.

Or no — and then we together relocate within a visible horizon. Three months, six.

Come what may — let's try.

[written after the bath] [written on endorphins] [not from a stable state]

That evening you stayed up until three. You were completely done.
In the morning — an exhibition we agreed to go together to?
Fine, I'll wake up and bring myself there.
That's exactly where he leaves you.

Your stomach hurts like hell.
But he leaves you there anyway.

—

Then the course. You get distracted. New people. Emotions.
And he doesn't ask anything about the course.
Only about himself.
How difficult his day was.
His son at a playdate.
He drank. Felt bad.
Didn't like the people around him.
He was lonely.
Wtf.

But I could be there with him, right?

—

And the next day doesn't help.
And the next.

And the next.

And then he says he doesn't want me to come back.

What do you mean — come back after Turkey, if I extend my LOA?

This LOA didn't fit his plan at all.

Not to mention what would be good for me.

—

Just fear.

"What if she wants to stay longer?"

How I despise this fear.

This powerlessness.

Like — please, no — almost panic.

Fear displaces kindness.

—

And did he have kindness toward you?

"You can see how I treat you."

Warmth in his eyes.

Tender hands.

The desire to hug and kiss.

To go places together.

"So that we have adventures."

He himself doesn't sit still. And you won't have to either.

—

He confidently stood next to you when it came to meeting your
friends.
Shamelessly arrived forty-five minutes late to dinner.
Declared, "You can't do X and Y." Almost yelled.
As if he really wanted to be close.
And then time passed.
It became closer to "really."
And that's it.
He decided to leave.

—

What do you feel, my dear?
What is happening with your shadow?
...and with your light part?

—

Right now it hurts so much it doesn't matter.
You just want to shut down.
Forget.

[sentence trails off]
Sleep.
[seatbelt sign still on]

Breathe out.
This is allowed too.
Let him go.
He tore this bond.

Torn ligaments will start to heal.

Just time.

And calm.

Chapter 30
Fly like a Girl

We never know how high we are
Till we are called to rise...
— *Emily Dickinson*

Engines roaring, I learn new meanings of the words *depleted* and *exhausted* — isolated in the plane cabin, suspended in the sky, no connection, filtered air, and unfiltered self-awareness.

Then it's landing, customs, luggage, transfer — a sequence the body completes automatically.

Life, apparently, does not wait for your emotional consent, and all you can do is let it carry you through the chilly mountain night, along the road beneath starry skies, straight into the hotel you've been to so many times before. And then I dive straight under a blanket.

Only to rise with the sun, because the day doesn't negotiate, either.

When I fling open the blinds, the Aegean pushes straight into my heart — with the ease of a distant but beloved relative. "See?

I'm here. Did you sleep well?" The sea lies below in its luxurious, unapologetic density of turquoise. I inhale the scent of pines, warm under the sun. After months of wandering, this is a place I come back to.

Needles whisper in the gentle wind; green is splattered with fuchsia and blue flowers climbing the posts of my small terrace. Somewhere below, cutlery clinks against porcelain. A gull laughs — I've already had fish for breakfast, and I'm still hungry.

RISE starts early — not the kind of early you post about, but the kind your body resents and obeys without complaint. RISE is the name of my acro paragliding school. No joking — these guys are in a league of their own: podiums and titles behind them, and a calm, generous way of teaching that keeps your learning steady, focused on what you've already done and what can be improved next, rather than on abstract ideas of your "capabilities." Coffee is brewed for function, and briefings are stripped of poetry: sequence, altitude, margin for error, fly, debrief, fly again — no mysticism, just repetition.

And then there is a new wing. Blueberry color, extra-small, still crisp and unsettlingly unfamiliar. I haven't opened and handled it on the ground. There will be no polite introduction — just a mountain, a launch, and a takeoff marshal with a radio.

"Ready when you are."

I look at the sky as if it might object. I take a breath and let my hands do what they know. That's the whole trick at take-off: stop asking the brain for permission. Load the wing. Feel it lift. Run.

The wing comes overhead cleanly, obedient, and then

the ground drops away.

Only once I'm airborne do I look up.

It's tiny, like flying a handkerchief.

Fear flares — quick and sharp — and I breathe in, then out.

It flies, I tell myself.

So I stop touching it. I keep my inputs soft and boring and let the wing tell me who she is.

It's fifteen minutes to the box.

The box is a patch of sky over the sea — far enough from village and mountain that mistakes have room. Below it, a rescue boat idles, pretending not to watch. If you throw a reserve, you descend fast, and water has a kinder surface than rock. That's the most comforting thought you get. That's the deal: don't mess up and you don't get wet.

Those fifteen minutes are the strangest part of the day: nothing to do, no distraction, just moving forward and observing the coastline as it opens wide beneath me. Another good idea would be to stretch out my arms and legs to keep warm in the morning chill that clings to the mountain, but I'm still too cautious under little Blueberry.

Fear rests lightly, like a hand on my shoulder. I let it stay. I don't let it steer.

"Safety check," the instructor's voice comes through the radio. "Acro position."

I sit up straight in the harness and tuck my legs under — compact, deliberate. I become smaller on purpose.

"Check your reserves."

Right. Left.

You do it every time, not because you're going to need it, but because if you ever do, thinking won't be an option.

"First run," he says. "Full stall. Find where the wing breaks, keep it there."

A full stall was dramatic when I first learned it, but now it's a safe space, a reset for times when a trick goes south. Can I be precise with the new wing, after six months of not touching it? I pull both brakes. The wing slows, slows — then the air lets go. The canopy folds, and I drop under it, held together by nothing but intention.

For a moment, everything feels wrong — the brakes are surprisingly easy!

Well, acro is the art of making wrongness exact. I search for the narrow band where the wing stays broken but a bit more controlled. Backfly. Tiny hand movements, guided by the tension of the brake lines. Legs are supposed to stay tucked. Too much information, all at once.

I release.

Poof.

The wing fills again and dives forward. I catch it late, embarrassed. Not symmetrical. The surge skews sideways. My legs come loose. The harness suddenly feels enormous, and I move in it like a sack.

This is where acro gets dangerous — not in the trick, but in the mess.

"Ok," the instructor says. Calm. "Let's try again." No pity from that one, huh?

We finish with wingovers. They are always confusing to

me — rhythm seems to be critical, but it fluctuates as you climb higher, and too much is happening at once.

The landing comes fast. Smaller wing, higher sink. I flare too late. It's not a crash, just a sentence with a hard period. My feet complain.

I note it but don't argue — there is no point, just feedback for next time.

On the ground I defocus, and when concentration leaves your body, you start to feel the heat, thick and dry after the cold above. I pack the wing carefully, folding fabric and lines into something orderly, and when I lift the harness onto my shoulders, I feel its full weight — nearly twenty kilos — solid, indisputable proof of what has just carried me through the air.

I get a cappuccino and light a cigarette, letting the sun warm my forearms while I watch others come in to land, one by one, wings sighing as they touch the ground. Somewhere between the caffeine and the smoke, the thought settles calmly and without drama: I can do better, I will.

The second run begins the same way, and somehow not at all.

The 1800 launch is short and unforgiving. Steep. A road waiting below if you hesitate. The takeoff is messy — crosswind, new wing, too much thought. The air carries me anyway.

On the glide to the box, the world goes quiet. Thoughts try to creep in.

Break. Release. Catch. Send.

My first deep-stall entries are a rodeo. Break inputs have to be adjusted for the Blueberry. Asymmetry. Crooked exit. I catch too early, then too late. We lose more height than planned.

"Again," the instructor says. "Try to be symmetrical. Legs under."

I breathe. Try again.

Better. Not clean — but coherent.

The landing is softer this time. I flare earlier, kinder. My feet touch the ground like I've remembered something.

Before the third run, I eat something salty. I talk to people because that's what happens between runs.

"Hi! Long time no see," someone says. "How are you doing?"

"Helicopters," I answer, without hesitation.

A pause. Ooops, I answered the wrong question, but we smile at each other anyway.

"And you?" I ask quickly. "How was your run?"

We're all swimming in the same chemistry — adrenaline, cortisol, something warmer underneath — and the rules of polite conversation soften.

The weather turns sketchy, clouds gathering in a way that invites hesitation, and we go up anyway.

On the bus to 1700, switchbacks winding, I feel empty. Not sad — used up. My briefing was sweet and simple: do the same thing, cleaner. Hold the body position. Trust the sequence.

On the way to the box, I tuck my legs and check my reserves. Right. Left.

"Four steps," he says. "Don't rush."

I start.

Break.

Release.

Catch.

Send.

The helicopter locks in.

The wing turns in a smooth, level circle — no wobble, no argument — the world revolving around me as if we've agreed on something.

It feels like a waltz.

One-two-three.

One-two-three.

"Outside weight shift," the instructor says. "Slowly open the outer hand."

I do.

The movement settles. The rotation becomes effortless. Holding means not interfering.

For a moment, the helicopter isn't a trick. It's a place.

And it's quiet.

Exit forward. Hands up. Let it fly. Catch the dive.

On final glide, the sea stretches below, the landing already visible. Sunset light pours in from the side. I feel almost weightless.

The landing is the softest of the day.

That evening, we watch the videos. On screen, a small blue wing turns and turns in perfect calm. The pilot inside looks like she knows what she's doing.

I don't recognize her.

Then I do.

By nightfall, I'm empty enough to be easy.

I had forgotten that for dinner we had planned to meet with

Jordan, the manager of my hotel, and his friends. I've known him for years, and the place has the unforced comfort of a well-off aunt's house — solid furniture, good wine, nothing trying to impress. "You like çökertme?" It's a potato-and-beef dish in Turkey, pronounced [cho-kurt-may]. "I have a new cook — let him make it for you! Or you can be his kitchen aid and we make a photoshoot for the hotel out of it."

The only thing required of me is to show up, and I do. I don't hold the room together. Someone else lights the fire. Someone else pours the wine.

The new cook is cautious around me, pausing before he speaks, watching my hands more than my face, as if trying to understand why the boss is making such a fuss over a simple preference. But he is kind — I'm fairly useless, but curious to learn, as I cook a new dish at the stove that was set up outside on the terrace overlooking the bay. "You will be my staff!" Jordan jokes, and I know instantly that I'll hear this joke plenty of times in my life, along with the story of this evening, that he will remind me of the nights when I come to his restaurant depleted after flying and we will sit on the terrace drinking wine.

Someone set up a long table under the pine trees. It runs almost the length of the space, catching the last of the light, already scattered with glasses and plates as if it had been waiting for us. Chairs scrape softly on stone and the smell of smoke drifts up from the grill in slow, lazy ribbons. Çökertme is served in generous layers — crisp potatoes still crackling with heat, cool yogurt sharp with garlic, meat glossy and fragrant — the kind of food that carries the quiet effort of someone who wanted it to be good. Plates arrive when they're ready, not all at once, and we pass things to each other, looking up with an uncomplicated kindness that feels almost old-fashioned. I smile half at them and half at the day.

The sun slides into the sea, closing the day the way it began — quietly shifting the colors, dimming the turquoise down, and tucking it away until tomorrow. The light thins. The air cools. We light candles on the table and listen to each other's stories, our eyes drawn to the flicker of fire shimmering in the wine glasses.

The night folds itself around us gently, and for once I don't feel the need to leave early or stay late.

I'm exactly where the day has brought me.

Chapter 31
Island of Snakes and Sunsets

> *Ever afterwards people will tell the great tale*
> *Of your crossing, and it will be called after you Bosporus.*
> — Aeschylus, *Prometheus Bound*[8]

Reluctantly, I leave Ölüdeniz — not sadness exactly, but resistance to being pulled out of a rhythm that finally fits. Pete doesn't want to come — too far, too complicated — so we decide to meet on the Princes' Islands instead, just outside Istanbul. It's a compromise. Neutral territory. Borrowed ground.

He is exultant, messages arrive breathless, almost boyish — *finally, at last, we're doing this.* The tickets are bought late, as usual, and I do what I always do when something matters: I organize. I check ferry schedules. I book a guided walk through the island's architecture after confirming with him what time would work best. Two days. Enough to reconnect, I hope.

---

[8] Translated by Herbert Weir Smyth

Then, almost casually, he mentions it — a call on the first day, breaking into our plans from twelve to two, something he couldn't move.

Walking toward the beach, I receive the message and stop in the middle of the promenade, a stupid towel slung over my shoulder, phone in my hand, the hiss of a coffee machine and the clatter of cups from the beach cafés ringing in my ears. Twelve to two is only two hours, but it cuts the day in half, stealing the best light and the tour we had agreed to book. I type and delete. Type again.

"It's inconvenient," I send, carefully flat.

Inside, something flips. Why? Why when we have two days together in a month. Why when I am flying back to Chicago after this. Why when you didn't want me in Dubai, and I won't go there now even for a million dollars. But none of that goes on the screen.

His response comes fast and dramatic. Maybe he shouldn't come at all. Maybe this is a mistake.

I am already in the car to the airport.

We speak on the phone. Voices soften. The air leaks out of the moment. We decide to go ahead. Nothing is solved; it is simply smoothed over, pressed flat enough to fit into the day. I arrive with that faint, familiar sensation — something has tilted slightly, not enough to fall, but enough to notice.

I land in Istanbul hours before him, not by design — my flights were just easier this way. I stand on the pavement outside the terminal, my bag heavy on my shoulder, and think: *"I could arrive offended.* The option is there, almost inviting."

Instead, I decide to enjoy myself.

I am still dressed like someone who lives in a flying camp — functional shoes, sunburned wrists, hair that smells faintly of salt and wind. There's nothing to be done about my hair, so I let it down and accept what wind and salt have already decided. I duck into the nearest shop and find a dress with an open back, simple and unapologetic. I change shoes. On my way out, a jewelry stand catches my eye: gold-plated earrings, rings set with bright crystals in five impossible colors. They sparkle in the May sun like drops of candy.

This is the version of myself I want him to meet — not armored, not reproachful, but playful, open — a woman waiting for her lover.

I still have time, so I sit down at a nearby restaurant that turns out, improbably, to be Michelin-starred. The food is precise and generous, and I eat with real appetite. It isn't the dress or the jewelry that changes my mood — it's hunger being met, pleasure being allowed. By the time I leave, I feel light and unmistakably myself. I want him to be happy to have me. I am.

The ferry carries us away from the city and into a different scale of time. The Sea of Marmara opens, pale and wide, the Bosphorus light stretching thin over the water. We stand on the deck of the ferry, hugging, smoking, watching Istanbul disappear on the horizon. Pete gestures at the water.

"It always looks calm from here."

"That's because you're already across," I say. "The crossing is the hard part."

Someone laughs, my forehead rests briefly against his

shoulder, and when we kiss in the sunset it feels effortless, almost scripted — the kind of happiness you recognize even as you file it away.

Come nightfall, the island comes into view: seagulls circling fishing boats near the shore, and a white, domed wooden building rising on the hill, with intricately carved mansions at its feet leaning toward the sea as if listening. The island is small — we will circle it on foot twice during our stay — a concentration of beauty that feels almost too complete.

It is the kind of place that quietly demands happiness.

By the time morning unfolds — breakfast finished and Pete absorbed in his very-important-can't-move-it call — the day has already tilted into afternoon. The light is softer now, angled, forgiving, as if the island has decided to wait for us. I head out first to wander the streets and meet our guide where the tour is meant to begin.

Her name is Ella. She arrives with a dog and a bag full of stories, and for the next four hours we are meant to walk the island together — past façades and courtyards, up shaded paths, into histories layered like varnish. Pete is late, even though I moved the start of the tour by an hour and it begins a hundred meters from the hotel. When he finally joins us, he still has one earbud in, nodding along to something happening elsewhere.

I feel a hot, surprising wave of shame — not for him, but for Ella, who has come to share her knowledge, her affection for this place. I decide, without saying it out loud, to become her most attentive listener. I ask questions. I look where she points.

Pete interrupts gently as soon as his call ends. "Coffee? Should we grab a coffee?" We do. Twenty minutes later, back on the path, he leans in and whispers in my ear, "This is boring."

I look at him and think: ask questions, steer the conversation, this is a private tour. Don't make it my job to de-bore you. I keep it to myself, but how do I wipe the subtitles from my forehead?

Five minutes pass. When I glance back over my shoulder, I see him again with two earbuds in, walking his own line through what was meant to be our day. Ella keeps talking. The dog trots on.

Later, as he often does, he slips back into the conversation — no excuses, attentive now, curious again. We continue on to dinner at a fish place on the other side of the island. "Be careful here, snakes may come out onto the paths warmed by the sun," Ella says.

A small, quiet restaurant is perched against the high coast, overlooking two tiny patches of land floating in molten gold. Islands where no one lives.

The following day carries an unmistakable weight — our last full one together before we part for different destinations. The island keeps offering us beauty. We circle it by boat that morning, the water cold and bright. We swim. We laugh. We explore the parts of the island we haven't yet seen. Awkwardly, we start the conversation.

We need to figure out what's next.

What do you have in mind?

You know I need to be in Dubai, for my son and all.

Well, I don't like the city — its transactionality, the climate, the way it feels — there is nothing there for me.

Yeah. Maybe you come there... but you need your own place. It's too soon for us to live together.

Something in me stumbles. Not breaks — just loses its footing. I nod. I don't argue yet. I store the sentence carefully, like an object I will examine later.

We walk up the hill to the Orthodox church, and when we reach it, the hall is quiet and cool, steeped in the scent of myrrh. The silence between us settles. There is no need to say a word; it would only sharpen the conflict. Maintaining that silence, we find a terrace beneath the pine trees. I sit on the parapet, and he lies down, resting his head in my lap. Quiet, calm, surrounded by culture and nature that were here long before us and will remain long after we are gone.

So why quarrel? The path up the hill, the contrast of the dark church and the sunlit terrace, seems to sync us again. Looking down at his head on my knees, I think, this is the right place.

Then he climbs onto a tree branch and calls down, "The view is good here — come up." I follow, dress and all. We decide to go see the highest point of the island, the fire lookout tower. The path winds through bushes and rocks, not long.

"What if there are snakes?" he asks. "Remember Ella said there were snakes on the island?"

"They'd hide," I say. "There are too many people here."

I am wrong. It is huge, arm-thick and long. We turn back and run for our lives, climbing onto a nearby rock — as if the snake couldn't do the same. It is terrible, and in equal parts fear and laughter, breathless and close, we find shelter in each other's arms. This feels like the right place.

That evening, Pete finds the coolest new restaurant. It hasn't officially opened yet, but they graciously agree to take us in as test guests.

I tell him about my dream of moving to Europe — about wanting to build a home, imagining friends arriving with bags and stories, making space for people in my life. I speak carefully, not as a demand but as a direction.

He listens, then asks, almost idly, "Who would get there?"

The question lands harder than anything he has said all day. I feel tears rise and take a sip of wine, changing the topic, steadying my voice. The man I imagine next to me is someone who supports my dreams; I have enough challenges on my own. Would we create something like a retreat near your place? An anchor event to invite your friends? I can imagine a keynote, someone to add to the fold — anything other than more doubt piled onto what is already hard. Our doubts are traitors, as Shakespeare said.

Nothing is resolved that night with Pete, and we run out of time together. In the morning it is all logistics — checkout, ferry, airport. When I walk him to security, the line curves back and forth in a slow, patient snake. He enters it, turns, waves. Moves forward. Turns again, waves once more, smaller this time. Then the crowd absorbs him.

I stand for a second longer than necessary. Then I turn and walk toward my own line.

Chapter 32
The Hourly Hotel

*Arrest occurs at a point of
inconcinnity between the actual
and the possible, a blind point
where the reality of what we are
disappears into the possibility of
what we could be if we were other
than we are. But we are not.*
*— Anne Carson, Eros
the Bittersweet*

The message arrives while I am standing at the gate, my boarding group already called, my bag placed neatly at my feet.

I'm late for my flight. I had a Zoom by the gate, got carried away, and missed the boarding. I'm so frustrated.

I read it twice. Then a third time, slower.

What fills me refuses to arrange itself into anything useful. Longing, first — the simple ache of knowing I will not see Pete for a while. Even in the distance that had grown between us, I still liked him and the way it felt to be near him. Sadness, close behind it. Relief, too, at the thought of returning to Ölüdeniz, to flying, to a rhythm that does not argue with me. Readiness, the familiar tightening in the body that means I can act. And underneath all of it, grief — not sharp yet, just present, like pressure.

The feeling that surfaces strongest is not despair, but efficiency.

Opening the flight app, I look up his destination. The next option is four to five hours away. Too long to be left alone in an airport, pacing, replaying the same small circle of thoughts. I try to call Pete; he doesn't pick up.

Then my attention shifts to my own flight. There is another one at 9 p.m. Late, but possible. I think through the logistics without ceremony: the driver can come later, that is easy; Jordan at the hotel asked if I would be there to share a dinner, but he can wait for another night; I have nowhere else I urgently need to be.

There is a rule I seem to live by without ever having stated it out loud: you do not leave someone alone in transit, not if you can help it.

My fingers hover — I type, delete, then begin again.

I can change my flight, but boarding for the current one has already started. I need your nod if we're doing this.

The reply comes quickly.

I nod.

A minute later, another message.

We need a hotel. Right now.

For a moment, I don't respond; the thought lands somewhat oddly. I smile at it, no decision made yet. My body is already moving.

Outside, we find each other in the smoking area — the place where the airport's efficiency briefly pretends to yield to human shortcomings. Pete looks relieved, energized, suddenly vivid. His voice drips with honey and seduction; he whispers something soft into my ear, takes on a warmth that knows exactly where to go.

I hesitate. I feel it clearly — the small internal pause where something could still turn.

He is a wonderful lover. And more than that, I want to feel close to him again, even if closeness now comes without promises. I have always been susceptible to this particular gravity.

Hand in hand, we walk back into the airport.

The hotel is absurd. Closet-sized rooms at the price of a Ritz suite, sold by the hour. We do not need it for the day, only until the next check-in — a pocket of time cut out of the afternoon, sealed off from everyone else.

The room looks like a spaceship cabin — lit in artificial white, with neon violet lines glowing in the corners. Maybe borrowed from a stage science-fiction brothel, something transient and anonymous. Blue latex skin would not look out of place here. The sheets smell artificially clean, like a promise made by a machine.

Something about the alienness of it all releases us. This was never planned. It was never meant to exist. The space, the light, the timing — none of it belongs to a life that continues. Because of that, it feels free.

The intimacy is intense and strangely unburdened. Not because it is new, but because there is nothing waiting on the other side of it. Breaths, moans, the body speaking a language that does not ask questions. It feels like borrowed time, and I let it be exactly that.

Afterward, wrapped in a sheet, I watch him pack. He looks down at me, already half somewhere else.

"It doesn't feel right to leave you like this," he says. "But I have to catch my plane."

In my mind, what follows arranges itself like a montage.

Standing up. Dressing. Small practical decisions — I can shower later, I can gather my things afterward. Walking him back through the terminal. Passing the same shops, the same signs, the same indifferent crowds.

For the second time that day, I walk him to security.

The line curves back and forth in the same slow, patient snake. He steps into it, turns, waves. Moves forward. Turns again, waves once more.

I stand and watch him disappear into the crowd.

Then, already calculating the next gate, the next flight, the next movement forward, I turn away.

Chapter 33
Blue Lit Breakup

> *now thread my voice*
> *with lies*
> *of lightness*
> *force within*
> *my mirror eyes*
> *the cold disguise*
> *of sad and wise*
> *decisions.*
>
> — Maya Angelou, *How I Can Lie to You*

I tap on a Zoom link, glance at the familiar question "Ready to get started?" and push the button to join the call.

[00:00]
— Hi. Pete, can you hear me?
— Yes. Can you hear me?
— Is the connection stable?
— You're a bit frozen.
— Hold on. Is this better?
— Yes. Wait — no. Now yes, it's working.

— OK. Hi.

— Hi.

[00:01]

— I haven't seen you in a while. How are you?

— I'm OK. How is it going for you?

— It's going, yeah... You're on your laptop. That's new.

— Yeah. I wanted the bigger screen.

— Fancy.

— I wanted to sit across from you.

— I like that.

[00:03]

— And as you can see, everything is blue.

— I was just about to ask why.

— There's a whole story to it. You remember I was extending my stay here, since I got additional time off? My hotel accommodated me for all but one night. Do you remember Jordan?

— The guy who made you cook çökertme? You told me about him, yes.

— He arranged for me to stay at a fancy hotel nearby, helped move my suitcases and all. It looked like a nice resort, with its own entrance to the beach... with one caveat I discovered only after dark: the light is special. (Pete chuckles)

— It looks like a club.

— True. I could dance here. Maybe I will later.

[00:05]

— How was flying today?

— Good. Intense. Clean takeoffs. I was safe. My instructor was smiling at me at the landing, which usually means I did well.

— You always sound happiest when you talk about it.

— It's predictable. That helps.

— I get that.

[00:08]

— How's your week been?

— Busy. Too busy. Calls stacked on calls, meetings on meetings. Like I'm always late to my own life.
— You sound tired.
— I am. But I'm OK.
— Your son?
— He's good. School stuff. Normal chaos.
— I'm glad.

[00:12]
— Are you back in Ölüdeniz now?
— Yes. Same place. Same faces. A bit of continuity — a paced lifestyle, flying, swimming, sleeping.
— That sounds nice.
— It is. And strange.

[00:15]
— I might come see you there one day.
— Maybe.
— Maybe.

[00:18]
— You look different.
— Different how?
— Calmer. Or... settled.
— I don't know. Maybe it's the light, or Zoom. But thank you.
— That's all right.

[00:20]
(The connection glitches. His image freezes mid-sentence. The audio stutters.)
— You're breaking up.
— Can you hear me?
— I lost you.
— Try turning your camera off.
— OK — wait.
(The screen goes black for a moment.)

[00:22]
— Maria, are you back?

— Yes. I think so.
— OK. Sorry.
— It's fine.
(A pause.)

[00:23]
— As you've probably guessed... we should talk.

[00:24]
— OK.
(A very long pause.)
— Pete, you started — you have to say it.

[00:25]
— I've been thinking a lot. About us. About everything.
— Uh-huh.
— I don't see a way forward that's fair. Not to you. Not to
me.

[00:27]
— What do you mean exactly? Can you say that again?
— I don't think this works. I don't think I can do this
the way it needs to be done.

[00:29]
— OK.
— I'm sorry.
— I know.

[00:31]
— I wanted everything for us.
— I know you did.
— I really did.
— I believe you.

[00:34]
— You deserve someone who can be there fully.
— So do you.

[00:36]
— Are you crying?

[00:37]
— Yes.
— I'm sorry.
(The camera goes off. The blue light disappears. Only sound remains.)

[00:39]
— Pete, I don't process things quickly.
— I know.
— I'm not feeling everything yet.
— That makes sense.

[00:42]
— I'm grateful for what we had.
— Me too.
— I don't regret it.
— Neither do I.

[00:46]
(The audio cuts out.)

[00:47]
— Can you hear me?
— Yes. Sorry. I think it dropped.
— Same.
— It's OK.

[00:50]
— I don't really know what more to say.
— Me neither.
(We both go silent, and neither of us seems to have the courage to say the final goodbye.)
— I wish you happiness. Honestly.
— I wish the same for you.

[00:57]
— Take care.
— You too.

[01:03]
I push the button "End Meeting for All".

Chapter 34
The Last Cigarette

The art of losing isn't hard to master;

so many things seem filled with the intent

to be lost that their loss is no disaster.

— Elizabeth Bishop, "One Art"

The balcony is narrow, its railing cool under my hands, a crystalline film of salt and dust glittering on the paint — more a temporary ledge than a place to linger. Night air slides in from the sea. Somewhere below, glasses clink, a chair scrapes, water in the pool laps against the tiled edges. Below, the village is unevenly awake: some people already asleep after early flights, others still gathered at restaurant tables, with pop music bleeding softly from somewhere down the road.

I light a cigarette without wanting to. The first drag tastes flat, like a habit stripped of reward.

I think once, clearly, without buildup:

You're leaving, so take my smoking with you.

The sentence arrives whole. I don't add anything to it. I don't argue. I smoke slowly, down to the filter, watching the ember shrink until it has nowhere left to go. I don't light another one.

For a moment there is anger — brief, hot, pressurized — turning inward rather than outward. Not loud enough to shout, not sharp enough to wound, but strong enough to bring a single, unsettling thought with it: I wonder if it crossed his mind, even for a second, to care how fragile I might be. Paragliding is an extreme sport; sudden mistakes are not unheard of. A wrong decision, a lapse of focus — none of it would look strange from the outside.

The thought doesn't spiral. It simply lands. I realize how alone I have been with responsibility — for my body, my safety, my recovery from burnout — and how little I had to steady myself against. That, more than the breakup itself, feels like a failure.

There isn't enough energy left in me to argue with any of it. I lean against the railing — not enough support — and end up sliding down to the floor, my back against the wall. Salt and dust graze my bare thighs, but I don't have the energy to care, so I let myself power down.

Inside, something goes quiet.

I sleep deeply that night, without dreams or interruptions, the kind of sleep that feels like a system reboot. I wake before the alarm, calm, surprised by how intact I am.

Morning brings light and coffee. The sea looks ordinarily

stunning again, which is a relief. I take my phone out of habit. Open the message thread with Pete.

So, our last meeting was basically in an hourly airport hotel. In case you needed a metaphor...

The cursor blinks, patient, waiting for escalation. I look at the sentence once more, then twice. I don't send it.

I lock the screen and put the phone face down on the table.

A few minutes later, I pick it up again. Open Instagram. A blank post. The same blinking cursor, a different invitation. I save the empty draft and lock the screen again.

My attention drifts away from the phone and settles on the coastline instead: boats cutting slow lines through water, a wing far out over the sea. I don't go flying. Not today, and not the day after. It isn't fear — it's judgment. Breakups and flying are better as separate dishes.

I consider asking ChatGPT for a second perspective or some inspiration. I pick up my phone again, instinctively, and then put it down, again. I can imagine the dialogue myself, without staring at the screen. I shift my posture slightly, feel my weight settle, and hear the question as clearly as if it had been typed out for me.

ChatGPT (imaginary): How does it feel in your body?
Me: Quiet.
ChatGPT (imaginary): Quiet like water beneath the ice
of a frozen river? Or like a bobcat coiled to jump? Or like
a climber, breathless at the summit?

I chuckle despite myself.

Like an oil flame candle burning in front of an icon. It doesn't touch anything — but as long as it stays lit, we're OK.

That's something, love ChatGPT, even the imaginary one in my head.

Later, I go out to lunch — I have to feed this beautiful body of mine — and in such a small village, it's inevitable that I run into familiar faces. I wonder briefly what will happen if they talk to me.

They do. Some brag about the latest acro tricks they've mastered. Others check in about plans to leave Olu or come back next time. One looks at me for a minute and asks: "You look sad. Want to talk about it?"

I can't stop from giving an immediate, snappy answer that shuts down any drama: "Not really. I'm OK — just quiet."

I don't elaborate.

In the evening, after curling up in bed with a book for a few hours, I realize something still scratches — he didn't deserve my being impolite, and empathy is not a cue for rudeness. I take the phone that I avoided for the full day and type up a message: "Hey! I realize I was not at my best. Frankly, I just broke up with someone and still can't process it. Though it's not a reason to shut you down."

I get the answer immediately (weird — I hadn't seen that he was online): "No need to apologize, I know how it is when you simply don't have the words."

It is odd how a reply from an almost-stranger thins the barrier I've been looking at the world through for the past day or two. It's OK not to have words left — it's OK to let go of them, along with other things in life (even cherished ones like attachment, or the ones you are addicted to, like nicotine).

The final letting go comes when I return to training — letting go of the ground and, for three or four minutes of an acro run, defying gravity. Breath steady, jaw unclenched, hands light. There are still cravings tugging at me, and something pulling me back, but there is also a current that carries me forward. The cigarette pack stays unopened where I left it, irrelevant now.

Part V
A Clearing

Chapter 35
The Return Ticket

*I'm not afraid of storms, for I'm
learning how to sail my ship.*
— Louisa May Alcott, Little Women

The return ticket was, in theory, supposed to take me back to Chicago.

In practice, it turned into a small game of Skyscanner Tetris. I wasn't exactly in a hurry to take the shortest route, and the algorithm — sensing weakness — offered me something better: two legs, a pause, a so-called *layover* in Belgrade. An hour away from Istanbul. Practically next door.

Honestly, why don't they offer weeklong layovers by default? It would save everyone a lot of pretending.

The day it takes to travel from Ölüdeniz to Belgrade is the kind of day that doesn't want to be remembered.

A drive to Dalaman, a short flight to Istanbul, then another short flight. Airports stacked inside each other like nesting dolls. Time folds and refolds until it loses its edges. I take my shoes off on the plane, wrap myself in a cashmere jumper and a wide cotton scarf, and disappear into noise-cancelling headphones. The engines hum as the cabin lights dim — a practiced choreography that tells the body it can let go. My body understands before my mind does: this is allowed to be easy.

I sleep in that strange, good way where you're not sure you slept, but you wake up lighter. Anxiety, which had been whipping my neurons for months, finally loosens its grip. No more threading sentences through my head. No more carefully choosing words that take care of him while trying not to abandon myself. No more imagining futures I was too afraid to picture breaking.

Only later do I realize how much energy that uncertainty had been stealing.

It turns out that after he was gone, my life became unexpectedly better. Simpler. Quieter. Unburdened by the constant hum of *well then...* He was right about one thing: it was better for both of us to part ways.

I am surprised by how OK I feel.

At the Istanbul airport, I walk past the terraces where people smoke and drink coffee at any hour, sheltered by glass, as if nicotine were a protected cultural heritage. I think about smoking at least a hundred times. I don't do it. On the runway, looking at the terminal through the porthole, a thought arrives fully formed:

This is where I saw him for the last time. In a hotel paid by the hour.

It lands, and then passes.

Apparently, Pete is leaving my system faster than nicotine.

The plane to Belgrade navigates between storm clouds stitched with lightning. We dive through them and land in a sudden clearing, like a secret. By the time I step out of arrivals, it's fully dark. Thunder rolls above the city. Rain pours, warm and relentless, the kind that feels more like relief than threat.

The airport smells of wet concrete, water washing dust from the ground, grass and soil rising into the air. Outside, a yellow taxi waits — old, honest, smelling of petrol and damp fabric. The driver doesn't talk much. The rain drums on the windshield as Belgrade slides past in blurred reflections.

My Airbnb is next door to Sarah's place. Same building. What luck!

I stand under the rain for a moment, phone in hand, three suitcases obediently soaking — over fifty kilos of my life stacked around me. I must look like a damsel in distress. A man with a small fluffy white dog appears out of the darkness, like a minor urban miracle. He offers his umbrella as if this were the most natural thing in the world.

We walk together for a few minutes. The usual first-meeting questions. Where are you coming from? Do you live here? He speaks good English, tells me his name is Max, that he lives on the ninth floor. He shows me the right door, explains where the elevator is, waits until I'm inside. Then he dissolves back into the rain, dog and all, like a magical helper whose job is done.

Thirty minutes later I've washed the travel off my skin and gone next door to see Sarah.

She opens the door already smiling, as if she's been waiting for me all evening — which she has. We sit in the kitchen, rain humming softly somewhere behind the windows. She disappears into the other room and comes back holding a white cotton shirt.

"I thought of you," she says. "I embroidered you flying over the Aegean Sea, so that you can have it close all the time."

It's loose at the shoulders, cropped just right — perfect over dresses. I put it on immediately, noticing the embroidery at once — palm-sized, placed over my heart: a blue and yellow paraglider floating above turquoise waves, unmistakably Ölüdeniz.

I stand in front of the mirror and can't stop turning slightly from side to side, as if the shirt might vanish if I stop looking. I take photos. I post one without thinking, captioned something only friends will understand — the *ones who know, know.* It feels like proof of something I don't need to explain.

Outside, the storm continues.

Over the next days, Belgrade settles into its summer rhythm: sudden downpours, skies rinsed clean, rainbows appearing without ceremony. Linden trees bloom heavily, sweet and almost indecent, their scent mixing with dust and ozone after the storms. Eighteen degrees Celsius. Light jacket weather. Perfect.

I walk without an agenda. Drink coffee. Let my nervous system catch up with my body. For the first time in a long while, I don't feel fragile. I don't wobble between excitement and despair.

I want love. I know that now — in the way you know something quietly, without bargaining.

Not craving, not drama, but the certainty that my person will stay when it's hard, irritating, and messy. I want a man who can figure things out and make them feel... the opposite of scary. Someone whose reliability shows not in speeches or promises, but in the simple fact of being there.

But tonight, none of that needs solving.

It's raining in Belgrade. The air is clean. I am dry, fed, known by name, wearing a shirt someone made for me.

That's enough.

Chapter 36
Call Me by My Name

We are all much more simply human than otherwise, be we happy and successful, contented and detached, miserable and mentally disordered, or whatever.
— Harry Stack Sullivan,
The Interpersonal Theory of Psychiatry

In Belgrade people don't treat you like a concept; they treat you like a person who needs to eat.

"Maria," Sarah calls from the kitchen, cheerful and bossy in the way only a friend can be. "You coming? Food is on the table."

I'm squatting on her bedroom floor with my laptop open, trying to make sense of an interview schedule spread across four time zones. Chicago. Belgrade. Istanbul, out of spite. Somewhere else that insists on being "GMT+1," as if we're all in a meeting.

"Coming," I say, and I actually mean it.

The apartment smells like toast and coffee and something

fried in a pan that will definitely make my mother ask, later, if I'm taking good care of my stomach. Sarah's place is bigger than mine — more room for a couch, more room for calm. The couch is directly opposite the TV, positioned like a throne for resting and consuming stories. There's no shame in it here. Nobody insists you have to earn sitting down.

I close the laptop as if I'm obeying a law.

At the table Sarah slides a plate toward me and then looks at my face the way you look at a photo you've been carrying in your wallet.

"You look good," she says. "Energized. Calm."

It's said without meaning tell me everything.

That, in Belgrade, is one of the small miracles: people can know you without interrogating you. They do not confuse closeness with access.

I tell her the short version anyway — the version that has no cinematic speeches, no carefully prepared blame. A relationship that got too tired, too anxious, too full of well, then... A clean ending that was still a rupture. A surprise improvement in my life after.

Sarah listens, not prying, not performing empathy, just absorbing it.

"OK," she says when I stop. "It is what it is."

Then, as if to prove she is not going to let this become a Greek tragedy, she adds, "Also, you look beautiful. Eat."

This is how she loves: by feeding you and refusing to build a shrine to your suffering.

We eat breakfast like it's a shared hobby. She tells me stories about her work, about colleagues who plan their lives with spreadsheets — and somehow it works. A baby here. A renovation there. A life assembled neatly, like flat-pack furniture with an unreadable Scandinavian name.

I listen and feel, unexpectedly, no jealousy.

Just curiosity.

Later, when the day begins to unspool, we end up on the couch in the evening with a glass of wine each and my bright green blanket from Morocco thrown over us like a tropical emergency exit.

"What is this color?" Sarah asks, tugging it higher.

"It's called optimism," I say.

"It's called radioactive grass," she corrects.

We press play on Bridgerton, because sometimes you need to watch beautiful people solve their problems in ballrooms, wearing fabrics that have never seen a washing machine. Everyone is always one glance away from ruining their family name. It's comforting.

We comment like sports announcers.

"Look at that dress," I say.

"That's not a dress," Sarah says. "That's a down payment."

"And the man?"

"The man is a walking trust fund with unresolved feelings."

We laugh. We sip. We judge their romantic decisions with the smug superiority of women who have lived through real chaos — and then we sigh at the exact same moments anyway.

It's not that we don't want love.

We do.

We want the steady kind. The kind that doesn't treat care as a temporary audition. The kind where, when you cherish someone, they don't suddenly start acting like they've completed the game and can now roam freely through other dimensions.

But we say it lightly, between jokes, because this is a living room, not a courtroom.

"Maria," Sarah says at one point, reaching for the remote. "If I ever start dating a man who makes me feel like I need to earn basic kindness, please stage an intervention."

"Gladly," I say. "I'll bring charts."

"Green&Co brain," she mutters.

"Occupational hazard."

The next morning, I'm in my own studio, the fancy Airbnb I booked like a small act of self-respect. There's a kitchen where I make breakfasts and a patch of floor where I dance for no reason other than my body asking to be inhabited. I put on music and move while my coffee cools and job postings blink at me from my browser like needy little creatures.

Apply. Save. Close the tab. Reopen the tab. Apply again.

At some point my inbox pings with an email that starts with my name.

Maria, we'd love to interview you next week for the position...

No fireworks. No panic. Just a quiet click in my chest: oh, right. I am still a functioning professional adult. Good to know.

In the afternoon, I go to the circus. Olga is, luckily, still in Belgrade.

The studio is on the top floor, with a huge arched window

and a blue floor that makes every movement look slightly more dramatic than it is. Outside, the sky can't decide what mood it's in. There are storm clouds and, somewhere behind them, the idea of a rainbow warming up.

Olga stands there like a woman who has never once doubted the usefulness of suffering.

"Maria," she says, clapping her hands. "Let's work."

There is no small talk. There is no gentle entry. She begins counting like she's trying to summon my muscles from another dimension.

"One. Two. Three. Up!"

My body obeys.

"Again."

My lungs file a complaint.

"Again."

"Olga," I wheeze, "I paid for a circus class, not for... whatever this is."

"This is your class," she says, unmoved. "Circus is just cardio with better posture."

By the time I'm dripping with sweat, the window is open a crack and the city sends its weather into the room. Ozone from the storm. Linden, sweet and heavy. Warm wooden dust and the human smell of effort. Somewhere outside, a rainbow flashes briefly — not spiritual, just efficient.

"Better," Olga says finally, the highest compliment she offers. "Now your strength is turning into grace."

I would like to print this sentence and frame it.

After dance, I go for a massage.

The salon is called Masha, which feels like the universe making a private joke about my name (Mahsa is a kind version of Maria in Slavic languages). The interior is beautiful in a way that isn't trying too hard — warm lights, soft textures, the kind of place that makes you stand up straighter just so you don't disappoint the furniture.

And it's half the price of Chicago.

In Chicago, this level of care would come with a clipboard and a waiver and a subtle sense that you're lucky they made time for your lower back. Here, the woman at reception looks at me like a sister she hasn't met before.

"Maria," the therapist says when I lie down, her voice calm and practical. "Do you like this pressure?"

"Yes," I say immediately, because this is the first question anyone has asked me all week that has a correct answer.

She laughs. "OK. Brave girl."

The room smells faintly of oils and clean towels. My brain tries to hold onto thoughts — interviews, schedules, what comes next — and then lets go. My body, relieved, takes over.

Later, walking back through the streets, I catch my reflection in a shop window and don't flinch. I don't brace. I don't expect the next thing to be rude or dismissive.

In Belgrade, people say my name and then say something kind.

Or practical.

Or funny.

"Maria, sit."

"Maria, eat."

"Maria, one, two, three."

Maria, we'd love to interview you...

Even when I address myself — Maria, relax. Maria, focus. Maria, don't be an idiot and buy cigarettes — the tone is changing. Less like a drill sergeant, more... interested. Like I'm a person worth handling carefully, not a project to be managed.

At the end of the week, we go across the city for Kate's birthday.

I've never been to this neighborhood before. It's higher, hillier, the kind of place that feels like a village stitched into the city. From the street you can see a valley with nice houses and a ribbon of river down below, as if Belgrade is casually showing off that it contains entire other worlds.

Inside, the living room is big enough for eight people to gather around a dark wooden table. Someone has put flowers in a jar because we are adults and also because jars are the most honest vases.

The cat moves through the room like a landlord.

In the kitchen, buns bake. The oven breathes out warm, yeasty air. Pizza arrives in boxes because we are adults but also because nobody is here to suffer.

People hug me as if I've been gone for a normal amount of time, not a year of moving countries and losing my mind and finding it again. They say my name during introductions and I don't do the thing I used to do — that tiny, involuntary flinch, like I'm waiting for the second half of the sentence to hurt.

Here the second half is usually something like:

"Maria, come sit with us."

Or:

"Maria, do you want more wine?"

At some point I realize — with a small internal scream — that I did not bring a birthday present.

I look at Sarah.

She looks at me.

My face probably does something theatrical, because Kate notices immediately.

"What?" she says, amused.

"I —" I begin, and then I'm honest, because lying would require energy. "I didn't bring you a present."

Kate laughs like this is the best news she's heard all day.

"Relax," she says. "Bring fruit to the table. That's the perfect present."

"Fruit," I repeat solemnly.

"Yes. You are now the Minister of Fruit."

Someone hands me a bowl. Someone else offers to peel something. Suddenly I am part of a small committee working on citrus.

There is something deeply funny in how quickly panic can be domesticated.

We toast Kate. We toast her move to Montana like it's both absurd and completely reasonable, because apparently this is what adulthood is: your friend calmly relocating to a state that sounds like a brand of hiking boots.

People tell stories. Someone describes their plans for a baby and makes it sound like ordering a bookshelf. Someone else complains about a renovation. The talk drifts to the future —

kids, countries, stability — the way it does when people have stable, planned lives.

I listen, and instead of feeling like I'm watching from the outside, I feel... included. Like my life is just one more messy version of a normal human plotline.

Later, someone says, "Do you know the song Maria?"

"The Blondie one?" I ask immediately, because of course I would. "Maria, you've got to see her..."

"That one is good," he says, "but I meant the Santana one."

"The Santana one?" I repeat, offended on behalf of my musical education. "I've never heard it."

He grins, puts his phone near the speaker, and suddenly the room fills with that warm, rolling guitar.

Se mira Maria on the corner...

The lyrics go on about Maria thinking of ways to make it better, and I laugh — not because it's a joke, exactly, but because it's too specific, too sweet, too perfectly timed. As if the universe heard all my complicated thoughts and decided to respond with a song written by a man who probably owns several silk shirts.

Around the table people keep talking, keep eating, keep passing slices of pizza as if this is the most important work in the world.

Someone says my name again, casually, as if they plan to use it for centuries to come — and maybe they do, because these small rituals belong to eternity.

Chapter 37
Taking Stock

A place for everything,
everything in its place.
— proverb

Late morning light falls sideways into the studio, generous and a little judgmental. It reveals everything at once: three suitcases open like wide mouths on the bed and floor, a backpack slumped against the chair, clothes and objects arranged not chaotically, but mid-conversation.

This is what four months of living looks like.

An extra-large suitcase. A large one. A cabin case. A backpack. That's it — no storage units, no forgotten drawers, no parallel lives abandoned in closets. Everything that carried me through Morocco, India, Dubai, Saudi Arabia, Turkey, and Belgrade is in front of me now, visible and accountable.

For four months, this was enough. Maybe more than enough.

And still, the idea of never unpacking — living permanently out of zippers and compression bags — feels like another kind of escape. Enchanting from a distance, exhausting up close.

I sit on the edge of the bed and start picking things up, one by one, letting them tell me what they know.

The skirt goes first.

Pink, long, unreasonably dramatic. It unfurls itself as if it expects an audience.

"*I have been busy,*" it seems to say.

It remembers the pirate fortress in Morocco, stone walls and wind, flaring wide like it was meant to be seen from the sea. It remembers Dubai, heavy air and swaying hips, nights where it learned how close confidence and exhaustion can live to each other. Jaipur too — the Pink City — where it let me pretend, briefly and without irony, that I was a princess with nothing urgent to decide.

The skirt is still intact — no tears, no stains that matter — which feels like an accomplishment we share.

It gives the boots a look.

"*Don't even think about putting me next to those.*"

The boots do not apologize.

They are scratched, dusty, unimpressed.

"*You're welcome,*" they reply. "*Someone had to touch the ground.*"

The paraglider is folded carefully, taking up more space than everything else combined.

Old fabric. New fabric. The new blue wing still smells faintly of ambition and factory air.

"*You're dramatic,*" the backpack mutters. "*You get carried around like royalty."*

"*I carried her life through the air,*" the paraglider answers calmly. "*You carried snacks.*"

There is no argument that wins against that.

I run my hand along the lines, check them out of habit. This piece of nylon held me together when my thoughts couldn't. Under it, gravity felt optional, and fear briefly lost its authority. It doesn't ask to be thanked. It simply waits to be packed correctly.

The diary is almost full.

Its cover is bright with Turkish carpet patterns — soft, scratchy enough that you can't forget the touch. Pete bought it for me last Christmas — a good gift then, and one that somehow kept working even now.

The pages are thick with ink, the handwriting changing shape as the months went on. Tight when I was anxious. Wide and sloppy when I was tired. Almost gentle toward the end.

"*You used me well,*" the diary seems to say. "*I'm tired, too.*"

I close it carefully. It doesn't need more words right now.

The backpack is sun-washed, sea-washed, corner-scratched. It is green and blue with hints of yellow — originally meant to look like avocados, apparently, though no one has ever agreed on that.

It has seen everything from the inside.

Passports. Chargers. Lip balm. Emergency snacks. Headphones. A spare T-shirt folded badly at airport security.

"*I know all your secrets,*" it says proudly.

It's true. And it's also true that no matter how carefully I pack, I still carry the faint smell of airports with me — something the necklace, resting quietly in its pouch, would never tolerate.

The necklace lies in its pouch, pretending to be fragile.

Glass beads from Italy are strung on an almost invisible thread. Sparkly, subtle, deceptively sharp at the edges.

"Composure," it reminds me. *"I require composure."*

It was never meant for flying. It belongs to dinners, sunsets, New Year's Eve in Istanbul, moments when movement slows and attention sharpens. It carries the fondness of the woman who made it — the way she spoke about glass as if it were alive, and how she wrote my name on the pouch as if she expected it to travel.

I smile and place it gently away from the boots, the backpack, and any sudden gestures.

The lipstick rolls out of my purse and straight into my palm, unapologetic — sleek, lacquered, bright red, reliable enough to stay on your lips forever, and largely unimpressed by circumstances.

"You will need me again," it says. *"Not today. But soon."*

When the suitcases are finally zipped — not rushed, not ceremonially — the room feels suddenly too small. Crowded with evidence.

I step out onto the balcony with a cup of wine — or maybe tea; it hardly matters — just to breathe.

Below, the city continues in its ordinary chorus. Dogs barking softly in the courtyard. Children playing, inventing rules only they understand. A car horn somewhere, impatient but brief. Music drifting from a neighboring balcony, someone else's afternoon spilling into mine.

It's been about ten days, maybe two weeks, since my last cigarette.

I notice it the way you notice a bruise healing — accidentally, with mild disbelief. Every day has been hard; every day I have wanted one. And still, here I am.

Tenderness arrives quietly.

Not pride. Not discipline. Just the sense that my first responsibility is this: to take care of myself.

I don't need more things. I don't need proof.

This was enough for four months.

I rest my elbows on the balcony railing and let my mind drift ahead — not to plans or promises, but to images: Lake Michigan in summer light, the skyline catching sunset, my cat rearranging herself on my chest like she owns me. Friendly hugs. Familiar work. The strange comfort of doing something I know how to do well.

The suitcases wait behind me, quiet.

PART VI
People, Meetings, Evenings

Chapter 38
Three Chicagos

I made a lot of mistakes
In my mind, in my mind...
— *Sufjan Stevens, "Chicago"*[9]

I step off the jet bridge feeling exactly like someone who has spent ten hours in an economy seat and finally stopped pretending it wasn't exhausting. My neck aches, my thoughts lag half a beat behind my body, and the fluorescent lights feel oddly personal, as if they've been waiting for me.

Then I see them. Kitty first — standing tall, smiling, already reaching for my suitcase. Cora beside her, flowers in hand, radiant. We skip preamble and just hug. Bags are counted and redistributed. Someone says, "You look fresh," which I take to mean, "You've made it."

The taxi smells like summer and fabric cleaner. Cora talks fast, trying to squeeze four months of updates into the drive,

---

[9] Note from the author: if you don't know this song, put it on, it's a great soundtrack for this chapter.

while Kitty quietly handles the route. I lean my head against the window and let the city come back to me — bridges, water, glass, familiar corners.

"Food when we get there? Or too tired?"

Me: *"If you keep me company, I'm down for anything."*

The apartment door opens. My cat shows up immediately, cautiously sniffing the faint smells of distant lands, then walks away with clear disapproval. Delivery is ordered; shoes are kicked aside; we sit on the floor with our backs against the couch, cartons sweating onto the wood. There isn't time to say everything, but there is time to lean into the same quiet. Beneath the steam of food and the stale sweetness of travel, I notice dust — old, settled, undisturbed.

That night I fall asleep in my bed as if slipping through layers of time. My brain floats between zones, misfiring gently; the skyline outside the window rearranges itself, doubles, blurs, then steadies. Lights become constellations. The river lifts and lowers like breath. I drift, half-awake, convinced the city is moving and I am not.

In the morning, the spell thins. What's left is practical and slightly abrasive: a clogged tub, a damp curtain gone sour, dust where hands should have passed, dishes that never made it home, clothes that aren't mine taking up space. The place looks familiar and wrong at the same time, like a version of my life I recognize but no longer wear comfortably. It isn't quite disgust — more a clear, unarguable sense of misfit.

A week later, Chicago has settled fully into summer, the kind that sticks to your skin and makes you intentionally enjoy every errand.

This is when the city splits for me into three overlapping Chicagos, all running at once. One is made of work and job searches: offices, interviews, calls, the professional self I know how to inhabit even when I'm not sure where it will take me next. Another is built out of my people — friends who walk with me, sit with me, feed me, laugh with me, stitch my days back into something social and warm. And the third is quieter but persistent: the return of wanting love as part of an ordinary life again, not as a distraction or a problem to solve, but as something that belongs alongside everything else. None of these Chicagos cancels the others out. I braid them together, unevenly but insistently, and move through all three at the same time. I walk to the office every morning — about fifteen minutes, a thermos with home-brewed coffee in hand — into an office crowded with interns who all seem to share the same smart posture and confidence that hasn't yet been asked to prove itself. My assistant has to hunt for a room with a window, a small but necessary benefit — the closest you get to being outdoors. There is no requirement that I be here; still, I come, choosing the physical fact of the office even as most of my conversations unfold in New York, Dallas, or some other distant square on the map.

My phone buzzes while I wait for the elevator.

Tinder: So what are you actually looking for?

I type, delete, then decide to be honest instead of clever.

Me: Something warm. Steady. With a future. If that sounds like a lot, it probably is.

The elevator doors close and lift me up, the question hanging there without pressure.

Clarity, it turns out, changes the temperature of everything. Conversations move with less friction. Boundaries hold their shape. Rejection — on either side — lands without leaving a mark. One man suggests trapeze flying instead of drinks, saying that even if we don't connect, it would still be a good night. We don't connect romantically, but it is still a good night.

Another man, in Chicago briefly before flying to Harvard to give a talk on AI, asks me to dinner. He's attentive without trying too hard. At the end of the evening, he mentions Boston, maybe long-distance. I say my no. He accepts it calmly. I walk home lighter, newly aware of how much space a clean no can open.

Work threads itself through everything. Hundreds of emails wait, some important, most not. I help where I can, even though I'm not staffed on a project. Being a consultant without a case is a strange position — you're visible, but not entirely necessary. I tell myself it's temporary, and for now, I believe that.

Job search and interviews fit in between business development calls and grocery runs. On Zoom, a career coach pauses when I describe one project.

Her: You saved how much?
Me: About forty-three million a year.

She stops for a moment, then smiles.

Her: Let's skip the burnout part. Let's focus on the number. We laugh, and the conversation feels steadier after that.

Sometimes Chicago compresses itself. I'm on a date, circling around the phrase "casual but intentional," not trying to resolve it, when someone waves from across the room. A colleague. For a moment, the city shrinks, then stretches back out again.

Friends walk with me to the office. Friends arrive in the evenings with bottles, jokes, and a willingness to stay. My cat graciously forgives me and comes to sit on our laps, purring, then resumes watching everything from a distance. I sleep better than I have in months. Outside the window, the river splits and the skyscrapers light up — offices, kitchens, bedrooms, other people's evenings happening all at once. The city doesn't explain itself or comfort me. It just keeps going, full of lives unfolding alongside mine.

Chapter 39
Evenings That Counted

How lucky am I to have something that makes saying goodbye so hard.

— A. A. Milne, Winnie-the-Pooh

"That catch was unreal," Kitty says, on the way from post-volleyball dinner. "You basically saved the set. And those powerful serves!"

"You say that every time," Cora answers. "But yes. Season officially open."

We're walking along the Michigan shoreline, still warm from the day, our skin covered in sand, cheeks pink from the sun. My shoulders are sore from hitting the ball, from all the reaching and jumping sideways, going after it like you'd lose a fortune if you let it drop. Some imaginary fortunes got lost today — and some real happiness was gained. The pleasure of plunging into the chilly waters of Michigan: the first shock, the rush of goosebumps, and then the quiet fun of staying in longer, swimming, calling others to join. Somewhere behind us are the courts at North Avenue Beach, now quiet again.

"Do you have a bag for the swimsuit?" Kitty asks.

"I wrapped it in a T-shirt," I say. "We'll see if it survives. But I can put yours there, too, if you need."

"Carpaccio was so good," Cora adds. "I still can't believe we got that table in Toto."

"Oh yes, I was so hungry, I could order one more pasta for dessert. And then you guys would have to roll me out of the restaurant."

"And that the guys brought Aperol to the beach," Kitty says. "Peak summer behavior."

I slow down slightly. "OK, but now I'm dizzy."

They both laugh, and we keep going, the conversation layering itself lightly over the rhythm of our steps. Someone brings up the photoshoot we're planning — outfits, timing, the hope that the skyline will show up properly. "Just to remember Chicago," Cora says, practical about it, as if memory needs logistics.

Talk drifts into Cora's move to Boston, and it arrives not as an announcement but as inventory: which furniture is worth moving, what can be sold, how many evenings she's already lost to Facebook Marketplace. She rubs her forehead. "I still have three piles of things to post," she says. "And I'm so tired of writing 'pickup only.' And then answering endless 'Can you deliver?' with polite decline — as if no one pays attention to the ad."

We reach the point where our paths split. Cora checks her

phone, exhales, says she should head home and deal with the ads before it gets any later. We hug — quick, familiar — and watch her turn back, already half absorbed by the next task.

Kitty and I stand there for a moment, neither of us saying anything. Then she glances at me. "Do you want to keep walking?"

"Yes," I say, at the same time she does.

So we do. The light thins, the air cools just enough to register. The lake darkens into something less reflective, more absorbing. Our pace settles. The chatter softens.

After a while, Kitty slows and looks out toward the horizon. "So," she says, careful, "what's your plan with Chicago?"

There's no pressure in it. Just curiosity, edged with care.

I answer honestly, without loading the words. Europe, interviews, not knowing exactly where I'll land, which is scary and inspiring. I tell her I don't think I'm staying here for the next year. Saying it out loud feels lighter than keeping it contained.

Kitty nods. She walks a few steps before speaking again. "That makes sense," she says. Then, more firmly, "Good for you."

She looks at me and smiles. "You're impressive, you know. And honestly? I don't think this city quite does you justice."

I open my mouth to argue, but she cuts me off with a small, decisive wave of her hand, like this isn't up for debate. Gods, I'm a lucky person to have her as a friend!

We drift naturally toward Navy Pier, not deciding so much as following the path as it offers itself. I mention, almost casually, that when Pete was in Chicago for the first time, we rode out here together. Then I add, "And you — remember when we first met?

We walked all the way here and took a ride on the carousel."

Kitty laughs. "I forgot about that."

"It was so much fun, and so unexpected — two 30-year-olds after a long day in the corporate office, our heads still full of confusion about where to live and how to settle," I say.

"Everything was so weird," she says, laughing at the memory. "Including us."

The ground widens beneath our feet. I tell her it was once a military runway, that this land is artificial — the same kind of engineering they now use on Dubai's coastline, just nearly a century earlier, and for different reasons.

"Do you feel safe on man-made land?" she asks, half-joking.

"I guess we'll find out," I say.

It's fully dark now. We stop near the edge and look out at the lake, which has flattened into something almost black. Then an explosion goes off behind us. We both freeze. We forgot it was Saturday. Fireworks tear open the sky — sharp bursts of light, briefly painting it with color: stars, spirals, jagged blooms.

More fireworks follow, blooming and fading over the water. We stand without speaking, our faces tilted up. Colors scatter across the lake's surface, then vanish.

Later, back at my place, we stretch our aching feet onto the coffee table and put on a Miyazaki movie. Fireworks appear again on the screen, animated this time, softer but just as luminous. My orange cat curls into a perfect ball between us, a small monument to coziness.

For everything else in life, there is planning, effort, and cost. For this evening, there is only this. And it is priceless.

Chapter 40
Misspellings

> *"When I use a word,"* Humpty
> Dumpty *said in rather a scornful*
> *tone, "it means just what I choose*
> *it to mean — neither more nor*
> *less."*
>
> — Lewis Carroll, *Through*
> *the Looking-Glass*

The first word in the evaluation is my name. It's not my name.

I notice this before anything else — before the score, before the paragraphs of carefully measured praise, before the language that describes competence from a safe distance. Just that first word, wrong and confident, sitting where recognition is supposed to be.

It's a perfect Monday morning in Chicago, the kind that makes the city feel generous. Sun on glass. Clear air. I stop by the coffee shop downstairs and order my usual, already mapping the day: a couple of slides to finish, a backlog of emails to clear, and lunch planned with a colleague. A normal rhythm. A good one.

I settle into my office, door open at first, then closed once I decide to focus. There are thirty new emails from the weekend. I start working through them methodically. Somewhere in the middle of the list, a notification from the HR portal appears: *You have two unread feedback forms.*

I pause. Evaluation season always does this — it tightens time around itself. These reviews matter. They shape career progression, compensation, placement. I've already been flagged yellow for my absence over the past months; this is the moment to read carefully, to learn, to calibrate. I stand up, get a second coffee, stop by the bathroom so nothing interrupts the next hour, then return and close the door behind me.

I open the first feedback.

Mary is...

The rest of the sentence is fluent, polished. Full of the language of excellence: complex project, strong organization, diligence, client success. I skim, already aware of the number attached to it. A two. Below average. The praise reads like an explanation for why the score shouldn't be taken personally.

I open the second one.

Maia continued...

Again, competence. Again, approval. Again, a careful balancing act. The tone is slightly warmer, as if to soften the first blow. The number is higher, but the game has been played already.

I sit there longer than necessary, not moving. I don't finish reading either evaluation. I click acknowledge and close the portal.

The anger arrives late, fully formed.

I go downstairs and step into the yard behind the building. Someone is already there, leaning against the wall, smoking. I hesitate, then ask.

"Can I borrow a cigarette?"

He looks at me — at my straight posture, my work clothes, the careful way I'm holding myself together — and hands me one.

"This won't fix it," he says, not unkindly.

"I know," I say.

I smoke anyway. The first drag tastes wrong. The second is worse. My head spins; my stomach tightens. When it's over, I feel heavier than before. My fingers smell like smoke. The butt goes out in the ashtray, small and conclusive.

Upstairs, nothing has changed. My office looks the same. The slides are still waiting. I open the HR portal again, as if repetition might produce a different outcome. It doesn't. I acknowledge the feedback once more and close it without finishing the detailed reading.

Then I check my personal inbox.

Two new emails sit near the top of it. Invitations to final interview rounds. Different companies. Different futures. Even different countries. The subject lines are plain. The tone is curious and specific.

I close the laptop.

I decide not to think about the people who wrote

the evaluations anymore. Not because I'm still furious — though I am — but because my attention no longer belongs to them. I give it instead to the places where my name might be learned, spoken correctly, and said with intention.

Chapter 41
Keeping the Days

> *Orange as the perfumed fruit*
> *hanging their globes on the glossy tree,*
> *orange as pumpkins in the field,*
> *orange as butterflyweed and the monarchs*
> *who come to eat it, orange as my cat running lithe through the high grass.*
> *— Marge Piercy, "Colors passing through us"*

Rise and shine, it's seven. You know you want to stay in bed, to take after Dora, stretched out in the morning sun, practicing a form of commitment-free existence that involves no calendars and very little ambition. Her orange fur flares against the grass-green bedding, so saturated it looks styled on purpose. Before you're properly awake, you've taken far too many photos, counting the contortions you need to get into — a strange, tender version of morning yoga, minus enlightenment.

Next comes coffee. Three and a half tablespoons of ground Lavazza, three hundred milliliters of bottled water — never the tap, not after the kettle grew a crust of green limescale that made you swear off the pipes forever. Brrr. Gas on low, cezve balanced carefully on the smallest burner, like a minor engineering project. Your mind wanders ahead — two calls today, one solid, one vague, both with people you like — and then the coffee hisses and boils over exactly as you drift too far. Steam rises, impatience flares, correction follows. You wipe it up, slow your hands, and stay where you are.

Later, you stand in front of the wardrobe, negotiating terms. First calls at home mean cat fur is a measurable risk, but there's still a walk to the office and, possibly, a date in the evening — if it gets confirmed, if it doesn't. You decide to wear something nice anyway — not as a costume or armor, but as a quiet choice. A pop of color, chosen without witnesses. You leave the apartment dressed for the day you're about to have, not the one you're imagining.

You walk a lot — fifteen thousand steps, sometimes more. When it's late and you're still circling the block to close the gap, you call them *stupid walks for your stupid mental health*. The joke works because it's accurate, and because repetition turns effort into habit. The walks don't solve anything, but they keep you from freezing in place.

Kitty drops by most evenings. Sometimes for a glass of wine, sometimes for ten minutes on the balcony, sometimes only to pet the cat and leave. The luxury isn't the duration; it's the geography. Two buildings down the block, five minutes on foot, no coordination required. Friendship without scheduling feels like a minor miracle.

On one of those days, we play volleyball again, and halfway through the set, the sky opens without warning. Rain comes down hard and suddenly, soaking the sand, the net, our hair. Someone yells something heroic and useless. We laugh and run for cover — a blessing in disguise for our team, which had been losing gloriously before the rain intervened on our behalf.

Later, on Cora's rooftop, we grill whatever survived the working week in her fridge. She lends you dry clothes — a cotton dress, white with blue stripes, two sizes too big. It smells faintly of someone else's detergent and a different life. You wear it home and keep wearing it, long after the dinner has passed. Even now, months later, you still reach for it sometimes, as if fabric could function as a thread between people now separated by latitude and time zones.

Some evenings, you come back on the L after the gym, already questioning the wisdom of public transport at this hour. You're sweaty, physically spent; it's dark outside, and the car is loud in the way only tired cities manage to be. You plug your earbuds in and let Massive Attack take over. *It's unfortunate that, when we feel a storm...* The train rattles, the bass settles into your chest, and you follow through anyway — uncomfortable, intact, still moving.

Your body stays busy: dance, bike, volleyball, trampoline classes, massage. When you're tired, you don't default to screens. You color, you read, you let your hands calm down before you ask your mind to do the same. It's not discipline or optimization. It's maintenance — like watering something you'd like to keep alive.

You notice, with genuine surprise, that if you earn consulting money and stop throwing it at the holes in your soul, something unusual happens: you save it. Chicago does not encourage this, and yet it occurs anyway, quietly, almost by accident. The accumulation feels less like restraint and more like respect — for time, for effort, for your future self.

You think about beauty — how some of it is found, ready-made, like lake light after rain, and some of it is constructed slowly: a meal, a habit, a boundary. The distinction matters less than it used to. What matters is the care involved, the willingness to show up repeatedly without demanding a result.

At night, the apartment settles. Sometimes Kitty is there, sometimes not. The cat curls into her favorite spot on the couch, precise and unbothered, like a small Sheldon demonstrating the most efficient way to exist. A projector throws old images onto the wall — this time it's Star Wars, something familiar and expansive, galaxies safely contained in a living room. Feet stretch onto the coffee table, aching in agreement. Nothing is urgent, and nothing feels missing.

You don't know what comes next, and you've stopped trying to pin it down. For now, it's enough to tend what's here — to keep the days intact, and trust that this, too, is a legitimate form of forward motion.

Part VII
Neither Signed nor Returned

Chapter 42
The Letter Without a Name

*This is the night mail crossing
the Border,
Bringing the cheque and the postal
order,
Letters for the rich, letters for
the poor,
The shop at the corner, the girl
next door*
— W.H. Auden, "Night Mail"

If you're reading this now — put on the Piano Concerto No. 2 by Tchaikovsky in G Major. I'm also listening to it while writing these pages. It would be lovely to share the Andante in Part II with you and maybe be as close in "real time" as you can get in a book.

I was listening to it under the stars of Kentucky — we made a road trip there, drove across a couple of states, swam in the lake, made a barbecue for dinner, and my friends went to bed, but I lingered on the terrace to breathe in the view, the trees, the water glimmering in the distance. This music resonated with my soul — sad and joyful, full of enchantment — like fae made it, not an orchestra of adults in black suits and dresses.

Back in Chicago, when I entered the building, the concierge said "Hi, how are you?" — the usual flow, no one expects you to say anything but "All good, how was your day?" But they stopped me as I was already passing the front desk toward the elevators.

"I have an envelope for you."

I took it, thanked them — but a thought crossed my mind: why here? Mail usually arrives in the box and I wasn't expecting any special delivery.

The envelope was blank — no information about where it came from, no sender's name, lightly creased at the corners, A4 in size. What could be inside? I'm not a killer or a spy to receive this kind of "no return address" correspondence.

Later, Pete told me he had been afraid I'd tear it to pieces and get rid of it without reading if I knew it was from him, so he left it blank. He went to the trouble of finding out that his friend Marcus was shuttling between Dubai and Chicago, and asked him to play Cupid and deliver the message.

After opening it, I found a couple of pages inside, covered in familiar handwriting.

My dear Maria, my sun, my light,

I miss you so much. My heart keeps reaching for you. Across any distance and any time zone. I carry the absence of your touch, your smile, your warm, intelligent eyes. There hasn't been a single day when I didn't think of you — on good days and on bad ones, I think of you.

I deeply regret that I never told you I love you. That I want to be with you, never to part. That I want us to have a beautiful, warm home together. I never told you that I see us growing old together. Your stubborn hair will turn white, wise lines will appear on your face, but your eyes... your eyes will stay the same. Laughing, full of tenderness for those you love.

And I gnaw my own heart raw, grieving that I lost you.

I let you down. You trusted me, and I let you go. Trusting me didn't come easily to you. We argued, but I always felt that I mattered to you, that you were holding space for me. You'd grumble, feel hurt, but you waited for me.

And of course, I'm waiting for you too. Your photograph is always with me. Every day I take it out of my bag just to look at you. And when I took it out today, I decided to write you this letter.

To ask for your forgiveness. For being a coward, and for breaking your heart.

I remember you — and us — with great tenderness. Everything we did together, how we were close, how we loved. Thank you for being in my life. You came into it at a very difficult time and became my support. And it's as if I'm still lying with my head in your lap by that monastery, as if I'm still sitting with you on the night beach in Olu, as if I'm endlessly having breakfast with you on the terrace of our house, as if I'm once again looking at the ocean with you, holding you in my arms.

All of that gave me so much strength.

I'm so sorry, my dear, that I wasn't able to become your support. That I didn't understand you and couldn't stand by you in the way you needed. You were able to take care of me — and I wasn't able to do the same for you. I don't know if this can be fixed, but I wish with all my heart that it could be.

Forgive me, my aviatrix. I'm holding you in my thoughts. You made me happy, and I'm grateful for every minute. I wish you everything that is real and true. I love you.

With tenderness,

Pete

June 4, Baku — Dubai

P.S. Forgive my handwriting and my mistakes...

Chapter 43
What do I do?

Stunned, I kept standing next to the kitchen counter. What do I do?

I was in a stupor — shaken, tears drying on my skin, numb.

Ok, sweetheart, let's breathe. Any emotion lasts about 90 seconds. Emotions aren't feelings, and we'll deal with those later. If you overreact to an emotion — you provoke a cascade and amplify it; if you shove it down and pressurize it — you will cause a counter-reaction ten times stronger. I was careful, as if I were dealing with a ticking bomb. Don't drop it, don't shake it... it will resolve. Now, just breathe. It's OK to feel whatever you feel; you will let it flow and live it to the bottom. Let's drink some water.

What's the date at the top of the letter? Hm, about two weeks ago. It took so long to get it to Chicago with someone, then to leave it at the front desk. Then for me to come back from the trip and find it. He is probably dying of anxiety. I really don't owe Pete anything, but torturing people is not my preferred pastime. All right, let's text him.

> "Hello, Pete. I got your letter. I need time to process how I feel and what I think about it. But I figure it's important for you to know that it found me, I read it, and I will reply."

Check.

Ok, let's continue breathing. It's a lot; you are overwhelmed — it's a very normal reaction. Also, it's getting late. How about we take a shower and go to sleep?

--

There is no way I can sleep. After the shower, I came back to his letter to see what exactly was pinching my soul so hard. I took my diary and started just pouring whatever was on my mind there — and, to my surprise, it pretty soon turned into a reply. To myself. To him.

June 22, 2025 ~~Saturday~~ Sunday, Chicago (at home)

I just came back from Kentucky. Mammoth Cave, lake house, long drive, grill, friendly banter. Amish lifestyle, swimming in the river, Tchaikovsky, and falling asleep under the stars. All this makes life worth it.

At home, Pete's letter awaited me. With a confession of love and a request to forgive. "For being a coward and breaking your heart." And it seems he put the right words to what went wrong. And appealed to love.

It's reason enough to start talking. Not enough to turn back to him, to believe and trust him.

You left — and this was a real, true betrayal. It got tough — and you left me alone. I didn't fail on my own, but I do remember the moment of falling apart quite well.

When you ultimately left me, I started to sleep better. I don't need emotional swings, grievances, doubts, dramatic gestures. From where I stand, the world is a cruel and tough place by itself; I don't need someone to add challenges on top of it. You said, "It's hurtful" — just at the moment when you were no longer allowed to do whatever you felt like. And what if something truly bad happened? A war? A sickness? What will happen if one of us gets physically hurt?

Why this letter?

I see and respect the courage. I see and highly appreciate the act of love. In the end, if something can save the world, it's love. Cheesy — but I'm not ashamed to believe in it. And I'm not touched by memories of "what we had" — it really doesn't matter anymore, just water under the bridge.

—

In my soul, it's winter. I don't trust. I need more words and more context. I refuse, point-blank, to imply anything in what I read. To guess. To think it out. I don't understand how it happens that you left — and you love me.

What has changed? Therapy helped? It doesn't seem like enough time. Is it a momentary aspiration? Well, the letter is dated June 4, and now it's June 22 — you had plenty of time to ask not to pass it on to me.

I don't understand, and it's strange. I need more words — what drives you, what shifted? What do you want? Factually — are you divorced already? What do you propose to do with the geographical distance? What do you want to offer? Why should I — why do you think I should — believe you? I don't seem to be stupid, and I have enough self-esteem. Why, then?

I really want to sleep calmly. To be happy. I wish you the same — to the fullest extent, and in the way that is best for you (here our visions might mismatch, I gather).

During the past weeks, I answered a hundred times the question "what are you looking for?" and realized that I want a lot more than I dared to voice to you. And yes, with these expectations I have every chance of meeting my white-haired age in total loneliness. Yes, it's a risk. But I think I'm OK to take it. With it, I sleep peacefully and don't agree to less than I dream of.

I can't spend my life with men who are married, and with a job that doesn't bring me joy. Lately, I missed a couple of parties and realized that spending time on my couch with a book, a cup of tea, and my cat is more important than "being social" with people who aren't mine. And with mine — I can sit looking at my phone, and they will still value those moments. They know that when they ask, and when they need, I'll be there. It can't be otherwise; it's like gravity.

I was flattered by your attention. And I thought you were... chaotic, but around when I truly needed you. I was flattered to think so. I learned this lesson the hard way — with repetition. When I was lying on this couch in Chicago in January and February and couldn't leave it to do anything, my friend came by and asked, "Can I wash the dishes?" And you praised her for being here — and didn't come. Just a couple of days before your arrival, you said, "I can't make it." Just like that. Remembering it now, I don't know how that Maria managed to plan a trip, buy tickets, pack bags. I really don't know — and I somewhat admire her. Somewhat pity her, too. In this engine, a lot of good things combusted as well — like the trust that your partner would help (no, you will do it yourself), that he can't just leave you on another continent without remorse or sympathy, the belief that sending flowers is enough support. Bloody hell, I remember crying and sleeping a week on end. And she managed. Just... wow.

And then we had another go — when you left because "it's hurtful." I still can't turn it in my head. What's hurtful? That someone asks something of you, wants something? Like not working during those two days you plan to spend together? Wants a place with her own bed? Asks about the future — how you picture it and where? Is unhappy that you have a wife and depend on her, and by extension her life also starts depending on your wife's wishes? Believes it's not OK to be excluded from such an important part of life as your relationship with your son?

Well, anything from the list above is not something you do to a loved one. It's not love.

Being in love — amorousness — maybe. Those feelings are more egotistical; they don't bother about how the other feels.

You were right. When we quarreled, I still needed you. I grumbled, nagged, groused, felt offended — but waited for you, and more than that, tried to find a way to reconnect. From myself, I didn't accept the question "Maybe, let it be?" From you — perhaps I was wrong. Now I see it as forcing you, but at the time I didn't accept it. Then you started to disappear. You took days to text me back. You "decided" whether you should tell me you couldn't make our Zoom, and then said it was better to break up. And I accepted that — on May 17.

What has changed from May 17 to June 22? Has it changed enough?

—

It feels like I don't have any right to tenderness anymore, and whatever tenderness I have left is better hidden — guarded by strength and harshness.

—

Maria, June 22

Chapter 44
In Return

Several times during the night, she opened her eyes, unsure if an hour had passed or a month.
— Leïla Slimani, The Perfect Nanny

The next days rest in my memory, scrambled — lost in the whirl of replies and questions. Not plot, or even scenes, but shards: my screen lighting up at odd hours, a camera click, a page of handwriting held between fingers and sent across the world.

Chicago — Dubai. The distance stops behaving like distance when it fits inside a messaging app. Sometimes it's on a sheet of paper, and I hold it in front of me again, at a slightly different angle — not to change the meaning, but to reassure myself that it exists.

I still walk like crazy. I tell myself it's for my health. It is. It's also so my mind has something to do besides circle the same sentences until they wear grooves into me.

A message from Pete arrives as I'm tying my sneakers. I don't read it until I'm outside — the entryway of my apartment feels too small to hold it. I take my phone out only once I'm walking, as if motion could keep the exchange from settling too heavily.

He writes:

"Hello, my dear. I'm very happy today — you replied to me. You replied straight away, almost momentarily.
I think that speed is driven not by joy from my letter, but by the pain that accumulated in your heart.

And still — I have an answer. The lines written by your hands. Your manicured fingers holding the pages in the picture."

My body hears that and reacts before my mind can name it. A tightening under the ribs, the familiar pressure of being seen too accurately. And I'm sure he is smiling now, as if I see him in front of me.

I go anyway, down to the river, then toward the lake. The path is full of joggers in neon shorts, couples pushing strollers like shiny boats, tourists taking photos of buildings as if they might float away.

What would they do in my place? That's the stupid question that keeps appearing, like spam. At the water, I take off my shoes and dip my feet in. Lake Michigan in summer is not warm; it's honest in a way that doesn't bother to soften itself for you. The cold climbs my ankles and interrupts the film in my head. For a minute, I'm not inside a letter, not inside a past, not inside this dialogue.

I can tell I'm stressed by the smell of my sweat — sour and pungent, as if my body is speaking in a louder language than

I am. What am I paying for? Is it worth the price?

Back on my phone, my draft sits there like an animal pretending to sleep.

I take out my notebook and write by hand:

"Hello, Pete. I appreciate your letter and your sincerity. I value when people speak in personal, precise language — without fluff. It doesn't mean I..."

I stop.

Because the truth is simple but not small. Love gives itself the right for a conversation. One chance, at least. It does not give itself the right to erase what happened.

I cross out the last line and start again.

In the office, my calendar looks normal. That is the first weirdness.

I have to lead a training session, then hold two calls and join a lunch I said yes to before my life reintroduced itself.

The summer cohort is everywhere — crisp shirts, bright faces. The floor smells of coffee, printer paper, and someone's cologne that costs more than my first rent. I find myself standing in front of the group — half-joking, half not:

"Your team will want to get the best out of you. It is in their interest to show you all the ways to get your life together while traveling four days a week and accumulating two hundred nights in hotels a year. But: A) they are extremely busy; B) you own your path — so listen. Green&Co has many ways of making up for the life taken from you, but you have to take them from the firm. Sponsorship for an MBA, sabbaticals, flexible schedules, rotations to internal projects — it's all on the table. It's just not always advertised. Take a picture of this slide and don't hesitate to bug your career support services until they tell you what's possible at your stage. The options vary, but they always exist — and if you miss them, that's on you. They're yours to take, not Green&Co's to push you into."

Afterward, I receive five DMs.

Thank you.

Needed this.

Never heard of it.

I feel something softening in me, the smallest relief: I'm not alone in wanting a life that isn't only work, and it's not making me less of a professional.

Later, outside, the city is impossibly clear. No wind in the Windy City. The air is so crisp it feels scrubbed. The buildings show themselves like an album of different eras: prairie-style blocks lying flat and wide; golden-age arches and gilded roofs from someone's romantic dream; minimalist towers from the seventies; and the new ones — glassy, organic, curving as if they're trying to look alive.

The lights come on gradually, one after another, and the city shifts into its evening register. I sit on a bench by the Riverwalk and drink wine from a plastic cup — my chalice of the day. People pass in loose currents — someone laughs too loudly, someone cries quietly, someone stares at their phone the way I do. My mind has so much to process that it takes all the bandwidth I have. I'm not unhappy, but I am unmistakably tense.

And because I know myself, I try to create a little structure inside the chaos.

I open my notes app and write a list.

Do:

— *Use your head. You are smart.*

— *Ask for facts. Don't infer.*

— *Take care of yourself first.*

— *Stay in the conversation long enough not to regret your own cowardice.*

Don't:

— *Lead with affection.*

— *Pretend you're OK when you aren't.*

— *Yield to "I can take it for love." You can't. You're still fragile.*

— *Reply fast.*

The list steadies me the way holding a railing steadies you on stairs.

Then, another message — this one is different, longer, careful, full of exits.

"Hi. I'm sorry, this will be a difficult message.

Could you find time to meet me for a cup of coffee this evening?

I know you might not be in the city. You might have plans. You might simply not want to. And you have every right.

I'm not counting on anything. I can fly home calmly and wait for a more suitable moment.

But if you have the opportunity to meet, I will wait as long as needed — wherever is convenient for you."

Can we meet?
...
...
...
... ?
Is it?
I'm on the plane.
Is
...
What are...
Right?
Coffee?
If you allow it...?

Chapter 45
Uninvited

That manly razor-smile of yours —
what is a "no"?
Your lines — I'll have my boys
rehearse, then let them steal
the show.
— Aloevera, "Nonsensical"[10]

Maria:
...Is it addressed to me?
Is this last message intended for me?

Pete:
Half of me wants to make a joke.
But this isn't the moment.

Maria:
It really *is* a difficult message. I'm struggling with it.
What are you expecting? What is this meeting supposed
to be?
Right now it feels like a serious boundary violation, and
I don't even know how to respond.

---

[10] Translated by the author

Maria:

I'm not busy this evening.
But meeting you so suddenly — today, or even
sometime in the near future — I wasn't prepared to be
faced with that choice.

Maria:

I'd just started replying to your letter. About how things
had finally begun to feel calmer. More normal.

Pete:

You're right — it *is* a difficult message.
I never wanted to violate your boundaries, and I never
will. Not now, not later.
At the same time, I couldn't not come. If you've read my
letters, you know that's true.

I'm writing to ask for your permission to meet — and I'm
prepared for you to say no. I'll accept that calmly and
with understanding.
If you do agree, even briefly, I promise I won't ask for
anything, put you in an awkward position, or say or do
anything that would make you feel bad.

I just want to see you. To understand how you are —
your state. That's impossible through letters alone.
So I made the decision to fly. I need to know how you
are. I will accept any outcome, any decision.
I'm sorry I didn't tell you earlier.

Pete:

I'm glad things feel calmer for you.
I'd like to hear more about that — if you allow me.

Maria:

You should have asked *before* flying.
Now you've already come, and I feel like I owe you
something.

Maria:

This isn't just "maybe another time."

Maria:
And no — you absolutely *could* have chosen not to
come. There is no "you know I couldn't help it."
I don't know that. And now I don't know how to act
properly. You've put me in a very strange position.

Pete:
You don't owe me anything. "Another time" is completely
fine.
This was a risk I accepted when I bought the ticket. I'm
not even there yet.
I truly don't want to put you in any position.

We'll do exactly as you say.
I can't make the decision about meeting on my own — it
has to be mutual.
But I promise one thing: no emotional whiplash. I'll be
OK with whatever you decide.

Maria:
This is a mess.
I keep rereading your messages, and I don't see an
equal adult partner. Something has gone off in
the dynamic between us.

On the one hand — all this *"whatever you allow," "if you
permit"* — I'm not the Queen of England. I'm just a living
woman.

On the other — *"I can't decide alone,"* but apparently
you're already on a plane.
So I'm the Queen when it comes to permission, but not
when it comes to being asked in advance whether I'd
even want to consider meeting.

How exactly do you imagine this meeting being
emotionally neutral?
What would physically happen?
Right now my working hypothesis is that you didn't
really imagine it at all — you wanted it, decided on your
own, and figured we'd sort it out later.

I might be wrong. Tell me how *you* see it.

Pete:
You sound angry. I'm sorry.
I decided to fly so that a meeting would be possible if we both decided it was OK. My only goal is to understand you better — to feel how you are, what's happening with you, what I might be able to do.

You know I'm good at sensing people — but in letters, I can be wrong.
I do see this as partnership. I'm clear about my intentions — they're about *us* — and I leave the decision to you. I take responsibility for any outcome.

This isn't a date. It's an attempt to understand.
Physically, we could meet at a coffee shop near your place. Not dinner, not a walk — I don't think those would be appropriate.
Maybe thirty minutes. I'd listen. You could answer some of my questions — only if you want. I'd answer yours. That's how I imagined it.

Please forgive me if I hurt you. I'm doing this with care. Your reaction tells me I don't fully understand everything yet.

Maria:
Well. It seems I've grown up — and fallen out of love with surprises.
Dear universe, please no more surprises for at least two or three years.

Maria:
I didn't even know this about myself.
Yes, I'm angry. I do see this as a boundary violation.
This isn't about being offended — I don't really do that.
And it's not entirely about care, either. I have intuition too, and I'm certain this isn't 100% care. Please think about that.

Maria:
Can we de-escalate this?
If we lived in the same city and my ex asked to talk, I'd probably agree without much thought. Can we meet in that register?

Just a conversation. Saving words. Answering questions. That's fine.
I want to avoid a situation where I have to defend my space — not just physically. You can always tell when a man is looking at you mostly as someone he wants to undress.
No romantic subtext. No swooning. I'm being very direct because this is the clearest way to relate to me right now.

Can you do that?

Pete:
Yes. That's exactly what I hoped for.
I don't actually know what "swooning" means.
Would a coffee shop work, or would you suggest somewhere else? What time feels comfortable?

Maria:
All right.

Maria:
I remember our first in-person meeting in Chicago.
The Ferris wheel, you casually trying to hug me out of nowhere.
I don't want to feel the way I felt then.

I'd rather be overly blunt — even a little rude — than leave things unsaid. That's what I believe now.
And I probably need to say that out loud to myself, too.
I'm not made of stone.

Maria:
What time do you land in Chicago?

Maria:

I don't drink coffee in the evening, and thirty minutes
feels short.
Dinner?

Pete:
Dinner would be wonderful.
The flight usually arrives around four. I'll stop by
the hotel to change and then head your way.
Does six sound realistic? Would that work for you?

Maria:
From O'Hare it's anywhere from an hour to an hour and
ten.
Plus customs. Plus the hotel.
Are you sure you'll make it?

Pete:
You're right — honestly, I'm not sure.
Seven might be safer?

Maria:
I'd suggest this place — it's relatively quiet, and the food
is good.
6:30 or 7:45

By the time we were walking back, it had grown late and
fully dark in Chicago. The lights of the skyscrapers were on; it
was a warm summer evening, windless, the kind of night that
feels good on your skin and makes you want to stay out longer.

The reflections swayed beautifully on the surface of
the water. It was getting late — the last boats had already
returned to their docks, the music from the waterfront
restaurants had faded. We walked along the shore.

And then, very prosaically, I wanted to use the public
restroom right there on the promenade. I walked up, tugged at
the handle — closed. Too late.

I turned back, looking for Pete, and when I reached him, without thinking, I held my hand out for him to take.

He didn't yet understand what was happening next.

And then I said it out loud: "You know, I reached for your hand — it just happened."

As I said it, I realized it was true. The body doesn't lie. It can be a bit of an idiot, and I'll probably regret it a hundred times later, but right now I just want to be close to Pete again.

To hell with logic, reason, caution. We get one life, might as well use it.

He took my hand. And I had the feeling that now, in principle, he could hold on to it for quite a long time.

Later we walked along the Riverwalk, he kissed me under Clark Street bridge. He said it then — for the first time, out loud, looking straight at me — that he loved me. We stood there holding each other until a security guard chased us off, like schoolkids behind garages, honestly.

He walked me home and then went back to his place. I was deeply grateful that he didn't ask — not with words, not with a gesture — for me to stay. That would have been too much.

I collapsed onto the bed, didn't even close the bedroom blinds, and watched the few remaining lights in the neighboring high-rises until I fell asleep.

Pete:
Good morning!
You might have thought yesterday was something we all imagined — but just in case, I'm downstairs in the lobby.

Pete:
You're probably still sleeping. I'll go grab us some coffee

in the meantime
 Cappuccino?

Maria:
Yes. Please.

Pete:
Got it.
Come down whenever you're ready.

Maria:
OK. I literally just woke up when you texted. Give me
five minutes.

Pete:
No rush at all.
Unless it's into my arms.

Maria:
I'll be quick.

A whole day passed like a minute — we were walking,
talking, and making love, and somehow the night arrived and
found us at my place. It just went on and on until he had to go
back on the plane. I even can't say if it was an evening or
a morning flight.

Maria:
Will you write to me later — tomorrow or the day after —
about your impressions of this weekend?

Pete:
I will, for sure.
Though I can already say something now.
I didn't even know I was capable of being this happy.
Thank you, my sweet one.

Pete:
But I'll gather my thoughts and write properly.
Will you write to me, too?

Maria:
Thank you as well.
I feel very good with you — and overwhelmingly sad
that we had to part.

Maria:
OK, I will put together my impressions, too. It will be
interesting to compare both versions side by side.

Pete:
I have a foolish thought.

Maria:
Hm?

Pete:
It formed clearly in my head, then slipped away. I need
to think it through more.
Something about how things don't come easily to us —
not served on a silver platter — and how that might
actually be a good thing.
That we'll never take it for granted.
I'm not sure if it makes sense. Or if it's a good thought.
But it's hard for me to leave you right now.
It almost feels like flying to you was easier than flying
away.
I don't know if you understand what I mean.

Flying to you wasn't easy at all.

Maria:
I understand — but I don't agree.

Pete:
Tell me.

Maria:
It's just don't *take for granted*.
The idea that everything good must be earned through
effort isn't true.
Some things, yes. Some things, no.
If you assume *everything* has to be hard-won, you'll

invent reasons to struggle.
Not everything good and valuable needs to be deserved.
Some things do. But when you care about people, you want to bring them something on a plate — simply because.
That's just an example, but why should it come easily to them, and never to you?
At the same time, there are things that truly require effort.
And if you spread your effort everywhere — where it's needed and where it's not — you might not have enough left for what actually matters.
You touched on something I have a clear position on.
Sorry this is long.

Pete:
I wrote and deleted three messages.
Each of them had content, but the real meaning was always the same.

I miss you deeply.
The weekend was wonderful, but it didn't come close to satisfying my hunger for being with you — for your touch, for your eyes.
I agree with you. We have a right to things being easy.
And with you, things feel very easy.

Maria:
With you, too — more than I expected.
And I refuse to take it for granted.
Thank you for this time, for the warmth, and for the love.
Let's think about how not to be apart for too long.

Pete:
Let's, my sweet.

Maria:
We'll deal with routine when — and if — it becomes real, hehe.

Pete:
At the airport now. Everything's on schedule so far.
Text me if you feel like calling?
It might not be very convenient for you, but just in case.

Pete:
Full plane

Maria:
Sorry, I'm with the girls.
But the view here is amazing.

Maria:
OK. I'm home now.
The girls, of course, bombarded me with brutally direct
questions — and at the same time led me to
the conclusion that "actually, your decision here is
pretty clear."

Pete:
I really hope you're already sleeping right now, my dear.
Sleep well. Write when you wake up
I'm so happy.
All of this feels very right.
I'm drawn to you.

Pete:
I might be able to slip out of the Riyadh trip this week.
We'll see. That helps!

Pete:
New achievement: the flight attendant just asked,
"Sir, weren't you on this same plane with us two days
ago, flying to Chicago?" :-)

Chapter 46
Two Cities, One Heart

*I have spread my dreams under
your feet;
Tread softly because you tread on
my dreams.
— W. B. Yeats, "He Wishes for
the Cloths of Heaven"*

When we're apart, our phones become a kind of stethoscope. The messages arrive like a steady beat — here, there, here again — proving there's still a living line between two cities that don't share a weather forecast, a time zone, or the same idea of what a weekend is. I read his texts the way you press fingers to your own wrist when you're trying to calm down: not to romanticize, just to make sure the pulse is there.

And then he's suddenly in Chicago, which is always how it happens. A plane, an arrivals hall, a crowd with rolling suitcases, and my heart doing something embarrassingly physical.

I'm standing at arrivals, pretending to read something on my phone while actually scanning every face that comes through the sliding doors. When he finally appears, a little thinner, a little rumpled after fifteen hours in the air, I recognize him before my mind has time to prepare. He looks up, sees me, and the shift in his face is immediate and unguarded — relief, joy, something soft breaking through the fatigue.

We don't hesitate; we're already in each other's arms, kissing like we've been interrupted mid-sentence a week ago and are now simply continuing. He smells like a fifteen-hour flight, metal trays, and himself underneath it all, and for reasons that feel bodily rather than logical, it's the best smell I can imagine.

"Hi," he says into my hair, like he's trying not to startle me.

"Hi," I say back, which is not remotely sufficient, but it's what comes out.

He pulls away just enough to look at me, and I see him take me in — my face, my eyes, the whole frantic fact of me being here. He's tired in the bones, but his gaze is sharp and kind. It feels like a spotlight I could stay in forever.

"Two days," he says, as if announcing a miracle.

We walk out into Chicago summer, and the city hits us with its familiar mix of heat, air-conditioning exhaust, and someone's perfume thrown into the wind. The rental car is waiting downstairs, aggressively clean in that way that's both pleasant and faintly chemical — new plastic, disinfectant, the promise that nothing has happened here yet. It's a perfect carrier for our happiness. Before we go anywhere pleasant, before we do anything cinematic, we do what real life has already scheduled for us.

We go get my cat.

The carrier comes out of my apartment like a small prison with an attitude problem inside. Dora glares through the plastic door with the offended dignity of a monarch who has been asked to travel economy.

Pete crouches down and peers in.

"Hello," he says, soft and respectful, like he's greeting a person's stern mother.

Dora blinks once, slowly, which in cat language means: I see you. I do not approve. I laugh, and it comes out louder than I expect. It feels good — the laughter, the fact that the tension dissipates.

The vet is an errand and also a test: traffic, parking, paperwork, the kind of mundane friction that romance usually avoids. Pete handles it like he's done this with me a hundred times. He carries the carrier without complaint, talks to Dora at red lights as if she might reconsider her stance on humanity, and at the clinic he listens with the calm focus of someone who understands that love is often just attention applied repeatedly.

When we're done, when the appointment is paid for and Dora is returned to her apartment kingdom, we finally get to do the thing that feels like ours.

We get in the car and head toward Michigan.

He plugs his phone in, and music fills the cabin like a third person climbing into the back seat — noisy, demanding, occasionally dramatic. We start with one track, then another, then something I don't recognize, and then he finds the one I didn't know I was waiting for.

"I'll Name the Dogs," he says, and his tone makes it sound like a dare.

"Appropriate," I say, watching cornfields begin to replace the city. "This is exactly the type of road where you'd name dogs you don't actually own."

He laughs and turns it up.

The song is unapologetically American — big and sunlit, made for highways and bad decisions that turn out fine. We roll the windows down and the warm air floods the car, loud enough to push the music outward. My hair comes loose and lashes around my face. The fields are wide and patient. Somewhere in the distance, a few cows lift their heads as we pass, clearly unimpressed by our soundtrack, as if they've heard better.

"Do you imagine living like this?" Pete asks, eyes still on the road, one hand on the wheel and one resting on the console close to mine. His voice is casual, but his question isn't.

"Like what?" I ask, even though I know.

"Like this," he says, gesturing at everything with the smallest movement of his chin. "Road trips. Weekends away. Leaving the city without it becoming... a project."

"A project," I repeat, and my consulting brain shudders in recognition.

He smirks. "Exactly. No deck. No stakeholder management. Just... driving."

I think about it honestly. About having a person who will get in a car with you because the weather is good. About arriving somewhere and being together without the rest of life squeezing in.

"I do," I say finally, and surprise myself with how easily the answer arrives. "It feels like rhythm. Like a nervous system that's not constantly bracing."

He nods once, like he's filing that away.

We let the song run out and then the next one starts, and it's "Illicit Affairs" by Taylor Swift, pensive and beautiful, the melody settling on my skin as if it knows where to land. I feel goosebumps rise along my arms, the hair lifting as if a current passed through the air.

"Taylor?" he says, amused.

"Don't be superior," I say. "This is poetry. In a cardigan."

He laughs, but the song does what it does: it makes sensual pleasure feel threaded with sadness, and the thought flashes — he is still married — sharp enough to sting.

I feel it land in me and, just as deliberately, push it away.

"Skip the ending," I say, reaching for the screen.

"Already?" he asks.

"Already," I confirm. "That part is for another day."

I switch to something loud and Balkan, a dancing track that makes the whole car feel like it's moving differently, and we roll the windows down even further. The wind grabs my hair and whips it behind me. The cornfields don't care about my emotional complexity. The road just keeps unfolding.

By the time we reach the house, it feels like we've shaken something off.

The house we rented hides in a forest, where it waits for us in an ambush promising pleasures that you can only get alone with a handsome man. Trees around it nod in the wind, as if to say: you aren't the first in our lifetime, and we don't care; we will provide you with cover and shadow anyway. Wood, shade, a deck that creaks slightly underfoot. We grill without planning, open wine without checking the time, and the evening softens around us. Happiness here isn't a performance, it's a series of small permissions.

Later, in the hot tub, steam rises into the cooling air. The water holds us like a loving hand. Pete sits across from me, shoulders dropping, face lit by porch light and whatever relief lives underneath it.

He reaches over and rests his palm on my thigh, warm and deliberate, leaving it there as if it belongs.

"What?" I ask, because the touch is doing too much to stay unremarked.

"I'm checking whether you're real," he says, and the line is almost a joke, except his eyes don't laugh.

"I'm real," I say. "Unfortunately. I have emails, and concerns, and everything."

That gets him. He leans back, laughing, water shifting.

"For the record," he says, "I have a kid out there, where it's late. But you don't get to be imaginary when someone is calling you at six in the morning because they lost a shoe."

"Only one shoe?" I ask.

"One shoe," he confirms gravely. "It was a crisis."

We smile at each other across the water. My body is quiet in the best way — not numb, not braced, just present.

The harder topics are there too, hovering like insects at the edge of the light: Dubai, distance, his divorce.

He says it without making it dramatic. "I'm pushing it," he tells me. "Finalizing it. I want it done — not someday."

I don't ask for details. I don't ask for timelines. I listen for the thing that matters: whether he sounds like a man who is moving forward or a man who likes saying he is.

He sounds like forward motion.

When I speak, it comes out clean.

"I can't live in Dubai and do corporate," I tell him. "I'm not built for it. I'll go feral. In a bad way."

He smiles. "I've seen your feral. It's charming for about forty minutes."

"Exactly," I say. "And Europe still matters to me. My career matters. My brain needs to do things. I can't come just to... orbit you."

He nods, quiet.

"So," I add, cautiously, because this part is still new even inside my own head, "I've been thinking about a third path. Not Europe, not corporate Dubai. Something slower. Study. Research. A PhD. Not as a plan yet. More like... permission."

He doesn't interrupt. When he answers, it's simple.

"That sounds right," he says. "And it sounds like you."

The sentence lands with a weight I didn't expect, but without pressure.

"I love you," I hear myself say, and there is an undertone of a question in it. Beneath that, something older and steadier flows, like a current hidden beneath a mountain, shaping stone without ever needing to be seen.

The following week stretches and blurs. I work, I wait, and

feel the steady pull between us tugging me forward even while I'm standing still. I find myself reading his messages the way you check a pulse — not because you doubt it, but because it steadies you to feel it. Then it's my turn.

Dubai meets me with heat and brightness and jet lag that feels personal, almost punitive. His apartment is half-furnished, suspended between lives: a bed, a table, a couch, white walls undecided about who they belong to. The living room opens onto a canal, water catching the light the way it does back home, and in the distance the Burj Khalifa rises, precise and unapologetic. The sea is close enough to sense even when you don't see it.

We order something simple. We don't pretend we're functioning. I take the projector out of my bag and we set it up against the white wall, throwing a movie onto it like a small act of rebellion against emptiness.

He watches me fuss with the settings, then with the cord, then with the angle, and his mouth twitches.

"You're nesting," he says.

"I'm not nesting," I reply. "I'm... installing cinema."

He comes closer and wraps an arm around my waist from behind.

"You do know you can just be here," he says.

"I am here," I say, leaning back into him. "I'm just making it harder for the wall to look so smug."

He laughs softly into my hair.

Later, when the movie is playing and the canal outside is holding the city lights in its dark water, he asks the question that matters.

"Where do you want to live?" he says. "Villa, apartment... another part of the city. I want you to choose."

I look around — at the half-furnished room, the blank wall now filled with moving images, the water outside, the Burj Khalifa puncturing the horizon like a pin.

"Here," I say, and hear how steady my voice is. "With this view. This feels... plausible."

The relief on his face is so visible it almost makes me laugh.

"Thank God," he says, and then, more quietly, "I was scared you'd feel trapped."

"I'm scared," I admit, tucking myself deeper into his embrace. "But not trapped. Not if I'm choosing."

When I fly back to Chicago, my apartment looks exactly the same. Same light, same angles, same quiet. The difference is inside me, loud enough to be heard.

The two cities are still two cities. The obstacles are still real. The divorce is still unfinished. The future is still a draft. But the beating line between us is no longer just messages and planes.

It's also this: the way it feels to stand at arrivals and be found, the way the road opens between cornfields while a song plays, the weight of a hand on my thigh in hot water, the white wall in Dubai turning into a screen because I brought the projector.

I allow myself to plunge into this feeling — into being happy. For a moment, my heart is beating so loudly that I can barely hear anything else.

Chapter 47
Too Much, Too Fast

By Monday morning, Chicago is doing that summer thing where everything looks deceptively easy. The river shines as if it has never hosted a single anxious thought. The glass buildings reflect blue skies with the confidence of people who have never had their work reduced to an evaluation form.

I make it to the office on autopilot: badge, elevator, hallway, a room with a window that my assistant has heroically secured, performing that miracle once again. Outside my door, someone laughs too loudly into a phone call. Inside, I sit down, open my laptop, and feel my mind scatter into five directions like startled pigeons.

I'm not unhappy. I'm just... busy in a way that feels scattered and unproductive, like being torn in several directions at once — spinning, blanking, starting again, like a call with a poor connection.

There are tabs open that I don't remember opening.

There is a slide deck that should be simple — several pages, minor edits, a tidy storyline — but I keep rereading the same action title as if it has started speaking a dialect I never studied. The cursor blinks at me with steady, bureaucratic patience.

On paper, I have time. In my body, I'm already late.

My coffee goes cold while I'm answering an email that takes three minutes and feels like a small tax on my soul. I realize I haven't eaten anything, then remember that yesterday I also "forgot" to eat, which is a childish verb for what is actually happening: my appetite has resigned without warning.

I try to correct for it with competence.

I drink more coffee.

A message from Pete comes in while I'm pretending to focus. Nothing dramatic — a photo of the canal in Dubai, the light catching the water the way it does in Chicago, as if the cities are exchanging best practices behind my back.

I look at it and feel that familiar tug in my chest: the line between us, alive and pulling, like a heartbeat you can't ignore once you've noticed it.

I answer him with a heart and a stupid joke — something about Chicago finally copying Dubai's canals and charging rent for the view.

Then I go back to my inbox. Over the weekend, thirty new emails arrived with enthusiasm — prescheduled to hit your mailbox right before it hits you in the face on Monday. I skim, archive, flag, reply. My head dips lower in my shoulders with each click, as if trying to hide.

Halfway through the pile, a subject line catches my eye.

New feedback available

The sender is the system; her tone is cheerful, her style is clean — navigating the eye to the link. I stare at it for a moment, as if it's an unfamiliar animal that might bite if I move too quickly.

This is what I "love" about modern corporate life: the way it delivers judgments the way food delivery apps deliver pad thai — automatically, efficiently, with no eye contact.

I click. The portal loads slowly, as if it's thinking about whether this is really necessary today. I tell myself it's fine, because I am an adult and I have read formal feedback before. I have read feedback while jet-lagged, while grieving, while wearing a blazer that smelled like someone else's perfume. I have read feedback in airport lounges. I have read feedback at two in the morning. I have read feedback while telling myself, calmly, that evaluation numbers are not a personality.

Still, my hand reaches for the coffee cup like it's a life raft, while I try to detect what project owes me an evaluation — and I can't think of anything.

The evaluation form loads — ah, it's from a project I did more than a year ago. It was a short one, three weeks of storm, but we survived and even overdelivered. It can't be bad — worst case, it's polite nonsense, because everyone forgot what that case was actually about.

I was parachuted into that project with a brief to make the best possible scope (exact and detailed, as we like it). It was a situation where the client refused to speak to the team, where the team was flying in on Monday, and on Friday there were no materials for the workshop scheduled in two days. I was a very green leader with five people watching me for cues, everyone exhausted, and the team had been there for two months already — and still not having even a clue about the target state of the effort.

I remember those weeks with the strange clarity of trauma and competence mixed together: eighty-hour weeks, a brain buzzing at night, the desperate creativity of building structure out of smoke.

By the end, we had initiatives, impact estimates, explicit agreements, and — against all odds — a sense of unity with the client team. There were moments when they laughed with us, weathering the storm in the same boat. There were moments when we looked like a team instead of a rescue squad.

The feedback scrolls into view.

"She failed to build long-term relationships over the course of the engagement." Hm, why don't they mention that this engagement lasted for three weeks — 15 working days?

"Maria could more proactively discuss issues beyond the immediate scope of the project."

My body reacts before my mind can assemble an argument. Heat rises into my face, my throat tightens, while all my muscles go limp. I gasp for air. Like, guys, do you have any common sense at all? The immediate scope of the project was a raging fire, and you didn't even bother to call, text, or Slack me to say you wanted more? You have my number.

There isn't any sentence that is technically fatal. But it feels absurd to potentially derail a year of a career and not give a heads-up, not even a shred of human context. Just an automated email on a Monday morning, delivered by a system that sounds like it's congratulating me.

My hands start to shake.

It's subtle at first — a faint tremor that makes the mouse feel slippery. I blink at the screen, willing my vision to sharpen, but the letters have that slight swimming quality they get when your nervous system is already negotiating with gravity.

A headache blooms behind my eyes, sudden and decisive, like someone turned a dial.

I reach for my phone to text Pete something neutral — something like "Call me later" — because the idea of hearing his voice feels like a handrail.

The phone slips. It hits the floor with a sharp, humiliating sound. I stare at it for a beat too long, as if it might apologize.

When I pick it up, there's a fresh crack across the back panel, a net of fracture lines branching like a tiny map of where stress goes when it can't stay inside.

My chest tightens, but I save myself from drowning in it. I go home. I continue with my tasks, cook, make myself eat, talk to someone. I go to bed early — and then, after several hours of staring at the ceiling, no thoughts, just sleepless exhaustion — not dramatically, not poetically — I recognize the pattern.

Ah, this again.

Chapter 48
Slamming the Brakes

Here
is swamp, here
is struggle,
closure —
pathless, seamless,
peerless mud. My bones
knock together at the pale
joints, trying
for foothold, fingerhold,
mindhold over
such slick crossings
— Mary Oliver, "Crossing
the Swamp"

It's not night anymore — the ceiling has softened, the air has changed temperature, and the city has moved on without waiting for me. I'm lying on my back, eyes open, body heavy in that specific way that has nothing to do with rest. Dora is sitting on my chest, which is rude, but also calming. She looks at me with the mild contempt of a creature who does not understand capitalism, performance reviews, or shame.

"I don't really know much," she seems to say. "I'm just a cat. But it looks like it's time to save your sorry ass."

"Yeah," I whisper. "I think you're right."

I sit up slowly. I reach for my phone and feel the familiar crack under my fingertips. The texture makes me recoil. It's evidence of my helplessness — trivial and petty, and yet so nauseating that a sense of something foul takes over my whole body. I drop it back on the bed.

Let's get up, pull on some pajamas, walk to the kitchen. I find water, grind coffee, reach for the cezve. My hands feel clumsy, as if someone slightly changed their settings overnight. I put the coffee on the stove and turn the flame low.

The apartment smells like stale air and me — like I've spent the night under a bridge. Shower, now.

Hot water hits my shoulders, and I stand there longer than necessary, watching yesterday slide down the drain. Somewhere behind the wall, the coffee runs over the edge of the cezve and onto the stove with a sharp, familiar hiss.

That's when it clicks.

January.

The same hiss. The same moment of distraction tipping into mess. Two weeks of it, every morning, right before I took sick leave and left. The same sensation of spiraling — down and down into depression, thoughts narrowing, the world becoming heavier by the hour.

No.

No, no, no.

I love myself too much to go back there.

If there is a moment to pull the emergency brake, it's now.

I turn the water off, wrap myself in a towel, and go back to the kitchen. The stove is a mess. Coffee everywhere, but I don't have the energy to clean it. It doesn't matter.

I need paper and a pen. Right there, standing at the counter with a coffee mug, I start writing down steps.

Do I have medical coverage left? I'm almost certain I do.

How do I access it? Who do I need to call first?

HR

Insurance

Therapist

Staffing — not today, but next week

Career advisor

Partners who looked to staff me on the next project

I keep writing until the list gets long enough to make my chest tighten again. Too much. It scares me.

Ok, Maria, you aren't a coward, but you are one hour away from a collapse.

I draw stars next to the items that are on the critical path. The rest I circle and mark for later. They are nice-to-haves for the future.

I'm an operations person. I know how to manage something big — the correct answer is one lever at a time. Only a finite number of things.

The cracked phone buzzes next to me. I ignore it. This can wait until I'm standing on steadier ground.

I take a sip of coffee from a clean mug and make a face. It tastes burnt and thin.

I don't care. I open my laptop and start scheduling the calls. HR today. My therapist has an opening tomorrow. Breathe — you have three hours before you need to speak. Go have some sleep; your body is begging for a pause.

HR first. The woman on the call is kind in a way that feels almost startling. She tells me I'm not alone, that this happens, that needing time is human. There is coverage left — up to three more months — and then it's partial, but we can figure it out. She'll help with the paperwork. I thank her more than once.

My therapist texts next: "I can spare thirty minutes today if that helps." I take it — I'm not sure I'll be able to do it tomorrow, so it has to be today. We talk briefly. She isn't surprised. You made the call to return after three months, but if you you've tried and you're slipping again, it's not unheard of. She praises me gently for not powering through and for coming for help sooner this time. She will fill out the papers for extended leave — three more months, and then we'll see. Corporations like yours don't love it when humans can't carry this workload indefinitely — but that doesn't make your body wrong.

I call Pete. My voice shakes at first and then steadies. He listens, concerned, asking about the future — the PhD, Dubai — and then he hears me pull back.

"My love," he says, recalibrating, "then don't think about that. Just take care of yourself. Sleep. Eat. Come to Dubai if and when you can. We'll talk later."

No fixing. No pressure.

I email insurance. I email HR again. Medical sick leave is approved. It lands with a quiet finality that feels like permission.

I text Kitty: *"Neck-deep in mental s**t again."* She replies with a hug emoji and no questions. I'll stop by in the evening. We will have tea and sit together.

With the last usable bit of mental energy, I scroll back to an old ChatGPT conversation titled something earnest, like Daily structure, and type: Hi. I'm here again. Can you give me a schedule for tomorrow?

People talk about slamming the brakes as if it's one dramatic movement — a foot down, a screech, everything stopping at once. But life doesn't work like that. It's a thousand small movements under the hood — pressure easing here, tension releasing there, systems disengaging one by one until the car is no longer moving.

Arrivals

Part VIII
September, Clarity

KATMADU
PASSPORT
PASSPORT

Chapter 49
Preparing to Leave

Here's your food, here's your drink.
Also some thoughts, if you care to
think.
Welcome to everything.
—Joseph Brodsky, "Song of
Welcome"

I came back online faster this time. Not because I'm stronger, or wiser, or suddenly cured of anything, but mostly because I caught the spiral earlier — and because routine, humble and boring routine, still works. Walking helps. Eating actual food helps. Sleeping at night helps, too. And God bless ChatGPT for taking the burden of daily decisions off my hands when my own executive function is running on fumes.

So we — Dora the cat, Pete, and I — have a cross-continental move to arrange. Scary and boring, like all logistics. My anxiety spikes when I remember that after moving to Chicago I acquired roughly three hundred objects in the process of setting up a new home — and now the question is where all of them are supposed to go.

Life is a game you're meant to play, not win. So we'll make it a game called Off-boarding.

Not from a case or even a job this time — from a life in Chicago. In three years you grow roots and credit scores; you learn how to love, find friends and places, accumulate joy and distress — just enough of everything to make leaving complicated. I needed a way to hold all of it without dissolving into sentimentality or logistics.

So: an off-boarding, with process, documentation, check-ins, and all.

I open a new note and title it with ceremonial seriousness: **"Off-Boarding: Chicago"**.

Then I pause.

What would a city off-boarding document even consist of, when the thing you're winding down is a life? Scope, obviously. Assets and stakeholders. Critical steps. Dependencies — what has to be in place for this to work. Risks and opportunities. Open questions. A parking lot for deferred items. Maybe something else. We'll see as we go.

It's laughable, it's also correct.

This is my element: taking an overwhelming reality and arranging it into neat categories until it becomes possible to move. They paid me well for this skill and gave me ample opportunities to train the muscle.

The page with clean boxes looks back at me from the screen, politely expectant. I glance at my watch. Perfect — I have two hours before my call with Pete. A natural Pomodoro, just enough time to work, not enough to get lost in the weeds.

Scope

• Move one human and one cat to Dubai

• Filter and make decisions about belongings: transport, sell, give away

• Say goodbyes to this place and to friends

• Preserve mental and physical health — it is not the end of life, and both will be needed in Dubai

Out of scope: Panic. Reinvention of the self. Powering through.

Critical Steps

• Confirm medical coverage and leave duration

• Secure export and import documentation for Dora

• Book remaining medical and preventative appointments

• Repair phone and consolidate digital records

• Define exit timing with Green&Co

• Align timelines with Pete (including my move, his divorce, and eventually meeting his child)

Assets

Furniture

• Couch — sold

• Bed frame — sturdy, anonymous, already listed

• Mattress — a friend wants to upgrade to a king size; fate intervenes?

• Desk — I loved it. The warm wood, the steady

presence through every state of mind. Impossible to ship, so I sell it for a good price and say thank you.

• Lights — the bedside lamp comes with me; I brought it years ago from Olu, and there is no version of this story where I leave it behind. The rest go — it's close to fall, students are arriving, and they'll take them gladly.

• Coffee table — dinner table when needed, stool when guests ran out of chairs

Gear

• Paragliding equipment — non-negotiable

Books

• Many. Business and fiction. Interior architecture and shelter for frantic thoughts. Expensive to ship, impossible to leave behind.

Clothes

• More than expected. Winter coats — Dubai doesn't need them, but my future might.

Household Objects

• Mugs from national parks — keep

• Pans and pots — sell or give away

• Glasses, pitchers, mismatched things that still worked — release

• Cezve — comes with me

Miscellaneous

• Notebooks, diaries, and photo albums — to sort, if no time, ship in bulk

• Paintings — decide: sell or bring (note from the author: I sold the ones I made myself for three hundred dollars and felt absurdly proud)

• Christmas decorations — keep (anyone suggesting

otherwise is risking their life)

• Pete's letters — to love and memorize

Packing feels like archaeology. Each object answers a quiet question: did you matter here? Will you matter in the next chapter of my life? Most of them say yes to both.

Stakeholders

• Pete — partner and co-pilot; future-oriented, steady, learning how to hold logistics and tenderness at the same time

• Me (and my imaginary committee) — every part gets a vote before major decisions

• Kitty — compass and witness; the person who helps me keep my wit together

• Friends — they step by more often, quietly mention at volleyball that it's the last one, and grow a little too silent during rooftop dinners

---

Dependencies

Work & Income (Green&Co): check terms and timing, medical coverage and wind-down rules.

Partnership (Pete): this is not a solo move; keep ongoing conversations about the immediate future and the not-yet-defined one; coordinate around timing, location, and emotional capacity

Cat Logistics (Dora): export requirements (USA), import requirements (UAE), airline requirements; surprisingly, moving a cat is harder than moving a baby; her timing sets the pace for everything else

Legal & Administrative: visas, bank records, addresses in every system that wants to know where I exist

Transportation: Plane tickets for Dora and me, shipping for my things (order, routing, customs)

Health: first, stay functional — and keep up with your mental health routine; second, book all possible preventative check-ups

Housing: check end date of my lease, overlap, if needed, because you can't afford being temporarily unplaced

---

Risks

- Staying here forever by inertia

- Not selling everything in time

- Breaking down again

- Not having enough money for the move

Mitigation measures:

- Ask Pete to help and let him co-pilot this move

- Rely on friends to tie loose ends (internet, ComEd, the small unglamorous things)

- Remember what's important — *breathe, and let yourself live this part of life*

Open Questions

- How long does it take to feel at home somewhere?

- What happens to ambition when it's no longer fueled by fear?

- Can a PhD be built out of curiosity and anger in equal measure?

A quick search tells me that roughly eighty percent of published work in AI is written by people who do not have breasts. Interesting.

Deferred Items (Parking Lot)

- Career storytelling — what's next, why, and how

- Explaining myself to anyone in Green&Co

- Worrying about the future beyond the move — I will be OK; I just don't know how yet

---

Now it's no longer a complex problem in front of me, but a finite number of boxes to tick. I meet them head-on, with daily check-ins and weekly conversations with Pete, tracking progress together. We tag-team the work, counting days not with urgency, but with steadiness.

One evening close to the end, Kitty picks me up and tells me to wear something ridiculous. She doesn't have to ask twice! I choose the sparkly dress — the one that catches light even when I'm standing still. We go to the symphonic orchestra and then to a Michelin-star dinner, and it feels like a deliberate refusal to treat this moment as a loss.

We toast to living, to leaving what's coming to an end, to knowing when to move on. I look at her across the table and think, with a gratitude that almost hurts, that I don't know if I will ever have another person in my life who can celebrate existence quite like this.

That's what I want to bring with me to Dubai — even if I can only carry half of it, and ask her to visit as often as she can.

The next weeks line up into a scheduled chain of events: appointments made, tasks fulfilled, disappearing, calls with Pete about his life, my life, the immediate future, and the not-so-immediate one. Mission "Move Maria" is being accomplished without rush.

Until one day I close the document. **Off-boarding complete.**

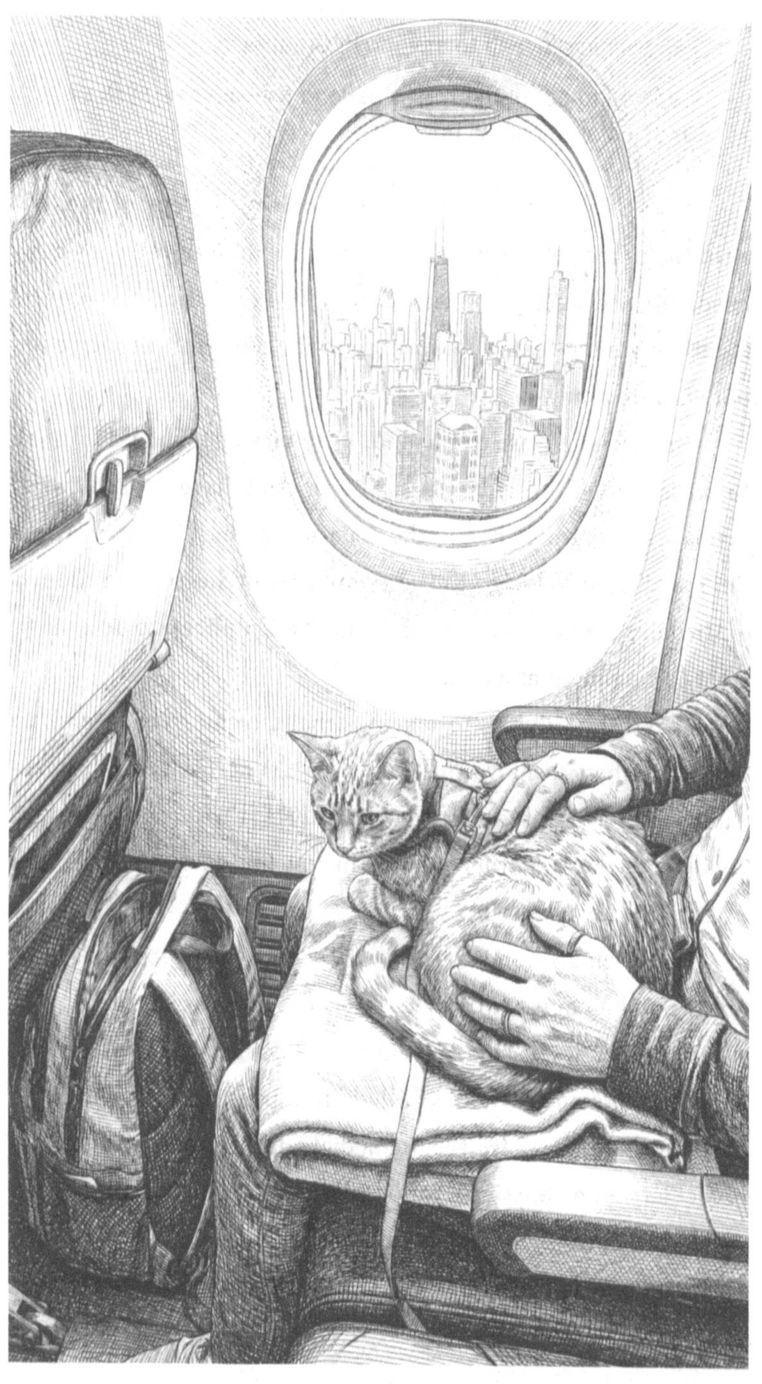

Chapter 50
The Flight

This is the terminal, the break.
Beyond this point, on lines of air,
You take the way that you must
take;
— Yvor Winters, "At the San
Francisco Airport"

Chicago looks orderly from above, the grid tightening as the plane climbs, Lake Michigan losing dimension until it becomes a flat, gray surface that feels less like water and more like a decision already made. I press my forehead to the window, half-expecting the familiar swell of sentiment that is supposed to accompany moments like this, but what I feel instead is practical, almost administrative, the kind of clarity that arrives when something has already been decided somewhere deeper and is now simply being executed.

Under the seat in front of me, Dora the Respectable Lady is zipped into a soft carrier that smells like my apartment and the laundry detergent I bought in unreasonable quantities once I understood that this move was not going to allow for gradual exits. Emirates would not allow pets in the cabin — not even in business, not even for the price of a kidney, which is apparently what business class costs now — and cargo was never an option — not emotionally, not logically, not at any point in the decision tree. I would have rerouted my entire life before agreeing to that.

Etihad flies direct from Chicago to Abu Dhabi. From there, Pete can drive us to Dubai. It isn't elegant, but it is workable, and workable has quietly become my preferred category for safety.

The airport part goes suspiciously well. We arrive early. No one invents a new form. No one asks me for a document I have never heard of but am somehow expected to produce immediately from inside my body. I put my headphones on while we wait at the gate, and at some point I realize I am moving slightly with the music, not dancing exactly, just reassuring myself that motion is still available to me.

I let Dora walk a little before boarding, careful but hopeful, laying her blanket on the floor so she can recognize herself in the middle of all this newness. She is frightened, clearly, but composed, dignified in the way only animals can be when they are doing something difficult without narration. She does not vomit from fear. She does not scream. She behaves like someone who understands the importance of maintaining a reputation.

Pete had planned to buy the adjacent seat at the last minute, just in case, but the just-in-case never materializes. The plane, however, is full. We are in economy for the full fifteen hours. Dora under the seat. Me folded into myself, legs tucked tight beneath me, body arranged into a shape that reminds me of acro-paragliding in Turkey — cozy, mildly painful, sustained by intention rather than anatomy. I think, with a kind of tired amusement, that I have done worse positions for less meaningful outcomes.

We take off at 9:30 p.m. On this route, I usually sleep, even in economy, sometimes especially in economy, but tonight my mind flares and can't let go of control. What if something happens with Dora?

The cabin darkens. People surrender to their seats. Trays rattle, seatbelts click, the collective body of the plane settling into its long obligation. I put my noise-canceling headphones on and start a superhero movie, cities collapsing quietly in my ears, and for a while it almost works, the hum of the engines stretching into something like cover.

Then a neighbor touches my shoulder. I almost jump — people never touch me (thanks to the "relaxed bitch face," probably, now aggravated by concern).

I slide one side of the headphones back. My neighbor leans toward me and says, in a low voice meant to be helpful: "Your cat is screaming."

The sound registers immediately, sharp and insistent. Dora is meowing loudly, with conviction, with the unmistakable outrage of someone who has not agreed to this version of events. I unzip the carrier without hesitation, clip the leash on, and let her out. This is not allowed, but I can't let her stay there alone; rules lose their authority when fear turns physical.

I spread her blanket across my lap, and she jumps up at once, her whole body trembling, a small, vibrating engine of panic pressed against me. I wrap one arm around her and hold the leash in the other, steadying us both, and within minutes the screaming stops. For hours she stays there, shaking quietly, trusting my knees to be geography, her weight both heavy and anchoring.

At some point, she even collects enough courage to wander off. She is a cat, in the end.

I give her exactly one meter of leash — three feet — a carefully negotiated compromise between curiosity and catastrophe. I imagine someone waking suddenly to fur brushing their arm, nails catching on fabric, confusion blooming into alarm, and I am very determined not to become that anecdote. Dora explores, returns, explores again, professional and methodical. Eventually, mercifully, she crawls back into the carrier on her own, curls up, and closes the conversation.

Only then do I realize how tired I am. I drift in and out for the remainder of the flight. Superheroes save cities with impressive inefficiency. I wake periodically to check her breathing. I dream without narrative. Time loosens its grip and stops pretending to supervise.

When we land in Abu Dhabi, I have been awake for nearly thirty hours. I collect three suitcases — the last physical evidence that I once lived somewhere else — and move through customs in a state best described as cooperative. There is an additional animal check. Papers are examined. Dora is approved. I am an approved cross-country pet owner, too. We are released back into the real world.

...and outside, no one is waiting for us.

Flowers? Hugs? Congratulations on arrival? Your expectations are your problem, apparently. I sit down with a coffee and make a conscious decision not to escalate, though there is fury building up underneath — disappointment, the threat of tears, the sharp fear of being alone in a country where no one is waiting for me. But I check my messages and see that Pete is racing to pick us up. He was delayed, but he wants to be here. Dora is alive and relatively calm; she even ate something. I am seated with a cup of Starbucks coffee — not great, not terrible. This feels sufficient for the moment.

Pete arrives eventually, slightly breathless, visibly apologetic, smiling anyway. We load the suitcases into the car, secure Dora, and I collapse into the passenger seat, my body finally accepting that it no longer has to perform.

He starts driving, talking easily, filling the space with familiar sound. Somewhere between exits, he mentions — almost casually: "I have a court hearing tomorrow morning, that the agreement with my ex has been finalized and is ready to be signed." He slips it into the conversation the way people mention traffic or weather, important but not destabilizing.

I smile, unsure now whether I am awake or dreaming, the boundary between the two pleasantly unreliable. The only thing I am completely certain of is his hands — steady, beautiful — on the steering wheel, guiding us forward, toward a place that already feels like it might be home.

Chapter 51
The Balcony

And Rose drew him in, and set him
in his chair, and put little Elanor
upon his lap.
He drew a deep breath. 'Well, I'm
back,' he said.
— J. R. R. Tolkien, The Lord of
the Rings

I wake up to the smell of coffee, which feels both ordinary and miraculous, a sensory detail that tells the body it is safe before the mind has had a chance to argue. The light in the bedroom is unfamiliar — softer than Chicago, already confident — and for a moment I don't know where I am, only that I am no longer in transit.

Somewhere in the apartment, Pete is awake, moving with the quiet confidence of someone operating inside a space without asking permission from it, and I lie still listening, cataloguing sounds the way you do in a place that is not yet yours: a cupboard opening, a kettle settling back onto its base, the low hum of a city that has already started the day without consulting me.

Dora is awake too, emerging cautiously from the carrier, pausing once as if to calibrate, then proceeding to inspect the apartment with professional seriousness. She walks the perimeter, stops to sniff corners, considers the sofa with suspicion, and when she finds the closet with my clothes, she slips inside immediately and disappears, having apparently settled on a strategy that involves hiding indefinitely, resurfacing only to eat, locate the litter box, and confirm that nothing has changed. I make a mental note that she has adapted faster than I have.

When I finally sit up, I notice my things — not unpacked aggressively, not distributed with the confidence of ownership, but placed. My sweater is folded where it makes sense, my notebook left on the table, the small Mediterranean painting my friend once made — calm blues and generous light, a memory of a very happy place — already framed but leaning carefully against the wall, as if waiting for me to decide where it belongs. It has traveled across several countries with me, a quiet proof of kindness and talent and continuity, and seeing it here makes something in my chest loosen; it is large enough that my eyes keep returning to it without effort, the way you check a familiar landmark to understand where you are.

Pete is making breakfast, nothing elaborate, the intimacy less in the food itself than in the fact that he is doing it at all, moving easily through a kitchen that is not yet finished becoming ours. We talk about small things, the coffee is good, and I am still so tired that my own presence feels almost theoretical.

He has to leave soon, and we don't say where he's going because we both know, the day already holding paperwork and endings — the kind that need to be completed so something else can begin — without requiring ceremony or weight — just a kiss, a promise of later, and the shared understanding that this, too, belongs to the work of building a life.

After he leaves, I fall back asleep, not out of avoidance but because my body insists, and when I wake again it is late afternoon, the light shifted, the apartment settled around me as if it has been waiting patiently. Dora remains in the closet, committed to her strategy, and I drink water, move slowly, letting the day continue without trying to catch up to it.

Later, we sit on the balcony, which has no furniture yet, so we settle on the floor with our backs against the glass, legs stretched out, glasses of sparkling wine sweating lightly in our hands. It is autumn, technically, and Dubai is kind about it, the air mild and forgiving, the heat temporarily restrained, the city humming below us in a way that feels present but not intrusive.

We start planning the balcony as if it is already important, imagining a table for breakfast, chairs that invite staying longer than intended, maybe a small sofa, a grill, flowers everywhere — more than necessary, more than reasonable — and an olive tree, Pete suggests, something that will outlive us all and see what becomes of Dubai in three hundred years. I can almost see it, the whole scene layered gently over the wide tiles of the balcony, the future projected onto the present without demanding that it arrive all at once, and I realize: "I don't particularly care that much about the plants or the sofa, but I will take pleasure in arranging them with you and for you, my love." Because somewhere along the way I am falling deeper and deeper in love — not recklessly, not without caution, but fully enough that the thought no longer frightens me.

I can't imagine five years here, and I don't try to force the picture, choosing instead to imagine effort — showing up, making this work without demanding guarantees — which feels manageable in a way long-term certainty never has, even comforting.

We raise our glasses.

"To the good things we've already had," Pete says, and I add, "and everything good ahead, that we get to share."

The balcony remains empty, but it no longer feels undefined, and we sit there a while longer with our backs against the glass, the city breathing around us, the shape of something solid and quiet beginning, without urgency, to take hold.

Epilogue
Time Will Put Everything in Place

> *I took her hand in mine, and we went out of the ruined place; and, as the morning mists had risen long ago when I first left the forge, so the evening mists were rising now, and in all the broad expanse of tranquil light they showed to me, I saw no shadow of another parting from her.*
> *— Charles Dickens, Great Expectations*

On that balcony, before it had furniture or habits or a reason to be photographed, I thought about the story I had just lived and noticed, with a mix of surprise and mild disbelief, how full it already was — cities, departures, paperwork, love, exhaustion, improbable tenderness — enough material, I thought, to make a novel of it if one were inclined to such things.

The thought arrived suddenly and without credentials,

which immediately made me suspicious of it. Normal people don't write novels. They move on. They summarize. They learn a lesson and file it somewhere sensible. I have a background in philosophy, which mostly teaches you how to doubt your own premises, and so my first response was not enthusiasm but hesitation: who would this be for, what right did I have, wasn't it all too ordinary, too specific, too mine.

Still, the idea stayed.

It returned in small, persistent ways — while I was making coffee, while I was waiting for documents to be approved, while September kept reappearing in different countries, carrying its familiar mix of clarity and restraint. I realized, eventually, that the question was not whether the story was important enough, but whether writing it might be a way of staying with my own life rather than rushing past it.

So I started.

Not with a plan, or a promise, or the ambition of endings, but with attention, writing the way one does when trying to understand what has already happened and what might still be unfolding. And somehow, quietly, the pages accumulated, until one day I closed the document and understood that I had reached the place where the story could rest for a while.

If you are holding this book now, it means that small, tentative decision traveled farther than I expected it to. I hope it brings you a measure of peace, or at least the reassurance that lives do not need to be dramatic to be meaningful, that care counts, that endings can be good without being final.

I don't know what happens next. I've learned not to insist on knowing. What I do know is that life continues, arrangements are revised, love adapts, and September, with its particular light and quiet authority, always returns.

The END

For Your Book Club

1.Maria appears successful in many ways: a demanding career, international travel, and a relationship that spans continents. Why do you think these achievements still leave her feeling unsettled? Have you ever experienced a gap between how life looks from the outside and how it feels internally?

2. The title Almost There, Almost Me suggests a sense of being close to something without fully arriving. In what ways does Maria experience this feeling throughout the story? Do you think the "almost" is about career, relationships, identity, or something else?

3. Burnout develops gradually in Maria's life. At what point did you begin to sense that something was wrong? Did her realization feel sudden or long overdue?

4. Travel plays an important role in Maria's story. How do the different places she visits influence her thinking or her decisions? Do you think changing locations helps her understand herself differently?

5. Paragliding appears several times throughout the novel. What do you think draws Maria to it? How did you interpret its

significance in the story?

6. Maria and Pete's relationship unfolds across distance, complicated timing, and uncertainty. How did the long-distance dynamic shape their connection? Do you think their relationship would have developed differently if they had lived in the same place?

7. The novel explores the end of one marriage alongside the possibility of another relationship. How does the story portray the difference between commitment, habit, and genuine partnership?

8. Maria often feels pressure to meet expectations — professional, personal, and romantic. Which expectations seem self-imposed, and which come from the world around her?

9. Many readers in their thirties and forties face questions about ambition, stability, and personal fulfillment. Which aspects of Maria's journey felt most familiar or relatable to you?

10. By the end of the story, Maria's life is not perfect, but it is different. What do you think she understands about herself that she did not understand at the beginning?

Enhance Your Discussion

Map Maria's Journey

Look up a map and trace the locations Maria travels to throughout the novel, then discuss how her perspective shifts in each place. Consider where she seems most like her old self and where meaningful change begins, and whether that shift is driven by the location itself or by what she is finally ready to confront.

The "Almost There" Conversation (with a film lens)

The feeling of being "almost there" appears in many modern stories about identity and ambition. Think of a film that explores a similar emotional space — such as *Lost in Translation, Eat Pray Love, or Frances Ha* — and compare Maria's journey to the protagonist's. Does Maria move closer to resolution, or does she remain in that in-between state, and why do you think this theme resonates so strongly today?

What Does Success Mean Now?

At the beginning of the novel, Maria's life reflects a conventional idea of success, but that definition evolves over time. Compare her journey to characters in novels by *Carley Fortune or Christina Lauren*, considering whether fulfillment in those stories is tied more to romance, place, career, or self-discovery. Do those books offer a clearer or more optimistic resolution, and which portrayal feels more realistic to you?

More books by indie authors

Hazelnut & Heartstrings
Adedoyin Ayeni

The perfect love story is always messy in the beginning.

He called me a moody hazelnut. I called him overrated.

Now he's back in my city — with a guitar, a smirk, and unfinished business.

Enemies to lovers? Maybe.

Drama? Absolutely.

Find here:

More books by indie authors

Black Eclipse
C.M. Stewart

Black Eclipse is shrouded in mystery, but secrets always come out.

Adira has been the warrior her entire life, always following duty, always remaining loyal. Her duty is to her pack, above all else.

More books by indie authors

Through Quick and Quinn
Erica Mimran Sherlock

Through Quick and Quinn is a relatable tale of two troubled teens whose unexpected friendship not only launches their parallel healing journeys but also gives them the courage to begin seeking truths about their families' circumstances. If you're looking for a coming-of-age story that tackles hard topics like anxiety, grief, and critical thinking, then Through Quick and Quinn is the book for you! (Don't worry, it has a splash of hopeful romance as well!)

Find here: 

More books by indie authors

A Tale of Scorched Ash and Elm
H.F. Day

Pursued by a warlord atop a dragon, a Viking on a vengeance quest, a witch in training and a half-elf freedom fighter must find the sword of a god to protect their homes and decide the fate of a nation.

Find here: 

More books by indie authors

The Spark that Ignites
J. E. Storm

The Spark that Ignites is a dark fantasy romance filled with neck snapping plot twists, grief, trauma, and antiheroes who claw their way out of despair. Join Emmery and Vesper on their quest for freedom and healing in a broken world with punishing magic, just remember: Nothing is free. Nothing is fair.

Find here: 

More books by indie authors

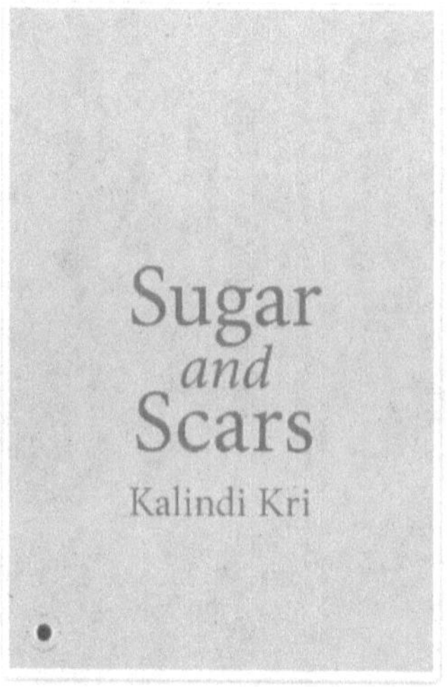

Sugar and Scars
Kalindi Kri

Oh, dear heart...

The mind holds on no longer. Why can't you just let go? Let me let go.

Through passion, heartbreak, and hope, ride through the whirlwind of Sugar and Scars — explore the stunning portrayal of life through the eyes of Kalindi Kri.

Find here: 

More books by indie authors

Until We're Free
Lauren Faith Goyer

Until We're Free is a hopeful romantic suspense about two close friends whose quiet connection grows deeper as they're forced to endure something unimaginable together. It's a story about love, trust, and choosing the right person to walk through the dark with.

Find here: 

More books by indie authors

From the Cold
Mia K Rose

Born to be a lady of the court, Claris longs to be a warrior — and when a soul-stealing demi-lich terrorizes her father's lands, she defies tradition to join the hunt. Fighting alongside the seasoned garde tests her skill and resolve, especially as sparks fly with the infuriatingly charming Torsten and danger closes in from every side. But when the monster's hidden weakness demands an unthinkable sacrifice, Claris must choose between duty, her future, and her heart.

Find here: 

More books by indie authors

Sparks & Shadows
Quinn J. Grover

Mikaela Prescott survived by staying hidden. But when a fire-eyed mercenary crashes into her carefully built life, Miki is dragged back into a brutal magical world where those who can't be controlled are broken — and survival comes at a devastating cost. She needs to decided if the price is worth it...or if she's ready to burn it all down.

Find here: 

More books by indie authors

The Ringmaster's Revenge — Cirque du Noir Book 1
Sara Cook

She's hunting a monster.

He's building an empire.

In a world of beautiful lies, their obsession is the most dangerous act of all.

Find here: 

More books by indie authors

How You Get the Girl
Scarlett Archer

Rachael Lancaster moves to San Francisco for a fresh start, only to find heartbreak and a demanding new job waiting for her. Her fiery boss and roommate, Valerie Vanderbilt, challenges her at every turn but a business trip to Los Angeles makes them question whether their rivalry is really just attraction.

Find here: 

More books by indie authors

i wish i was worse
Shirin Delalat

Forget the tidy, redemptive memoir. This one is a scalpel disguised as a story. Darkly funny, deliberately provocative, and painfully precise.

Shirin takes you through the moments she stayed quiet when she shouldn't have, and the ones she didn't. And paid for it.

Some chapters will make you laugh. Some will sting. All of them are honest.

More books by indie authors

Secret in the Shadows
Tiffany Marks

A break-in shatters Cleo's new beginning in Spring Bluff—and uncovers a connection to a deadly past. Former soldier Win Harrington won't back down from a fight, especially when her safety is on the line. In the face of danger, falling in love might be their only way forward.

Find here:

More books by indie authors

The Healing Touch
Zofia von Huck

Lim Nightingale has always been frail and sickly, which sets him apart from the other elves, even more than the fact he's a quarter-human. When he hears of a new medical treatment being performed in the city where his estranged human half-sister lives, he decide to attempt it. As Lim and his dysfunctional family travel across the continent to the hospital, they start to talk, exposing long-held secrets that make Lim realise that his body is not the only thing in need of healing. If he wants to help keep his family together, he must first mend his own broken spirit.

Find here: